We
Are the
Brennans

We
Are the
Brennans

TRACEY LANGE

CELADON
BOOKS
NEW YORK

WE ARE THE BRENNANS. Copyright © 2021 by Tracey Lange. All rights reserved.
Printed in the United States of America. For information,
address Celadon Books, a Division of Macmillan Publishers,
120 Broadway, New York, NY 10271.

www.celadonbooks.com

Designed by Michelle McMillian

The Library of Congress has cataloged the hardcover edition as follows:
Names: Lange, Tracey, author.
Title: We are the Brennans / Tracey Lange.
Description: First edition. | New York, NY : Celadon Books, 2021. |
Identifiers: LCCN 2021005982 | ISBN 9781250796226 (hardcover) |
    ISBN 9781250796202 (ebook)
Subjects: LCSH: Catholic families—Fiction. | Irish Americans—Fiction. |
    Family secrets—Fiction.
Classification: LCC PS3612.A566 W4 2021 | DDC 813/.6—dc23
LC record available at https://lccn.loc.gov/2021005982

ISBN 978-1-250-79621-9 (trade paperback)

Our books may be purchased in bulk for promotional, educational,
or business use. Please contact your local bookseller or the
Macmillan Corporate and Premium Sales Department at 1-800-221-7945,
extension 5442, or by email at MacmillanSpecialMarkets@macmillan.com.

First Celadon Books Paperback Edition: 2022

10 9 8 7 6 5 4 3 2 1

To Freddy
For making everything possible

Monday's child is fair of face
Tuesday's child is full of grace
Wednesday's child is full of woe
Thursday's child has far to go
Friday's child is loving and giving
Saturday's child works hard for his living . . .
And the child that is born on the Sabbath day
Is bonny and blithe, and good and gay.

—OLD ENGLISH NURSERY RHYME

We
Are the
Brennans

CHAPTER ONE

Sunday

The grinding noise and vibration of the rumble strips under her passenger-side tires snapped Sunday to attention. Getting behind the wheel had been a bad idea. She tightened her grip at ten and two. Then she worked her eyes a bit, blinking and widening them, because a passing "Construction Ahead" sign briefly doubled. Her exit was coming up, just a few more minutes. She checked her speed and nudged the accelerator. Denny used to tell her the cops looked for cars going too slow, a sign of drunk driving.

She'd ordered an Uber, but the estimated time of arrival kept getting pushed back. Probably some Hollywood event going on, which always played havoc with the traffic. At some point she looked up from her phone to realize she'd been left alone with the bartender. That's when she rushed out of there and decided to chance it.

It had been a last-minute invite that afternoon. Mia—or was it Maia?—another waitress who'd only been at the diner for a couple months, asked Sunday to come out for her birthday. She almost said no and went home. Like she did most nights. But if she went home she would open the email from Jackie and stare at the photo again, and that thought was too damn painful. She wanted to be anywhere other than her lonely apartment that night. So she'd gone to the annoying hipster bar with the LED ice cubes to attend a birthday party for a girl she barely knew.

She leaned forward in the driver's seat and slowed her speed. This work zone was tricky. There were tight lines of orange barrels along both sides of the road, shifting lanes around in some random way. The lights on top of the barrels blurred and blended with the electric speed signs.

That bartender must have thought she was flirting with him because he'd been chatty, offered some cheesy compliment on her dimples. But she'd only been watching him pour her drinks, trying—and failing—to keep count. It was probably mixing alcohols that had put her over the edge. Denny would shake his head and call her an idiot. Her brother always said that was just asking for trouble.

Early in the night she'd had a get-to-know-you-better talk with Mia/Maia, and afterward Sunday had just wanted to quiet her mind for a while. Mia/Maia was turning twenty-four that day, soon to complete her graduate degree, and had recently gotten engaged. The diner job was just a stopgap because her real life was about to start. Everything Sunday learned about the younger woman was a by-contrast commentary on her own life. If Jackie's email had started her down Regret Road that morning, the conversation with Mia/Maia had sped up the trip.

When the world started to spin in a scary way, along with her stomach, she cursed herself again for drinking so much. What the hell had she been thinking—she knew better. She looked for a place to pull over but there was none. She didn't know what the hell this road project was about, but her car was pinned in between the barrels, which seemed to be taking her through a maze. The swirl of lights and painted lines in the wrong places on the road only made it harder to thread the needle. She bumped up against one of the barrels on her right side and the car jerked back and forth a bit before she steadied the wheel.

All she had to do was make it home. Her exit was up ahead, though it was difficult to spot the turnoff among the sea of orange markers. She'd drink a gallon of water, down a couple ibuprofen, and head straight to bed. No detour to the laptop. No opening Jackie's email again.

When a concrete barrier materialized before her out of thin air she slammed on the brake with both feet. She heard the roaring squeal of tires, felt the violent resistance of her old Toyota as the seat belt dug into her chest and shoulder. But she knew it was too late.

Another Denny-ism came to her: "You have fucked this up on a grand scale."

Then she slammed into concrete and everything went black.

CHAPTER TWO

Denny

"You have fucked this up on a grand scale," he told himself.

He was staring at the spreadsheets and statements that comprised the pub's financials. No real purpose in doing that. Glaring at them some more with his hands shoved in his hair was not going to intimidate the numbers into changing from red to black.

The sun hadn't risen yet. The only light came from the stained glass pendant chandelier hanging above the kitchen table, which was dimmed to a medium glow. He'd given up on sleep an hour before; he could only stare at the ceiling for so long. After making a pot of sludgy coffee—Theresa usually made the coffee and he hadn't gotten it right since she left him four days ago—he decided to take another look at the ledger. See if he could finagle the loan payment that was months past due from some hidden reserve he'd overlooked. But as his mother used to say, *You can't get blood from a stone, son.*

He jumped when his cell phone rang in the 4:26 A.M. silence and assumed it was Jackie. Middle-of-the-night calls from his younger brother were not unheard of, though Jackie only called him as a last resort, when he was out of options for a ride home and too far or too shit-faced to walk.

Denny would never say no, but Jackie would have to sit through a gnarly lecture about growing the fuck up the whole drive home.

He grabbed the buzzing phone before it woke anyone else. "Yeah?"

When the crisp male voice on the other end asked if he was Mr. Dennis Brennan, his gut twisted. It wasn't Jackie. But maybe it was another collect call from Westchester County Corrections informing him that Jackie had been arrested again. He sat up straighter while he confirmed his identity to the caller.

"Mr. Brennan, this is Officer Becker with the LAPD. I'm calling about Ms. Sunday Brennan. There's a card in her wallet that identifies you as her emergency contact."

A low ringing started in Denny's ears. He didn't have time to be relieved about Jackie. "Yeah." He swallowed. "She's my sister."

"Mr. Brennan, your sister was in a car accident tonight. Looks like she's gonna be okay, but she's on her way to Cedars-Sinai."

Denny took a breath. "What happened?"

"She hit a median barrier on the highway and flipped her car. Fortunately she was wearing her seat belt, and no one else was involved."

"But she's all right?"

"Appears so. She was conscious and talking at the scene. She was damn lucky."

Flipped her car? Jesus. When was the last time he even talked to Sunday . . . Probably last Christmas when she called and they each took a quick turn saying hello to her. She only bothered to check in a few times a year.

"I don't recognize this area code," Becker said. "Are you in California?"

"No, I live in New York." He glanced around the large, cluttered kitchen, laid his hand flat on the thick trestle table, as if to confirm where he was.

"Is there someone here in LA that can get to the hospital and check on her?"

They had no family out there. He didn't know any of her friends, didn't even know if she had a boyfriend. It's not like she kept them informed. "I don't really know much about her life out there. I'm not sure who can check on her."

"Well, maybe you or another family member should get out here."

Something sounding like judgment had crept into Becker's voice. Denny was tempted to describe how much he had on his plate, what would be involved in making a sudden trip to the West Coast right now. For a sister who had all but disappeared from their lives five years ago, he might add. And there was no one else who could go. Jackie would have been the only realistic option, but he couldn't violate his probation by leaving the state without prior approval.

"Mr. Brennan, you should know your sister was drinking heavily. We didn't even need the BAC to know she was drunk. We could smell it."

Getting drunk had never been Sunday's thing.

"She's pretty beat up," Becker said. "Her driver's license will be confiscated, and she'll be facing charges."

Nice. Another sibling facing charges. And how did anyone live and work in LA without a car? Denny wasn't even sure exactly what she was doing for a job, just that she had a position with some media company. Or maybe it was an ad agency.

His eyes drifted to the double doors of the stainless fridge, which were covered in calendars, Molly's drawings, and family photos. He sought out a particular picture, the one of him and his three younger siblings from nine years ago at their parents' anniversary shindig, a surprise party Sunday had worked like a dog to pull off. There was an obvious resemblance thanks to the thick brown hair, hazel eyes, and square chins. You couldn't tell from the picture that Sunday had gotten no sleep the night before, because twenty-year-olds could do that. Young and fresh in a breezy summer dress, the only girl nestled among her brothers in their khakis and white button-downs. Long wavy hair loose around her shoulders, infectious smile revealing deep dimples. But he remembered how, right up until their startled parents walked into the room, she'd been running to and fro, checking off lists, ordering the rest of them around. She'd wanted everything to be perfect for their parents. That was the kind of thing Sunday did back then.

Denny pictured her waking up. Alone. "Do you have any idea how long she's going to be in the hospital?" he asked.

"At least a couple days. And I'm guessing she'll need some help after that, getting home and whatnot . . ."

Who was he trying to kid, he was going to LA. He would get out there, make sure she was okay, maybe learn a little about her life. He was curious, particularly after this call. Perhaps things hadn't worked out for her quite as well as he'd assumed. Or maybe it was just too much partying. Either way, it seemed Sunday had received some of that comeuppance their mother used to warn them about.

"Okay," he said. "I can get there by tonight."

"I'll let the hospital know."

Denny thanked him for the call, which seemed an ironic thing to do, and hung up.

By any measure this was not a good time to be leaving, and more than once that morning it occurred to him that he was inconveniencing himself to such a degree for Sunday, who had checked out of this family long ago. He could have just called her at the hospital, sent some flowers. But that didn't feel right. Maybe it was knowing he was her emergency contact—that, despite the time and distance, she still wanted him to look out for her.

Arrangements had to be made for coverage at the pub since Kale was away—this all would have been much easier if his business partner had been home instead of attending a funeral in Ireland. Denny broke the news about Sunday's accident to his dad and Jackie, who both had a lot of questions Denny couldn't answer. Most of them amounted to: *What the hell was she thinking?* They all agreed not to tell Shane until they had more info on her condition, though there was a possibility his dad might slip. Lately his short-term memory was inconsistent. Denny called his auntie Clare and asked her to check on his dad each morning, make sure he took his pills. He couldn't afford to mess with his blood pressure meds. Clare said of course she would check on her brother, didn't she always? And, she added, she'd known living in that debauched city would do Sunday in. Denny could practically hear the sign of the cross over the phone.

In the middle of all that he paused to take Molly to kindergarten. It was the highlight of each morning and he wasn't about to give it up just because Theresa had taken their daughter and left to stay with her sister, Angie, because he "wasn't communicating" with her. But it meant he had to drive to Angie's place first to pick her up.

He lit and relished a long-awaited Marlboro—if Theresa was going to take a break from their marriage, he was going to take a break from his vow to never smoke again—while he drove through the neighborhood he'd lived in his whole life. West Manor leaned toward upper middle class. It was thirty miles north of Manhattan, largely a commuter town because the high-paying finance jobs were in the city. There was a lot of Colonial and Shingle-style architecture, traditional homes that were roomy but close together. His parents had found West Manor thirty years ago while looking for relief from the growing younger crowd of McLean Avenue in Yonkers, the self-proclaimed thirty-third county of Ireland. Located twenty miles farther north along the Taconic State Parkway, West Manor was a family-centric suburb with good schools and athletic fields, a thriving construction industry, and the small but strong Irish Catholic community Denny's mother had craved.

Angie lived in the Manor Condos on the far west side of town, along with a lot of other divorced people, which, to Denny, didn't bode well. Before pulling up in front he tossed his cigarette out the window and popped in some gum.

His entire mood lifted in a single instant when Molly came bounding out to greet him, her little arms wrapping around his neck as he scooped her up high. Her soft black curls were pulled into a long ponytail, and she wore denim overalls and her favorite jacket, a black parka with her soccer club name, West Manor Strikers, embroidered across the back in red letters. It was too warm for April, but Molly would not be parted from it. Theresa followed her down the walkway in a long cardigan over a tank top and the yoga tights he liked to watch her move in, her wild hair gathered high on her head.

He busied himself wrangling Molly into her car seat, which gave him a moment to choke down the emotion that surged through him. The initial relief at seeing them was followed by some combination of panic and anger that rose up every time he had to drive to this fucking condo complex on the other side of town to *visit* his family.

"Daddy . . ." Molly rolled her wide eyes. "You're not doing it right." She pointed out where he'd gone wrong with the car seat straps. He deliberately went wrong again and she laughed at him, the dimples she'd somehow inherited from her aunt digging into her soft round cheeks.

After he had Molly buckled in, he closed the door and turned to Theresa. She stood with one arm across her middle, a coffee mug in the other hand. Theresa was five foot nine, just a couple inches shorter than him. She had a boot-camp-workout body and an attitude that dared anyone to mess with her. But the skin around her eyes looked tender, like she hadn't been getting much sleep either. He wanted to ask questions: Why was she putting them all through this? When would she come home? How much longer did she think it would take Molly to realize this wasn't just a visit with Aunt Angie? But he could tell from her arched brows and the no-nonsense set of her mouth that she would just give him the same answer he'd already heard—*I'll come home when things change.* So instead he told her about Sunday's accident, hoping it would prompt some sympathy, maybe even an offer to come back and help out. But all she said was, "You better go check on her. That doesn't sound like Sunday."

Once they were on their way Denny explained he would be gone for a couple days and Molly started in with the questions.

"Daddy, why don't I know Aunt Sunday?"

"Because she moved to California before you were born." He glanced in the rearview mirror to see Molly's forehead scrunch up.

"Why doesn't she visit?"

He'd asked himself that one many times. "She's very busy with work."

She considered that for a moment, her little arms crossed while she looked out her window. "Well, if I had brothers I would visit them."

He let that sit.

"Daddy?"

"Yeah?"

"Did you give Granda his pills this morning? I don't want him to forget since Mommy's not there."

"Yeah, baby. I gave him his pills."

"And did you check Shane's calendar?"

He'd forgotten about that. "Yep. Don't worry."

She spent the rest of the drive telling him about a boy in her class who was "super annoying" because he wouldn't settle down during reading time. Apparently Molly was trying to counsel him, AKA tell him what to do, but he wouldn't listen to her.

Most parents pulled up to the curb and watched their kids run inside, but Denny parked and walked with Molly, like he did every morning. As soon as they were out of the car her little hand burrowed into his. He would have stopped time if he could, and listened all day as she prattled on about her art projects and plans for recess. At the front steps he knelt down and gave her a hug.

When she stepped back her perky nose wrinkled. "You smell funny, Daddy. Like the guys who smoke outside the pub."

Jesus, she didn't miss much.

She kept her hands on his shoulders. "Maybe when you get back it will be time for us to come home."

Denny swallowed through a squeeze in his throat. "That would be great, Molls. But it's nice you and Mom are helping Aunt Angie out for a while."

Molly nodded and rolled her eyes. "Yeah. She needs it."

They hugged again, then Denny watched her jog up the steps and into the school before he headed back to his car.

Taking this trip right now was a bad idea. He should stay here and meet with Billy Walsh about missing another loan payment. He should stay and make sure there were no more delays with the opening of their second location. If one more thing went wrong at the new site, one more unexpected expense came up, he was sunk. Not only would he lose the business, he'd likely lose his family as well.

• • •

He arrived at LAX around 7 P.M. and Uber'd straight to the hospital, a half-hour ride through the congested highways and streets of his sister's adopted city. It was hard to picture her there, among the hazy sprawling metropolis that went on as far as the eye could see. If she'd been looking for the complete opposite of their hometown, with its population of ten thousand and village-feel, she'd found it.

Once Denny had been alone on the plane, nursing a beer with nothing but time to think, it had really sunk in. Sunday could have been killed or killed someone else. She'd always been so responsible, annoyingly so at times. This just didn't fit with the sister he knew. Truth was he didn't know her anymore. Whenever they spoke it was all surface info, fleeting and forgettable. Everything she said indicated she was living the dream.

The dream had brought Sunday to the West Coast in the first place. She'd always wanted to be a writer, and five years ago she up and moved to LA after receiving a job offer to write content for websites. Anyone who knew her was dumbfounded by her decision. She'd never so much as mentioned leaving New York. Her entire family was there, and they were a tight-knit group.

But what truly stunned everyone back then was that she left Kale. Not a family member or friend saw that one coming. Certainly not Kale.

The Uber dropped him in front of the vast medical complex that was Cedars-Sinai and it took him a few minutes to locate the non–intensive care unit. A nurse looked Sunday up in the computer and pointed him in a direction with a room number, informing him that visiting hours were over soon. He wheeled his carry-on down the wide, hushed corridor. His hope was to get a key to Sunday's apartment and stay there, avoid the cost of a hotel. Though she didn't know he was coming yet; he'd decided to surprise her. And maybe he'd been a little afraid she'd tell him not to bother.

The door to her room was open, the lights lowered for the evening. He parked his case under the window, turned to her, and sucked in his breath.

Fading sunlight streamed across a sleeping Sunday, who looked small and shrunken in the adjustable hospital bed with the side rails. The first thing to grab his eye was the large splint on her left arm that ended above her elbow. It was propped on a pillow beside her. As his gaze moved upward, he couldn't help the "Jesus Christ" that slipped out. Her face was covered in varying shades of deep red, which, he knew from personal experience, would turn lovely hues of purple. There was a white bandage across her nose; maybe she'd broken it. The longer he looked, the more details seeped in: small cuts on her cheeks, presumably from glass. Lacerations on her arms, some creeping out from under the splint. An angry gash on the left side of her forehead that had been stitched up. They had an IV going into her arm and a heart rate monitor clipped to her finger.

Without taking his eyes off her battered face, he lowered himself into the chair by the bed. Memories hit his gut like tennis balls from a machine: Sunday running to him in tears in grade school because Bobby Brody flipped up her skirt. Denny and Kale had made Bobby pay sorely for that one, and it had been well worth the parent conferences and detentions. The time she had to serve a three-day in-school suspension in junior high after punching a boy who called Shane a retard. Throughout her sentence Denny, Kale, and Jackie had taken turns giving her the thumbs-up and making faces through the classroom window for moral support.

He thought about what a good sport she'd been, up for a Hot Wheels session when he had no one else around, letting the boys rope her into ball games and skateboard stunts. How she would stand with her arms crossed and hip cocked when she meant business. The way she cheered louder than anyone else at his and Kale's soccer games, and spent endless hours helping Shane.

Floating just under the anger was the stinging realization that he missed her. Or maybe that was part of the anger. He didn't know.

Dr. Kelley, thatch of white hair on a tall rumpled frame, stopped in a few minutes later to provide a report. Her arm was fractured and would be put in a hard cast the next day. She had sustained a concussion that could cause short-term migraines or nausea. The cuts on her cheeks and nose would heal, though the gash on the side of her head would leave a scar. And the bruising would fade over time, but first it would get worse. Dr. Kelley—Dad would be glad to know her medical care was in Irish hands—wanted to see how she was doing with the head injury, but she'd likely be discharged in two to three days.

When the doc mentioned her blood alcohol level had been 0.19 Denny felt his shoulders slump. He'd assumed she was over the limit, but not by that much. As the owner of a pub he was well versed in BAC levels. At around a hundred and twenty pounds, Sunday had probably consumed five to six drinks, possibly more depending on how long she'd been at it. Maybe this was a thing with her now, this kind of drinking.

He ended up spending the night in the hospital, dozing in the chair next to her bed. But he'd had to work for it after the nurse initially said no.

"I'm so sorry, Mr. Brennan—"

"Please, call me Denny."

The young brunette in blue scrubs smiled up at him. "Denny. I'm sorry, but it's against hospital policy."

"I totally understand. The last thing I want is to get anyone in trouble." He ran a hand through his hair, mussing it slightly, and stepped closer to her, glanced at her name tag. "It's just, I traveled across the country today, Amy, so I could be here when my little sister wakes up. You know, so she's not alone, and scared."

She glanced over her shoulder and leaned in. "Tell you what. I'll try to be the one to check on her tonight so no one else comes in here."

He gave her a broad smile. "Thank you."

"But, if someone else catches you . . ."

Denny touched her arm. "You were never here."

She pointed at him and grinned. "I'll see if I can find an extra dinner tray for you."

He winked at her as she turned to go.

"Some things never change."

It took a moment to realize the raspy voice belonged to Sunday. She peered at him from the bed, her eyes so puffy it was hard to tell they were open.

He pointed after Amy. "She's going to bring me dinner."

One side of his sister's mouth curled up. "Course she is."

He sat down in the chair next to the bed. She was like someone he hardly knew and yet so familiar. Strangers with shared memories.

"I can't believe you came," she said.

"Thought I better see what the hell was going on out here. How're you feeling?"

She took a breath and winced. "Like it's all about to start hurting." Her voice cracked and her speech was slow, probably due to her swollen everything. "How do I look?"

"Like hammered shit."

She tried to smile.

He crossed his arms.

After a moment she turned toward the ceiling and swallowed, blinked several times. Tears spilled down toward the pillow and Denny's body deflated a bit. He had planned to keep his distance, fulfill his obligation in a cool and professional manner. Be the big brother and make sure she was okay but allow his disapproval to leak through.

Instead, he reached out and gave her good hand a squeeze.

She squeezed back. "Thanks for coming."

When the Uber turned off the highway the next morning and headed into an industrial area, he questioned if he'd gotten the address right. He didn't know LA, but he knew a sketchy part of town when he saw it.

He was glad he had stayed with her overnight, even though actual sleep was impossible in the rigid plastic chair. They didn't talk much. She was exhausted and even minimal movement caused pain. Besides, she had no memory of the accident, had trouble sustaining a simple conversation. But throughout the night she woke for short intervals, turning to him each time, as if to make sure he was still there before she drifted off again. When someone came early in the morning to prep her arm for a cast, he figured that was his chance to catch a shower at her apartment.

He was dropped off in front of a nondescript two-story stucco building crisscrossed by a rusty metal fire escape. There were bars on all the lower windows. Over the years Sunday had hinted at a nice building, a trendy neighborhood. He had no idea when she moved to this shithole. Maybe she'd always been there.

His concerns were confirmed when the key she'd given him actually fit the exterior lock. He climbed a flight of stairs, walked down a dim, narrow hall, and entered her studio apartment—or was there a name for something smaller than a studio? It was barely a room, with a phone-booth-sized bathroom and a "kitchen" that amounted to a mini-fridge, a microwave, and a hot plate.

But as he soaked it in he had to smile: tiny as it was, she'd made it hers. The walls were painted a light gray, and the large area rug was a swirl of muted pastel colors. A double bed sat along one wall, the comforter covered in large blue butterflies. The opposite wall was occupied by a gold retro love seat and a simple desk, which held a laptop and a pile of yellow legal pads.

There were more signs of his sister in the narrow jam-packed bookshelves, with more books stacked on the floor, and a linen bulletin board hanging above the desk. It was covered with photos, most of them pictures of family. Him and his siblings at various ages. Their parents in front of the Cathedral of the Holy Cross in Boston a few years before Mom died. A large picture of the exterior of the pub, the Gaelic translation of their name front and center over the door: Ó'Braonáin. There were also pictures of Kale and Sunday together, a couple from high school, others from years later. None of the photos were recent, and none with faces he didn't recognize.

Several small framed drawings sat on the desk—a sketch of their house in West Manor, simple portraits of each family member. Jackie's work. He must have sent them over the years. With a little prick of resentment Denny wondered if Sunday stayed in closer contact with Jackie than she did with the rest of them.

He sat in her desk chair and swiveled around to take a closer look. Some landscape prints on the wall, probably Impressionists, because those were her favorite. A clothing rack that was less than half-full, but Sunday had never been big into clothes. A corner shelf with a few basic dishes. He picked up a black polo shirt that was lying on the arm of the love seat. A badge pinned to the upper left side read "Welcome to Dick's Diner!"

None of this jibed with the life he thought his sister was living, with her intimations of a developing career and busy social life. How many times had he lambasted her in his mind while he schlepped Mom and Shane to all their appointments, tried to save Jackie from himself, moved his family back into the house because Dad needed help . . . Visions of her soaking up sun at the beach or partying on some roof deck, living the life of Riley. No one to worry about but herself. At least in that scenario he could understand why she left and stayed away. This was worse. Her life here appeared downright lonely, but she still chose it over coming home.

After she was discharged the next day they both took an Uber to her apartment. She was quiet on the drive; she had been most of the morning, like she was deep in troubled thought. It had started when she carefully heel-toed to the mirror in the hospital bathroom to survey the damage up close.

"My God. I look like something from a horror flick. Look at my eyes." Her irises were swimming in pools of crimson and her face was moving into full-stage blue-purple bruising, darkest at the bridge of her nose. Her choice of a black cast exacerbated an already bleak picture.

"You burst a bunch of capillaries," he said. "They'll go back to normal."

"Are you sure?"

"Yeah. It happened to me once after a fight in high school."

Shortly after that they were visited by a brusque LAPD officer who skipped all pleasantries, officially cited her for driving under the influence, and confiscated her license, replacing it with a temporary driving permit that was only good for thirty days or until her court date. Given her uneasy expression since then, the consequences seemed to be truly dawning on her.

Her movements were slow and unsteady as they climbed the stairs to her apartment, and as soon as they got inside she collapsed into her chair, resting her bulky cast on top of her desk.

"You hungry?" he asked. "I could run out and get something."

She shook her head. Her face and body sagged as she looked around her apartment. He could almost watch reality setting in. She'd be thinking about her next steps: calling work, losing her license, lawyers' fees, and hospital bills.

He sat on the love seat and made a decision he'd been deliberating about for the better part of a day. "I have an idea I want you to consider."

She raised her ruined face to him and he tried not to wince. It still caught him off guard to see her that way.

"I think you should come home."

Her eyebrows pushed down and then shot up. "To New York?"

"At least until you get back on your feet. Hear me out, Sun. The doc said you need time to recover. I would assume by now you lost your job. At the *diner*. But even if you haven't, you're going to lose your license for a long time and have no way to get there."

"I can figure all that out." She gestured around her apartment. "This is where I live. I can't just leave."

He sat forward, his elbows on his knees. "Everyone's worried about you. You haven't been home in almost four years, and that was just two days for the funeral. And now, you get into this accident—"

"No one needs to worry about me. I'm fine."

He tilted his head and gave her a pointed look.

"I made a bad decision the other night, Denny, but I like my life here."

He sensed that was true, to a degree. Her signature was all over this apartment and, based on the notepads on her desk filled with longhand, it seemed she was doing some kind of writing. But in the three days he'd been there he'd only seen evidence of loose friendships—an old guy next door checking on her, a couple of brief calls she received at the hospital—but no signs of people that were a significant part of her life. Meanwhile she had a house full of family back in New York who needed her.

He pulled out the big gun. "I could really use some help at home."

She flinched, almost as if he'd yelled at her.

"Dad's getting worse," he said. "He refuses to get evaluated, but I'm afraid it might be early-stage dementia. He's forgetful, and he can't drive at night anymore. He gets confused and his vision sucks. A month ago he hit the big beam in the middle of the detached garage, took out the electrical. The ceiling almost came down."

She turned to look out the small window over her desk, like she didn't want to hear any more.

"Jackie's checked out," he said. "Shane's doing pretty good, but his anxiety acts up a lot. Kale and I are trying to open the Mamaroneck location, but we've had major setbacks—"

"That's enough."

"Sorry if it's hard for you to hear, Sunday. But some of us are in it every day, taking care of things."

She thrust her face toward his and pointed to her chest. "I have been there and done that. I gave everything I had to this family. And look what it got me."

"What the hell does that mean? You *chose* to leave." He glanced around her apartment. "You chose this life."

She shook her head. "I'm not going to let you emotionally blackmail me into coming back."

Maybe that's exactly what he was doing. But she'd stayed away for five years. If he couldn't get her to come home now, she probably never would. "Theresa took Molly and left to stay with her sister," he said. "She said there's too much going on at the house, and with the business. That I'm stressed out all the time and things need to change."

She drew a sharp breath and for the first time since they started this conversation, her eyes softened. "I'm so sorry, Denny."

Sunday was the last one in the family to know about the separation. There'd been a time when she would have been the first person he talked to about it. Just sitting with her now, sharing all this, provided some degree of relief. Like he wasn't totally alone in it. For a second he was even tempted to tell her about Billy Walsh and the loan. But she could do nothing to help with that.

When she spoke again it was so quietly he wasn't sure he heard her. "Maybe I could go. For a little while."

"Seriously?"

She didn't answer. Instead her eyes roamed around the room while she chewed her bottom lip.

"Look, I know it wouldn't be easy, coming back. You had your reasons for leaving. But you have no idea how excited everyone would be."

"Not everyone."

He shrugged a shoulder. "Don't worry about Kale, I'll talk to him."

"What about this DUI? I don't even know when my court date is yet."

"I got a lawyer buddy back home. He said you're free to leave the state while all that is resolved, and he hooked us up with a DUI guy out here."

"I don't know," she said. "I just got out of the hospital. I need a little time."

"What you need is your family. And right now, they need you too."

She stared at him for a long moment before sighing in surrender. "Okay. I'll come home."

He slumped back against the couch. Thank Christ.

CHAPTER THREE

Sunday

O kay. I'll come home."

A certain comfort came with making the commitment. She couldn't back out after that.

The instant Denny had mentioned the idea of going home, there'd been a lifting in her chest. And even while she argued with him part of her wondered if it was possible. The truth was—and she hadn't seen this coming—she didn't want to say no. When she had woken up in that hospital room to see Denny standing there, his big solid presence filling and warming the space, a potent homesickness had hit. Listening to him talk about their father and brothers the last couple of days had only sharpened the ache.

But really it had started the morning of her accident, when she opened that email from Jackie to find a link to a local newspaper photo. It was a picture of Denny and Kale standing in front of their brand-new pub, big smiles on their faces. Denny sported his usual frat-tastic look—untucked button-down and cargo pants. Kale wore a T-shirt and jeans he might have picked up off the floor that morning. They were both close to six feet, but Kale wasn't as thick as Denny. He was mindful appeal and softer edges to

Denny's raw charm and rough corners, in both appearance and manner. There was a large "Opening Soon" banner hanging above them and the caption read: *Owners Denny Brennan and Kale Collins plan to offer Mamaroneck locals the same ambience and flavor of their popular first location in West Manor—which has won Best Local Pub in Westchester for two years running!*

Only after reading the caption did Sunday let her eyes land on the other two faces in the photo, like her brain knew she needed time to prepare herself. Sitting on Denny's and Kale's shoulders were their kids, Molly and Luke. Molly, the niece she didn't know, and Luke, Kale's son. Who looked just like his dad, the same curly hair and sweet smile. She stared at the little boy until the constriction in her chest became too painful. Then she had slammed her laptop shut.

She'd been on a mission later that night at the bar, to soften the severe sting that came with realizing how much everyone had moved on without her.

It turned out to be depressingly easy to close out her life in LA and pack up the few things she wanted to take with her: clothes, photos, her laptop, and journals. Five years reduced to a suitcase. She called the small circle of friends and coworkers who would notice she was gone, and two days later they were on a flight to New York.

The fluttering in her stomach became very pronounced once they landed at JFK. Specifically, when she was looking for their luggage in baggage claim while Denny ducked outside for a quick smoke. She'd given him a load of shit about starting up his dirty habit again. He'd quit almost ten years ago after meeting Theresa, who was a nurse-in-training at the time and said it was a deal-breaker. But he promised it was just until Theresa came home.

A chill hit when they stepped out of the airport, but the sky was blue and the sun strong. Unlike the general sameness of LA weather, spring in New York fluctuated wildly. Denny hailed a cab and she soaked in the cityscape as they crossed the Triborough Bridge, the massive cluster of towers and spires, sleek high-rises mixed in among historical architecture. By contrast she'd never thought of LA as a true city, with its clumps of tall buildings surrounded by a vast network of squat ones. Not to mention the ever-present layer of smog. The Manhattan skyline was clear and crisp, like her world had come back into focus, and there was a surge of exhilaration at being home.

But when they arrived in West Manor forty minutes later and the cab wound its way through town, all the doubts slithered back in, twisting her insides into knots. She hadn't allowed herself to think this through, how she was going to find her way back into the family. At least she had some time before she had to face Kale, who wasn't due to return for over a week.

Her hometown hadn't changed much, but that was by design. This part of New York was rich in history and there were countless historical societies committed to preserving it. In grade school she had learned all about the rich and powerful Philipsburg family, who acquired over fifty thousand acres north of Manhattan in the 1600s. They imported slaves to develop the land and make Philipsburg Manor a thriving center for agriculture, before it was confiscated during the Revolutionary War and used as collateral to raise funds for the Colonial cause. Like other towns in the area—or hamlets, as they liked to call themselves—West Manor had its fair share of structures listed on the National Register of Historic Places, including the Episcopal church, an old cemetery, and an out-of-commission railroad station. It was a quaint, comfortable town that came with a high cost of living. Most people either worked on Wall Street or fought for jobs in construction, health care, or retail.

Her heart hammered against its cage as they rolled past houses that had served as the backdrop to her childhood. Sunday had only been back once, for her mother's funeral. It was a brief trip, and she'd stuck to the house and immediate family. Now she'd have to settle back in, reacquaint herself with people. It would be harder to avoid the faces and places she didn't want to see. At least the one face that was still long gone; Jackie had confirmed it. In fact, that family's house in West Manor had been sold. And the Penny Whistle Pub was closed down now, converted to a small market. That helped.

Her agitation settled a bit when they pulled up to the three-story white

Colonial that had always been home. Black shutters, red front door, four dormers poking out of the roofline. It seemed larger than Sunday remembered, probably because her whole apartment could fit in this house ten times over. "You need a big house for a big family," her mother used to say with a touch of defensiveness. But they all knew she had secretly loved having one of the largest houses in the neighborhood.

Her father was waiting in a rocker on the front porch. She could see the flat tweed cap above the newspaper he was reading. When he closed the paper and stood in his cardigan and khakis, she drew in her breath.

"I know," Denny said. "He looks a lot older than when you were here last."

There was a touch of frailty about her dad as he laid his paper on the chair, navigated the porch steps, and walked down the path. He moved with less certainty. His wrinkles were more defined, and the thick hair was much more salt than pepper now. But then he adopted his Dad Pose, the same one her brothers often used: wide-legged stance, arms crossed, hands tucked up under armpits. While Denny settled up with the driver and grabbed the suitcases, she climbed out and met her father at the curb.

"Well, look what the cat drug in." A smile broke across his broad, ruddy face, but as he got a closer look at her it faded fast.

"Hi, Dad." She offered a one-armed hug.

He hugged her back. "Christ Almighty, Sunday."

"I'm fine. It will all heal."

After looking to Denny for confirmation, her dad nodded and cleared his throat. "Come on in now. They're all waiting on you. Except Shane. He's at work."

As she followed him up the path she noticed the trim rosebushes lining the front of the house were still well cared for, green shoots starting to wake up after a winter's sleep. Her mother had loved those roses, every one of them a deep scarlet color. After she died, Shane became their caretaker, and he clearly took his job seriously. The house looked okay. But there were areas of peeling paint and tarnished spots here and there, conditions that would not have been allowed to exist under Maura Brennan's watch.

Sunday climbed the porch, stepped across the threshold, and slammed into the familiar mixed aroma of old wood, black tea, and fresh laundry. Maybe even the slightest scent of her mother's rose perfume. The first thing she noticed was a large banner that read "Welcome Home Sunday" in bright multicolored paint strokes. Had to be Jackie and Molly's handiwork. It was strung up between the living and dining rooms. The old paisley sofa and armchairs were in remarkably decent condition, no doubt because they'd been protected in those awful plastic covers, at least until her mother died. The old cherry dining table and chairs were more scuffed up. The built-in shelving nook in the living room that had long been her mother's shrine to Denny hadn't changed much. It was still filled with soccer trophies, team pictures, laminated newspaper clippings, though some Molly paraphernalia had been added.

Beneath the welcome sign stood her aunt, her niece, and her brother Jackie. She felt her bruised face bend and pull into a smile at the sight of them. However, their expectant smiles all faltered in unison.

"Come on, everyone," her dad said, waving them over. "Don't be shy."

Clare recovered first, stepping forward in her white blouse, long dark skirt, and simple pumps. As close to a nun as possible without the habit and veil. "Hello, pet." She put her hands on Sunday's shoulders, her eyes riveted to the damage. "My God, child."

"It's not as bad as it looks."

Denny walked in the front door with the suitcases and Molly ran to wrap her arms around his legs. "Daddy!"

"Hey, Molls." Denny picked her up like she weighed nothing and wrapped his arms around her. The way his face eased into pure relief made Sunday tear up. After he settled her in his arms he asked, "Did you say hi to Sunday?"

Sunday walked over and poked Molly's stomach. "I know I look scary, but you'll get used to it."

Her small features scrunched up as she studied Sunday's face and arm. She had Denny's intense gaze, but Theresa had given her the restless hair and touch of Italian olive to her skin tone. "Is that from your car accident?" she asked.

"Yes, it is."

"Auntie Clare said you were half-cut."

Everyone turned to Clare, who waved it off. "I said no such thing." But her face flushed. Only she would use such an expression for drunk.

"Yes, you did," Molly said. "When we were at the store—"

"Who's ready for some tea?" Clare asked. She spun and headed for the kitchen.

Sunday turned to Jackie, her Irish twin at only fourteen months younger. He was a few inches shorter than Denny, and had a slighter build, all lean muscle and refined features. His hair had grown long enough to pull back into a man bun, which Denny and her dad probably had a field day with, but his face was clean-shaven. He stood underneath the banner, hands jammed in his pockets, just staring at her.

"What the hell, Jackie. It's not that bad," Denny said. "You look like you're seeing a ghost."

He probably was, in a sense. This had to be dredging up an old dark memory in his mind, one they'd both tried to bury long ago. Sunday stepped toward him.

To her alarm, his eyes watered.

"It's okay. I'm fine, really." She put her good arm around him.

He raised his arms to hug her back. "Hey, Sunday," he said into her shoulder. Then he held on for a good long minute.

"I can't believe you didn't tell me about the accident," Grail said. "Or let me know you were coming back. I had to hear it all from Mom." She lifted an eyebrow. They were first cousins and, despite an eight-year age gap, they'd been close growing up.

"Sorry. It all happened so fast. You know Denny. He's a force of nature once he gets an idea."

Grail just nodded. She'd always said it was one of the things women loved about him.

They were unpacking Sunday's suitcase upstairs in her old bedroom later that evening. Clare had freshened it up, but the room looked the same as the day Sunday left. Her twin bed was still covered in the plush white bedspread with delicate violet flowers. The writing award she'd won sophomore year in high school still hung above her old rolltop desk, and the tall built-in shelves were crammed with her books. The intricate three-level Victorian dollhouse her dad had made for her fifth birthday sat on the dresser, and a crate full of her high school cross-country jerseys still sat in a corner of her closet. Nothing had changed, as if the room knew she'd be back someday and had faithfully waited for her.

"Sorry I couldn't be here for the homecoming," Grail said, hanging a couple shirts in the closet. "My shift didn't end till six." She was still wearing her work clothes, a professional pants suit and flat dress shoes with a thick rubber sole. Her dark hair was cinched back in a low bun.

"I know it was a couple years ago but congrats on making detective," Sunday said. "How do you like it?"

"It's good. Most of the guys treat me fairly, with the exception of one or two jackasses who are threatened by a woman in their midst."

Sunday dropped down on the bed, put her right hand under her left arm to provide support. The cast was itchy and awkward, and it pulled at her left shoulder.

Grail sat beside her and flopped back on the bed. Growing up, Sunday had wholly worshiped her older cousin, who was far wiser and braver. When Sunday got her first period in eighth grade, it had been Grail she'd gone to, scared and in tears, because her mother had handed her a church pamphlet that explained nothing and warned of the impure thoughts she might start to experience. Grail had also been the one to help her figure out birth control when she and Kale were headed in that direction.

"What the hell happened out there, Sun?" Grail asked, staring at the ceiling. "I mean, you left here for some killer job. You never visited because you were *so busy*. We all figured you were living a fabulous life, with loads of money and men."

Sunday had never said any of those things, but she'd allowed them to make assumptions. "I was getting by," she said. "I had my own place. And the only reason I waited tables was because it left me with time to take classes, and read and write." She shrugged. "I just didn't want anyone to worry."

"Well, you kind of blew that with the whole drunk driving accident."

"True."

"Any boyfriends out there in LA?"

"A few. Nothing serious."

Grail sat up next to her. "You look exhausted. You shouldn't have been traveling so soon after the accident."

"Probably not."

"How's it been with everyone?" Grail nodded in the general direction of downstairs.

"A little awkward, especially with this." She pointed toward her face. "But we'll get past it. Although I haven't seen Shane yet. He works until nine."

Grail jutted her chin toward a photo that had sat on the desk all the years she was gone. "Does he know you're back?"

Sunday turned toward the picture of Kale from eight years ago. His dark, shaggy hair fell to his eyebrows, covered half his ears and the top of his neck, the ends curling up in random directions. Crooked grin and eyes so light they were gray. "No, he doesn't." She reached over, lifted the picture, and put it in a desk drawer.

"Well, let me know when he finds out. I'd like to be a fly on the wall for that reunion."

After the whole family ate Clare's slow-cooker pot roast together, the place cleared out. Her dad had to "meet a guy"—a euphemism for placing bets with his bookie at a hole-in-the-wall bar in town. Jackie headed out to pick Shane up from Newman's Market, where he'd been bagging groceries and stocking shelves for almost seven years. Clare and Grail left together, bickering about something pointless like the polar-opposite mother and daughter they'd always been. That was when Molly asked to have a chat with Sunday.

Looking very grave across the table with her little arms folded on top, Molly first put Sunday on notice: *I'm gonna move into your room when*

I turn five. Mommy and Daddy already said I could. Though she offered Sunday her little room located next door to Denny and Theresa's master suite downstairs. Then she broke the news that the dollhouse now belonged to both of them. *We're just going to have to share, Sunday. And please ask before you move things around because I have it all set up just right.* While Molly talked—for quite a while—Sunday listened with a solemn face and nodded often, her heart breaking a bit over how infinitely adorable four years old could be. Only after Sunday reassured her they would work out an equitable plan for the bedroom and the dollhouse would Molly let Denny take her to Theresa. Even though he tried to hide it, Sunday sensed Denny's frustration with having to drive his daughter to another home for the night.

When Jackie and Shane got home, she initially just watched while Shane lumbered through the door, slipped off his backpack, and hung his coat on the rack. He sat on the small bench in the foyer, unlaced and removed his construction boots. He wore carpenter jeans and a flannel, like their dad had every day for decades. Shane was a gentle giant, even taller and broader than Denny, with his hair cropped close to his head. At twenty-five, he was the youngest of them all. He'd been diagnosed with an intellectual disability over twenty years ago, but it had never held him back. Shane was a hard worker and generally had one of the sunniest dispositions Sunday had ever come across.

Jackie followed him in. "Look who's here, dude." He nodded toward the living room.

Sunday stood from the couch. "Hi, Shane."

"Oh boy. Sunday?" He stood and his right hand went up to twirl the hair on that side of his head, a habit that kicked in with confusion or anxiety. They had told him she was coming home; it was best to avoid surprising Shane. But they couldn't have prepared him for her face.

He backed away when she started toward him. "What . . . what happened to your face and your arm? Is that from the car accident?" His voice was deep and always slightly louder than everyone else's, because of the mild hearing deficiency he was born with.

"Yes," she said. "But I'm fine."

He stared at her. "Oh boy. You look . . . all messed up." He rocked from one foot to the other.

"I know it looks pretty bad. When the car flipped over my face hit the steering wheel and I cut my nose." She pointed to the white bandage that resided at the bottom edge of her vision. "I burst capillaries in my eyes too." She used two fingers to pull one eye open wide. "That's why they're red. And I broke my arm against the door."

He stopped rocking and leaned in for a closer look, pointed at her arm. "You got a black cast. Tony at the store broke his arm, but he got a blue one."

Jackie gave her a knowing smile over Shane's shoulder. She'd managed to convert his alarm to curiosity.

She swallowed a lump in her throat while she soaked in his sweet face. "It's so good to see you, Shane. I missed you."

He treated her to his huge, unreserved smile. "Me too." Then he gave her a bear hug. She didn't let on when he squeezed a little too hard.

The pain made it difficult to sleep through the night. No position worked for long, and when she was alone in the dark her mind gravitated to the accident. Her brain was piecing together what happened, just like the only other time she'd suffered a loss of consciousness. Of their own free will, mental snapshots were emerging: rushing to figure the right tip for the bartender, looking up to see herself careening toward a concrete barrier, flashing lights and the sensation of hanging upside down. She would drag her mind from the accident only to have it land on other upsetting thoughts. Old ghosts from the past, doubts about the future.

She headed downstairs when she heard movement in the kitchen early the next morning. Denny was at the table, wolfing down a microwave burrito. She poured herself a cup of coffee, leaned against the counter, and took a sip. Then she bent over and spit it in the sink.

"Jesus. How do you burn coffee?"

"You're welcome," he said, around a mouthful of food.

She poured out what remained in the coffeepot and made a fresh batch. While she waited for it to brew, she studied the calendars posted on the fridge. One tracked her dad's fairly quiet days: midday shifts at the pub, the Gaelic football schedule, card games with his buddies. The other, which had hung on that same door since she was a kid, listed Shane's shifts at the market, his medication schedule, appointments with his occupational therapist, and, of course, the Yankees game schedule. Keeping that calendar current used to be her job. Looked like it was a combined effort now. Each of her brothers' handwriting, as well as Theresa's, was splashed across it.

"What do you have planned for today?" Denny asked her.

"Nothing." She poured some coffee and sat at the table. "Why?"

"I could use some help with the ledger for the pub."

"He sure as hell could," her father said, shuffling into the kitchen in his slippers and flannel robe. "I'm to here with his griping about it." He brought his hands together as if in prayer and inhaled. "I smelled that coffee from my bed and knew it couldn't be the muck your brother makes." He poured a cup and joined them at the table.

"What's going on with the ledger?" she asked.

"It's in chaos," Denny said. "I've had trouble holding on to bookkeepers."

"For how long?" No way her brother was successfully tracking the details and numbers that went into maintaining accurate financial records. He just didn't have the patience.

"Hard to say. We hired a few, but they didn't work out. And then we'd go without for a while. Kale takes care of all the other administrative stuff so I tried to stay on it." He dragged a hand through his hair. "At this point, I can't even get anyone to consider taking it on because it's such a mess, or if I can, they want to charge out the ass."

"Well, I can try to help—"

"That's great."

"—but only for a little while, until you hire a new bookkeeper."

"Deal."

"I mean it, Denny."

He held up a hand. "Understood."

"Okay. I'll come to the pub in a bit."

"Thanks, Sun." He flashed a smile on his way out the back door.

"Good luck with that," her dad said, slurping his coffee.

"I know."

Jackie came down the stairs in boxers, a T-shirt, and a bedraggled mop of hair. "Is there any coffee left?"

Sunday nodded toward the pot.

"You working today, Jackie?" Her father had tried for nonchalant, but clearly this was a touchy subject.

"Shift starts in thirty."

"When will Shane be up?" Sunday asked.

"Not for a while," Jackie said, checking Shane's schedule. "He doesn't go in until noon today."

"Was he up late with the LEGOs?" her dad asked.

"I looked in on him around midnight. You should check it out. He just started Hogwarts Castle." He headed for the stairs, taking his mug with him. "I gotta go."

"Will you be home tonight?" she asked. "Maybe we can find some time to catch up."

He gave her a pure Jackie smile, expansive and youthful. "Definitely." Then he jogged up the stairs.

She pulled her legs up on her chair, sipped her coffee, and relished just being back in the house, with her dad and brothers, part of the morning routine. For the briefest moment it was possible to kid herself into believing she'd never left.

Her father, rarely given to gushing proclamations, looked down and spoke to his cup. "It's grand to have you home, Sunday."

And despite the lack of sleep, throbbing head, and nagging uncertainty about coming back to New York, a feeling swelled in her chest that she faintly recognized as hope.

CHAPTER FOUR

Mickey

I t's grand to have you home, Sunday."

He didn't look at her when he said it because he was a bit over-come. Part of it was her sad, broken face. Part of it was the smile she'd managed to pull from Jackie—a smile he couldn't remember seeing in a long time. But mostly it was knowing a missing piece of their family had come back into the fold after so long. Sunday being gone all those years had been like having a phantom limb. She still felt attached and her absence was painful. She'd been in the house less than a day and the atmosphere had already shifted, lightened and warmed up. The gentler voice, airier laugh, swish of hair. Mickey loved his daughter-in-law, Theresa, with her no-bullshit manner and gutsy opinions. But he had badly missed Sunday, including the soothing balance she was for Denny's blustery energy.

She had occupied a special place in his heart from the day she was born, which was a Sunday, the name he insisted on giving her much to Maura's dismay—*What kind of name is that? People will think we're mental.* Nor-mally Mickey had deferred to his wife in such matters. But what was the harm in blessing their girl with a name of good fortune, even if the idea did come from an old nursery rhyme.

He cleared his throat. "Call me when you're ready to walk to the pub. I don't have a shift today, but I'd like to go in. Besides"—he smiled—"two people shorten the road."

He went out to collect the newspapers he had delivered to the house each morning. It was one of his indulgences, along with OTB for betting on the horses, and his bookie for football and fights. Then he headed to his room to spend a few minutes talking with Maura, something he'd done each and every day since her death four years ago.

The first thing he told her was that Sunday had come home. Then he promised to do whatever it took to keep her there.

They walked the four blocks south and three blocks west to the pub later that morning. Their house was in the oldest part of West Manor, often in high demand because it was within walking distance to downtown, a half-mile strip of restaurants, shops, and professional offices. Lampposts lined the streets and displayed hanging baskets overflowing with colorful blooms this time of year. All the buildings along Saw Mill Road, the main thoroughfare, were in keeping with height and square footage limits. The zoning laws in this part of New York were stringent. No one knew that better than Mickey, after being a project manager in construction in this area for over thirty years. Many a palm he'd had to grease along the way, be it with money or favors, to push projects through the approval process.

Sunday scanned the streets while they walked, asking him about new or renovated houses, businesses she didn't recognize. She turned her injured face down or away when they passed people, mostly joggers or moms with strollers. When they rounded a corner and Brennan's came into view she halted.

"Everything okay?" Mickey asked, stepping back beside her.

She nodded. Her eyes, which may have been a little moist, skimmed the exterior. "The place looks great." He heard enthusiasm in her voice, but wistfulness too. She'd been a big part of the planning for Brennan's, which opened the year before she moved out west to take that job writing for the internet. Whatever that meant.

He never approached the pub without a fierce rush of pride. It took up half the block and was a class place, starting with their family name above the heavy mahogany front door. The Gaelic translation—Ó'Braonáin— had been Sunday's idea, and Jackie had designed the exterior, a deep emerald green with dark wood trim. When Denny and Kale told him what they wanted to call the pub all those years ago, Mickey insisted the loan he and Maura had given them didn't warrant such an honor. After all, Kale was an equal partner, had put just as much blood, sweat, and tears into the venture as Denny.

"That's okay, Mr. B," Kale had said. "Brennan's is fitting, and flows better than Collins's."

Kale was practically a Brennan anyway. He'd grown up four blocks away and spent the bulk of his time in their home. Mickey had never minded. What was another kid, especially one who was so unassuming, when there were already four.

He and Maura had met Kale's parents at St. Monica's Church in town, where many transplants from Ireland coalesced and celebrated the sacraments together so they still had meaning. Where all the children were baptized and their parents absolved of their sins each week, or when the wives could harangue the husbands into visiting the confessional. In his case that had been rare indeed. Mickey and Maura had been friendly with the Collinses, but not close. Keith Collins had been a fussy, priggish sort. It hadn't been a shock to hear his wife left him for another man when Kale was four years old, though she'd also cut herself out of the boy's life. The poor lad had no siblings, just a sickly father doddering around the house. No wonder he loved the warmth and bustle of the Brennan home.

Kale and Sunday had been together near eight years when she took that job in California. Initially Mickey assumed Kale deserved the blame, but after watching his almost-son-in-law suffer in the wake of her departure, he decided there had to be more to the story. Now that Sunday was back, he was determined to find out what it was.

As soon as they arrived at the pub, Sunday and Denny disappeared into the small back-corner office, leaving him up at the bar with a cup of coffee. Paul, the head bartender, was prepping for the day. He was a divorced fifty-something with an earring and tattoos, but he'd turned out

to be a solid employee for Denny and Kale after Jackie had to quit working at the pub thanks to the terms of his probation.

"The Yanks playing this afternoon, Paulie?"

"Not today, Mick."

Damn it. He could tell by the trace of weariness in Paul's tone that
he'd already asked that question. It was frustrating as hell. He'd always been
healthy as a horse, other than a mild heart attack years ago that had alerted
him to his high blood pressure. He could recall specific football games
from his childhood, the details of the day he came over from Ireland almost forty years ago, all the guys that had worked on his crew over the
years. But ask him what happened that morning and there was a chance
he wouldn't remember. And then there was the humiliation that came
with promising not to drive at night after hitting that support pole in the
garage. The worst thing about an aging memory was how people side-
lined him, not bothering to mention things that might be confusing or
upsetting. And it was as much for their sake as for his, to avoid explaining
and repeating.

On second thought, the worst thing about a failing memory was the
wondering if he'd brought it on himself, if it was a reckoning for past sins.
His mind was trying to keep secrets from him. Fitting punishment for a
man who'd long kept secrets from his own family.

"You must be thrilled to have your girl home," Paul said. He was drying and shelving pint glasses. "By the looks of her, that must have been
some accident."

"Aye, it was a bad one." Mickey had wanted to question Sunday more
the night before, push for answers about what was going on out there
in LA. But Denny had said to give her time, that she was embarrassed
enough without having to get into all that.

Besides, that dinner had been the rightest Mickey felt with the world
in a long time. Everyone gathered in the formal dining room, Sunday in
her old spot again, immediately to his left. Clare, seated at the other end
of the table in Maura's old place, had allowed herself a glass of beer and
had a flush to her cheeks. There was lots of banter, Mickey and Clare
told tales about their eight siblings and growing up on a farm. And their

children were always fascinated to hear about living through the Troubles in Northern Ireland. Though he had to be careful there, and he could feel Clare's eyes on him when he talked about their lives before they came to America.

Mickey's kids and Grail all believed Grail's father died in Ireland before she was born. They didn't know about Clare's out-of-wedlock pregnancy, the reason his parents shipped her off with him to live in the States. Being with child and without a husband was still a big deal in Ireland in the '80s, especially in the North when the woman was Catholic and the man was Protestant.

And none of the kids knew about the beating Mickey had given that bastard, to within an inch of his life. Married and twice her age, he'd used Clare and kicked her to the curb, pretended not to even know her when she went to him in tears for help. Mickey had enlisted friends to stand watch while he did the deed, and they'd had to pull him off the fella in the end.

For many years Mickey had helped the cause by running errands for the IRA. But transporting money and guns across the border from County Louth had required only mild strong-arm tactics. He had scared himself that night, the way he lost control with that man. He'd already been thinking about leaving Ireland for broader horizons. With the Orangemen after him for revenge and the IRA out to own him, that whole affair sealed the deal.

"Mickey?"

He looked up. "Sorry, Paul."

"I asked if you'd care to wager on the subway series this year."

"I'd love to take your money."

Paul laughed. He favored the Mets and Mickey was die-hard Yankees. So was Kale, who was usually there to back Mickey up.

Where was Kale anyway? Felt like he hadn't been around.

Mickey sipped his coffee and decided not to ask. He had the feeling he'd already been told.

Sleeping long and hard had never been a problem, though in recent years he was prone to waking during the night to go to the toilet. If it hadn't been for Mother Nature's late-night call, Mickey wouldn't have heard movement and voices down in the kitchen. From his angle at the top of the back stairs he could glimpse the lower half of Sunday sitting at the table, tapping away at a laptop. Jackie was taking the seat across from her. Mickey was tempted to join them, but didn't want to intrude. Besides, once those two got going about books and art he was lost anyway.

"You working on the ledger?" Jackie asked. "Denny's a bag of dicks for making you clean up his mess."

"No, it's okay," Sunday said. "I want to help, but I don't know how much I can do. It's like deciphering the Da Vinci Code. He kept track of almost nothing the last few months. And at some point a bunch of cash floated in and out of the account." She lowered her voice. "Do you think he's running up credit card debt?"

"No way," Jackie said. "He wouldn't do that. And Theresa and Kale would never go for it."

"You're probably right."

Mickey agreed. He'd raised his kids to know better than to spend money they didn't have. Looking down through the white wooden railing he saw Jackie's leg start bouncing under the table.

"Can I ask you something?" he asked. "The night you had your accident . . . Was it because of the email I sent you that day?"

"No," she said. "I was just out for a friend's birthday and had too much."

"Really? Because slamming drinks and getting behind the wheel doesn't sound like you. It's straight-up stupid."

"Kind of like getting busted with a giant bag of someone else's weed?"

At least Maura hadn't lived to see two of their children in trouble with the law.

Mickey sought out one of his favorite photos that hung among the many lining the stairway. It was of all the kids, standing oldest to youngest, ranging in age from Denny at eleven years old to Shane at six. Similar chestnut hair, bright eyes, and freckled cheeks, each a head taller than the one to their left. They had their arms about each other and wore wide smiles. Sunday and Jackie stood together in the middle. As two kids sandwiched between a can-do-no-wrong older brother and a disabled younger one, they had often seemed attuned to each other's state of mind.

"While you were in LA," Jackie said below, "did you ever talk to anyone about that night?"

Mickey expected "Which night?" But there was no response. He had to lean down to hear Jackie's next words.

"It's just I've read a lot about, you know, trauma. And you should talk—"

"Don't." Sunday didn't sound like herself. So sharp and final. But . . . *trauma*. What the hell was Jackie on about?

"It wasn't your fault, Sunday."

"Stop it."

"I just want to help."

She shut her laptop. "I don't need your help. I'm going to bed." The legs of her chair scraped across the floor as she stood.

Mickey was about to get caught eavesdropping. He ducked back into his room, quietly shut the door behind him. A few minutes later Jackie and Sunday shuffled past in the hallway, mumbling good night to each other.

When he was sure they were tucked away in their rooms Mickey got out of bed and went to his closet. He crouched down and peeled back the carpet from the far corner of the closet floor. Then he wedged a shoehorn between two floorboards and lifted one, revealing the little compartment that had always been a hiding place for him. He grabbed the spiral notebook and pencil from among the items he kept there, flipped to a clean page, and jotted a note: *S + J hiding old secret.*

Till recently he'd fought his doctor's suggestion to write down things he didn't want to forget, determined not to become reliant upon notes like some feeble old fart. But this was too important to take the risk.

One way to keep Sunday from leaving again was to find out why she left in the first place.

"Do you think the Yankees will win tonight, Dad?" Shane asked.

"I sure as hell hope so. They're overdue."

They were set up with ham-and-cheese subs on TV tables in the liv-

ing room, a tradition on the nights the Yankees were playing and Shane
was off work. It was the first evening they weren't eating as a family since
Sunday had come home.

"Where is everyone, Shane?"

He responded without taking his eyes off the game. "Jackie's working
late. Denny drove Molly to Theresa. Sunday went to the pub to do some
work."

Each one of his children was special, but there was something very
peaceful about Shane. His youngest son was uncomplicated, eager
to please, never in a rush or frustrated with his dad's memory slips. Of
course, Shane had never graduated to that phase when children realize their
parents are vastly imperfect beings.

When he'd taken longer to meet certain developmental milestones,
such as walking and talking, they hadn't worried much. Maura had delivered four babies in six years. By the last one they well knew each
developed at their own pace. When Shane continued to have trouble
communicating—not responding when they called him, garbled speech,
talking too loudly—they had him evaluated. Initially he was diagnosed
with a hearing deficiency. But even before he started preschool they began to wonder, and it was confirmed when his peers surpassed him in the
learning environment. The specialists diagnosed a mild form of mental
retardation, nowadays called an intellectual disability.

"My God, Mickey," Maura had said. "What will his life be like? We
won't always be around to take care of him. And I see how people look
at us now. Everybody knows." There had been panic in her wide eyes, a
mother worried her boy would face alienation throughout his life. But
also the panic of people knowing their business. By then Maura believed
she'd brought this on herself by daring to have a baby at forty-two years
old, which just wasn't proper. She came from a backwater town in Done-
gal, born into a frosty, highly judgmental lot who believed in the literal
letter of Catholic law. She'd watched her parents forever shun her older
sister for marrying a divorced man, never even knowing their own grand-
children. They'd taught Maura to hide weaknesses and flaws. But there
was no hiding Shane or his disability from the eyes of the world.

He'd put his hands on her narrow shoulders. "Shane has brothers and a sister that love him. We'll all help him to live a full life. And when you and I are gone, they'll always watch over him."

He couldn't have spoken truer words. After his children learned about Shane's disability they closed ranks, each of them taking on different roles with him. Denny, his protector, using his fists to punish any miscreant who dared look sideways at his youngest brother. He had Shane manage equipment for the soccer team, and found him jobs later on. Sunday told him stories and helped with his schoolwork, talked him through bouts of anxiety. Jackie built LEGOs with him, and took him on long walks. And it was Kale who introduced model cars to Shane and kept him in a steady supply.

Mickey had taken pleasure in bringing Shane to his worksites, where he'd been fascinated by the massive equipment. Tragically, though, Maura had never seemed to find her way with Shane. She often looked at him with a mix of distaste and fear, as if his booming voice and uneven gait were a reproach from the Lord Himself. She had no patience for helping Shane learn tasks or play a game. His exuberant demonstrations of affection, the powerful hugs and proclamations of love, turned her stiff as a board. The whole family was grateful when mother and son found one shared activity—Shane helped with Maura's roses. It required little conversation since he had a natural aptitude for it, and they could work alongside each other but focus on the ground beneath them.

When Maura died twenty years after Shane's diagnosis, she at least went assured that her youngest was well looked after. Mickey didn't know if Heaven existed, only that if it did his entrance through the pearly gates was far from guaranteed. If he got the chance to make his case to St. Peter for overlooking his many transgressions, he'd point down to his children and say, "I must have done something right."

When the phone rang, Shane was deep in his sub, crumbs and juices spilling over his hands, onto his tray. Mickey got up to answer it.

"Mr. B? It's Kale. We just got back. How's everything with the Brennans?"

On the TV, Boston scored a hit. "We're all good here," Mickey said. "Shane and I are just watching the game."

"I won't keep you. I was hoping to catch up with Denny. His cell went to voicemail. Is he still at the pub?"

Mickey looked around the living room, into the kitchen. Damn it, when had he last seen Denny. "Let me think . . ."

"Oh boy, Boston has the bases loaded, Dad."

"Ah, Jesus. That's not a good start."

"What was that?" Kale asked.

"Sorry, Kale. I was talking to Shane." Mickey couldn't recall seeing Denny for a while. "Denny must still be at work."

"I'll catch him at the pub."

Mickey hung up and sat back down. It wasn't until Denny got home from Theresa's a few minutes later that he realized his mistake.

CHAPTER FIVE

Kale

I'll catch him at the pub."

That's what he'd been hoping to hear, that Denny was still at work. Kale hadn't talked to him in twelve days other than a brief text conversation about Theresa and Molly going to stay with Theresa's sister. Kale had known things were tense between Denny and Theresa, with the ongoing problems at the new location and Mickey's recent accident in the garage. And Theresa was fed up waiting for Denny to be ready to have another baby. But their separation had been a shock.

He slid his cell into his jacket pocket as he pulled into their driveway, and he and Vivienne both breathed a massive sigh of relief. An hour's drive to the airport in Dublin, followed by a six-hour flight, was enough to make anyone wish for the day to be done. Never mind that he'd had to sit apart from his wife and son on the plane, beside a large, loud woman who snored like a freight train. There'd been another hour waiting in line to deal with a lost suitcase. All this on top of a big send-off the night before. He had imbibed more alcohol in the last two weeks than in the previous two years. At least it seemed that way. Denny would probably call bullshit on that.

"Thank God," Vivienne said, climbing out of the passenger seat, stretching, and scraping fingers through her long blond hair. She opened the back door and checked on Luke, who was dead asleep. "Now he's out. We could have used some of that on the plane."

Kale smiled at his three-year-old in the rear. Luke's head tilted sideways against the car seat and his mouth hung open in a perfect O. He'd inherited Kale's dark curls, but the bottomless blue eyes were all Viv. Luke never stirred while Kale reached in and pulled him close, carried him into the house and up to his room, removed his shoes, jacket, and pants. Next he collected the bags from the car—the ones that had made it to New York—while Vivienne moved through the house flipping on lights and turning up the thermostat.

"Want a cup of tea?" she asked when he came back downstairs. She removed her trench coat and hung it on the hooks by the door, winced as she slid off her shoes. For some reason she refused to leave the house in anything other than heels.

He left his jacket on and checked his watch. "I was going to catch up with Denny."

"Imagine that," she said. "Twelve whole days without Denny and the Brennans."

His nerves bristled a bit. "I just want to find out where we are with the new place."

She nodded in understanding; she knew he was worried about it. "Okay. I hope it's good news."

"Me too." He leaned forward to give her a peck on the cheek. "I'll try to make it quick."

He escaped out into the cool night air, got back in the driver's seat, but didn't start the car right away. Viv had been great about the trip, making all the travel arrangements and then spending almost two weeks around a big family she didn't know and couldn't understand half the time. She tried to ingratiate herself to his aunts and cousins, listened to countless stories. Though she'd pleaded with him to pay the cost to come home two days early.

Through the living room window he watched her climb the stairs to their bedroom at the rear of the little Dutch Colonial house. First on her wish list for their next place, which she'd been talking about more and more lately, was a main-floor master suite. And an open-concept design. Stainless appliances and quartz countertops. She had a long wish list.

He could go back inside, wait till tomorrow to catch up with Denny. But her sarcasm about being away from the Brennans had irked him. He started the car and headed for the pub.

It took less than five minutes to drive into town; he usually walked. Brennan's was closed this time on a Monday night, so Denny was probably working on their ledger, trying to get it in some kind of order. God help them if they didn't find another bookkeeper soon. They ran a great bar and restaurant, but they had no business doing their own books.

Saw Mill Road was almost empty so he parked in front of the pub rather than pulling behind into the parking lot. He pulled open the door, inhaling the smell of polished wood and quality beer.

"Denny?" It was fairly dark, but a lamp was on in the small office behind the bar. "I'm glad you're still here. Let me get a beer." He poured a Guinness just the right way—forty-five-degree angle, pausing at three-quarters full to let the surge settle. After taking a deep draw of the creamy beer, he took off his jacket and laid it on a stool. "That was a *loooong* trip. It was good to see everyone, but I am family'd out." He headed down the length of the bar and turned in to the office. "What's the word on Mamaroneck—"

He felt himself, at a cellular level, freeze. Standing before him, a kaleidoscope of purplish-yellow bruises covering her face, was Sunday. She stood by the desk, wide-eyed and stiff.

"Jesus Christ," he said.

She offered a lopsided smile. "Nope. Hi, Kale."

When her voice confirmed she was really there, some chemical flooded his brain and propelled pure excitement through his entire body, fingertips to toes. The urge to reach out and touch her was so powerful he took a small step forward before catching himself, causing his beer to slosh over the edge of the glass. He reached over to place it on a file cabinet.

"I didn't know you were in town," he said. All he could do was stare. It had been almost five years. Her wavy hair was shorter, ended at her shoulders. She wore an oversized T-shirt with colorful paint stains that had to belong to Jackie. But her face . . .

"It was kind of last minute," she said. "Denny didn't think you were back for a couple more days."

Which is why he hadn't received a heads-up yet, no doubt. "I came back early." He nodded toward her. "What happened?"

"I was in a car accident. But I'm fine." She waved a dismissive arm and he noticed the other one, a bulky black cast hanging by her side. Black. How very Sunday.

"How are you?" she asked. "How's your family?"

His family. Vivienne and Luke. For a moment they'd ceased to exist for him. "Good, they're good. We all are." He glanced at the desk, which was covered in paperwork. "How long are you here for?" He sounded awfully calm for being so spectacularly blindsided.

"I'm not sure. I needed a break from LA, and it sounded like Denny could use some help." There were pinkish pools of blood in the whites of her eyes, which glowed against the dark blotches.

He made himself look away. "There's no arguing with that."

"I thought I'd come back for a while and see what I could do . . ." She seemed to be gauging his reaction.

What did "a while" mean? My God. Had she moved back home? "Well," he said, "you might want to start with the books, before Denny and I end up in jail or the poorhouse." What the hell was he saying? He ran a hand through his hair and tugged on it a bit, a way of pinching himself.

But then she laughed that laugh he knew so well, low and soft, a little throaty. She gestured toward the desk. "I already started digging into some of it."

There was nothing else to say without veering into dangerous waters. All the safe small talk was used up.

"Listen, Kale, I know this is awkward, and I'm sorry for . . . For so many things." Her voice wobbled at the end.

Warning bells went off in his head. This conversation—this whole situation—was full of land mines. He felt shaky, light-headed. Untethered to reality. And he couldn't trust himself right then. "We don't need to do that," he said, holding his hands up. "I'm glad you're here to help out. Denny's needed it for a long time." He hadn't meant it as an accusation—or maybe he had a little—but she glanced down. "We'll see each other around, so let's just move on." He gave the next seven words some heft. "There's no need to revisit the past."

She nodded. "Right. Okay."

But he couldn't pull his eyes away from her face. It wasn't just the bruises. Underneath those he saw the lively eyes that hinted at her curious mind and dry sense of humor. She was just a little beat up. From an accident, and maybe from whatever life she'd been living the last five years. A life he knew nothing about. "I'm going to take off," he said. "Tell Denny I'll catch him in the morning."

"I will."

It was time for him to go, but he wanted to stay, talk to her more. Sunday had ripped out his heart, but she'd also been the most important person in the world for a long time. And, for the moment, he was uplifted. The sheer relief at seeing her again transcended everything else.

Without letting himself second-guess it, he stepped forward and hugged her, wrapping his arms around her shoulders with a delicate touch. "Welcome home, Sunday." He felt her tense up for the briefest second before her good hand slid up his back.

"Thank you," she said into his shoulder.

He pulled away and said, "Good night," which was all he could manage through an acute ache in his throat. He left and was almost to the end of the bar when he turned back to get his beer. He stopped at the office door.

She was sitting at the desk, head in her hand. It looked like she might be crying. His first instinct was to walk back in there and make sure she was okay. But he didn't feel in control of his own emotions, and Vivienne and Luke were tugging at his conscience now. He walked away, grabbed his jacket, and went out to his car.

He'd known the day would come when they would have to face each other, make conversation. At least it was over. But now a barrage of questions were elbowing their way to the surface, ones that had haunted him for a long time after she left.

He stuffed them back down deep and headed home to his family. None of those questions, nor the answers she might offer, mattered anymore.

The next morning, after Vivienne and Luke left the house, he took an unusual route to work.

Since birth he'd lived four blocks from the Brennans, except for the few years he shared a dorm room and then a small apartment with Denny. His house was farther from downtown, where the homes were still classic but a little smaller. His normal route to the pub took him past the Brennan house where, most mornings, he stopped in to wait for Denny. He'd sip coffee with Mickey and talk about how the Yankees were looking, climb up to Shane's room on the third floor to check out the latest LEGO build, chat with Jackie if he was home. And, without fail, if Molly was around she'd sit Kale down and demand a card trick. He'd shown her the only two he knew last year, simple sleights of hand, and she made him do them over and over. After that he purchased a *101 Card Tricks for Beginners* book he found online.

But he wasn't up for seeing Sunday again yet, so that morning he bypassed Poplar Street altogether.

He'd slept little the night before, just tossed and turned, his gut doing gymnastics. Twenty-four hours ago he'd been looking forward to getting back to the calm of home. But it was all upended last night, the instant he laid eyes on her.

When he got to the pub Denny was already there, a sheepish look on his face. "Sorry, man." He poured two cups of fresh coffee and slid one across the bar. "I was waiting to tell you until you got home so you didn't worry about it on the trip."

"Yeah. Thanks for that." Kale pulled off his jacket and dropped onto a stool. "So what happened?"

Denny leaned forward on the bar. "She was drunk and got into an accident."

"Jesus." The Sunday he'd known never would have done such a thing.

"I went out there to check on her. But then I asked her to come home."

"Is she back permanently?"

"I hope so." Denny straightened up and crossed his arms. "I get how weird it must be for you. But it's good to have her back. Dad and Jackie are all smiles lately. You should see Shane—he won't leave her side except to go to work. And she's finally getting to know Molly."

So much had gone on lately in the Brennan family and, somehow, Sunday had been in the middle of it and Kale had missed it. Almost like she'd usurped his place. Which was silly. They were her family. "Is she really working on the ledger?" he asked.

"She's just helping out until I find another bookkeeper." Denny shrugged. "You know she'll do a good job."

Kale nodded but he wasn't sure how to feel about it. It would bring her into the pub, necessitate them working together. The thought of which caused an involuntary rush. Which, in turn, caused panic.

"Did you tell Viv?" Denny asked.

"Not yet, but I'm looking forward to it."

"She has nothing to worry about. That was a long time ago."

Somehow it didn't seem that simple. Kale already felt like he'd done something wrong. He felt guilty about his reaction to seeing Sunday again, and the fact that he thought about her all night. Not to mention he hadn't told Vivienne she was back yet because he wanted time first to process it himself.

He took a deep breath and tried not to sound pessimistic when he said, "Tell me where we are with Mamaroneck."

"Wait here. I got something to show you." Denny headed back to the office. Maybe a delay tactic. They'd been like brothers for twenty-five years and this subject had the potential to rattle their friendship if they didn't tread lightly.

The new location had been Denny's idea. He'd driven that bus from

the start and run roughshod over any concerns Kale brought up. Mamaroneck was too expensive and the building needed to be refurbished,
but Denny had an answer for everything: *This will open up a whole new
clientele. The place will be inspected before we sign off—I know a guy. Have
I steered us wrong yet?*

So they put 20 percent down on the new location—which meant
taking out a loan on his and Vivienne's paid-off house—and obtained
a large mortgage for the rest. Then they put the remainder of their cash
toward a total renovation. Which was just shy of completion when the
city informed them they had a massive leak under the building. Over six
months later, the second location still hadn't opened. The financed project sat on the mortgaged land, collecting dust and bills.

Denny came out of the office and laid a page from a newspaper down
on the bar in front of Kale. It was a large ad announcing the grand opening of Brennan's Mamaroneck location next month, complete with a copy
of their menu and the promise of a dozen beers on tap.

Kale looked up at Denny. "Seriously?"

"The city inspector comes in two weeks to confirm the foundation issue is resolved. I hired some staff, gave them their start date." Denny
turned his hands up. "I told you I had it under control."

Denny had taken out an ad and hired staff, betting on a successful inspection. Which they'd failed twice now. "We don't know that it will pass
inspection," Kale said. "And even if it does, we still have a lot of prep to
do out there."

"I'm going out this week to walk the site, make sure it's ready. They're
going to approve."

As his father used to say about Denny, in a not entirely disapproving
tone, "That one could talk you into cutting off your own hand and make
you think it was your idea." This was what Denny did—act now, apolo-
gize later. He'd done it when he signed the first offer on the new property
even though the price was too high. When he hired Paul without talking to
Kale first. Even way back, when he accepted a gun Mickey bought them
to keep behind the bar for protection, despite Kale's protests. Denny was
always sure he knew best.

"Look, Kale, I figured you had enough on your plate. I got us into this mess, I'll get us out."

While he was in Ireland Kale had decided to stop being the naysayer when it came to the new place. There was no point, they were stuck with it now. He just wanted to problem-solve and avoid further strain on their partnership. He wouldn't be a business owner and have a job he loved most days if it wasn't for Denny. Maybe he should be grateful he was shielded from some of the nitty-gritty.

"Okay." Kale sipped his coffee.

Denny's eyebrows pulled up. "That's it?"

"Yep."

"You're not gonna say 'I told you so' again?"

"Nope."

"Good. But it comes off you in waves anyway."

"Oh," Vivienne said.

"Yeah, I just found out."

It was later that night. Luke had gone up to get ready for his bath and they were finishing dinner.

"When did she get back?" Vivienne asked.

"Like a week ago I guess."

"And she's staying here?"

"I don't know. I didn't get details. Sounds like she came back to help Denny and the family for a while."

"Mm-hmm."

"Anyway, you'll see her around so I thought I'd mention it." He offered an easy-breezy shrug and started taking dishes to the sink.

She was quiet as he loaded the dishwasher. The air in the room seemed to get heavier while he worked.

When he was done he turned to her. "Viv, that was over a long time ago."

Her smile was weak.

"I should get Luke's bath going." He started for the stairs.

"Did you see her?"

"We ran into each other at the pub. Took us both by surprise."

She sat very still, hands in her lap. "When?"

"Last night. I didn't mention it because you were about asleep when I got home."

"Do I have anything to worry about?"

He walked over and took her hand, pulled her up, and put his arms around her waist. "No, you don't. You're my wife, and we're a family."

Her big blue eyes probed his. "I know. But you were with her a long time."

"That was five years ago. I have no idea what she's been doing all this time. For all I know, she's got a boyfriend."

She gave him a skeptical look.

"Or a girlfriend."

"I doubt that." But she smiled.

"Who knows. It just doesn't matter." Although he'd spent the better part of the day wondering about those things.

"Daddy?" Luke appeared on the staircase. He wore no clothes and carried a plastic shark. "Come up. It's baff time."

"Ba*th* time," Vivienne said.

"Coming, naked guy," Kale said. He turned back to Viv. "Are we good?"

"We're good."

He headed up with Luke. It would take a little more of that before she could rest easy, and he would be happy to do it. She didn't deserve to lose sleep just because Sunday decided to come back. Vivienne was a beautiful wife and a good mother, and he'd made a vow to her.

And she would never hurt him the way Sunday had.

He managed not to see Sunday again for four days, spending much of that time swatting away memories and rationalizing. Her return was no big deal. He was a husband and father now. He'd built a new life. As long as he maintained some distance, he would be fine.

It was after the lunch rush and before the happy hour throng, when he and Denny usually sat in a corner booth to debrief, plan for dinner, fine-tune their ordering process. Kale dreaded some of the changes that would come with the new pub, including losing this quiet time of the day. More staff and customers would mean more work and problems. Inevitably he and Denny would often end up in separate locations and this daily meeting would go by the wayside. And he wouldn't always be able to walk to work, which meant he and Vivienne would need to buy a second car. Kale would have been content to stick with one location and the level of income it afforded. But he'd been outvoted by his partner and his wife, both of whom had bigger goals.

Sunday and Mickey came into the pub while they were finishing up. Despite his self-talk about no big deal, his whole body tensed up while they all exchanged hellos. He needed to get past this involuntary reaction to seeing her. In the daylight she looked even more wounded, her skin pale against the dark bruises and black cast.

Mickey went behind the bar to start his shift, whistled while he turned on the TV and searched for an early game.

Sunday pulled a spiral notebook out of the laptop bag she was carrying and flipped it open. "You guys are up to date on the mortgage on the new place, right?"

"We should be," Kale said, looking at Denny. He was the one paying the bills the last few months.

Without even glancing up from his paperwork Denny said, "Yeah. Of course."

"I figured," Sunday said, biting the tip of a pen. A habit she'd had as long as he'd known her. He used to come across mutilated pens all the time and tease her about it—*What did this pen ever do to you?* "But a delinquency note popped up on the account," she said, "and I can't find the check number. I'll just call them."

"You don't need to," Denny said. "Ignore the note. The payment was a few days late, but it's taken care of."

"Are you sure about that?" Kale asked.

"Yeah. I was busy last week, remember?" Denny tossed his head toward Sunday. "The check's in the mail."

"Which is it?" Sunday asked. "'Taken care of' or 'in the mail'?"

"I *took care of it* by putting a check *in the mail*."

"Sounds like some famous Denny last words," she said.

Kale laughed. "No shit."

"Oh yeah?" Denny looked back and forth between them. "Just like old times, huh?" His tone was provoking, daring them to fall back into the familiar.

How easily it had happened. Kale had slipped right past his vow to stay aloof and taken his old place at her side. Denny used to complain that he never had a fair chance because it was always two against one.

Sunday cleared her throat. "I just came in to get some stuff from the back so I can work on the ledger at home." She turned and walked back to the office.

Denny checked his watch. "I gotta go."

"Hold up." Kale lowered his voice. "You're absolutely sure about opening next month?"

"Yeah, man. I told you. Why?"

"Just trying to plan." If it opened next month, according to their projections they would be caught up and edging toward the black by the end of the year.

"Plan away," Denny said, heading for the door. "We're opening next month. Bank on it."

Maybe it was time to tell Vivienne they could start thinking about a new house. She could probably use a little reassurance right now.

Frankly, so could he.

CHAPTER SIX

Denny

W e're opening next month. Bank on it."

It had to open next month. Everything Denny had in the world depended on it.

He hopped in his Jeep and headed south on the Taconic State Parkway to meet Billy Walsh at the new location. Mamaroneck was twenty miles south, located on the Long Island Sound. It had miles of coastline, triple the population, and a younger, more diverse demographic. Denny and Kale had maxed out their growth in West Manor. Mamaroneck was a town with growing industries of its own—health care, manufacturing, tech—that could take them to the next level, a proper restaurant that would support a couple dozen service jobs and up their profit margin substantially. They just had to make it to opening day.

But that meant Billy had to give Denny one more month's grace. If not, it would require drastic measures. Kale could pull together some money, but that would mean telling him everything. It might also mean the end of their friendship, let alone partnership. Because Kale never would have agreed to a hard money loan secured by using the West Manor property as collateral.

Denny pulled onto Mamaroneck Avenue, which wandered through a thriving medical corridor before heading toward the water. Once he reached the vibrant downtown, he parked in one of the diagonal spaces in front of the new Brennan's. Just laying eyes on it settled his nerves a bit. Hopefully it would ease any concerns Billy might be having too.

It was almost double the size of their first pub and sat in the middle of a busy thoroughfare lined with upscale restaurants and shops. A couple blocks away Harbor Island Park was surrounded by the waters of the East and West Basins, which were full of boaters in the summer months. The emerald exterior popped against the neighboring businesses, an antiques shop on one side and an old-school creamery on the other. There were striped awnings over the large plate glass windows, and rich wood letters spelled the Gaelic name above the door. No one would have guessed there'd recently been a raging leak underneath that threatened the building.

When he unlocked the front doors and stepped inside, there it all was: polished maple floors, bronze fixtures, leather booths. And smack in the middle, a large square bar and cocktail area. All of it just waiting for paying customers.

He headed back through the brand-new stainless kitchen and down into the basement, where, six months ago, during what was supposed to be a final inspection, the city assessors discovered the water main had been leaking long enough to compromise the foundation.

That's when he had started to panic. The last two years had been a continuous money suck, starting with the expensive lawyer who kept Jackie out of jail. No one knew about the home equity loan Denny had taken out to pay for her. Not even his father, who still owned the house and thought he was signing insurance paperwork. Why worry everyone; he planned to pay it off within months. But there'd been other expenses that quickly maxed out the line of credit—his share of the second location, Shane's new hearing aids, the late property tax bills and fines because his father had neglected to pay them for two years. Just to stay afloat Denny had "borrowed" from the business account without Kale's knowledge. He'd dug a deep financial hole, banking on the grand opening to start replenishing the funds.

He went back upstairs and took a peek out the back door. They'd had to jackhammer a wide swath of asphalt and bulldoze tons of dirt to replace the pipe and shore up the foundation, but now fresh white lines were painted on the smooth parking lot in the rear. Once the sun set a security guard would station himself there for the night. That was costly, and maybe paranoid. But his dad, who'd been in the construction business for forty years, had inspected the damage and firmly believed it was vandalism, maybe caused by competitors or bored kids. Denny wasn't taking any chances when they were this close. He went back inside to wait for Billy.

With no money to repair the damage, he had put the word out that he was looking for a quick unconventional loan from a source that would keep it quiet. He'd been doubtful when a member of the reno crew had made an offer, questioned how a laborer would have that kind of cash sitting around. But he'd apparently just sold his mother's house and didn't know what to do with the money. And it was a bonus that Denny knew the guy. Sort of.

Everyone had called him Belfast Billy when they were kids, a nickname based on his strong Northern Irish accent, the one that made everything sound like a question. Billy and his family had moved to West Manor from Ireland—or more specifically, according to Denny's mother, "the slums of Belfast"—when they were all in elementary school. Denny and Billy had been on the same soccer team a few times when they were young, and Billy's dad had worked for Denny's dad for years. But the two families had traveled in different social circles, particularly since Billy's dad was a raging alky who eventually drank himself to death.

Billy had been known for poor grades, smart-ass remarks, and frequent absences, but Denny remembered him being fairly wily too, often getting out of trouble with a smile and a slick story. And plenty of girls had been drawn to the aw-shucks bad-boy image and the lyrical lilt to his voice. There'd been talk of an arrest just after graduation, for domestic violence—some drunken fight with a girlfriend—but it might have just been a rumor. At some point Billy had returned to Ireland for a while. He'd only been back in the States a few months when he offered Denny the loan.

He turned at the knock on the door to see Billy standing there and waved him in. He was hard to miss in a crowd. He had Jackie's lean, muscly build, with thick hair somewhere between ginger and blond that swept across his forehead. And he always wore tight jeans, tighter T-shirts, and biker boots.

They sat at a table and Denny looked across at his . . . what—silent partner? "How's it going, Billy?"

He shrugged a shoulder. "Can't complain."

"You still living up in Katonah?"

"Yeah. The bloody boonies." He rolled his eyes. "My aunt needs a bit of help around the place."

"I get it. Family."

Billy hunched over the table and looked around the restaurant. "Place is looking good." He hadn't seen it furnished and decorated yet. The reno crew had finished at the site weeks ago. He pointed behind the bar. "You've any inventory back there yet? I could do with a beer."

"Sorry. Can't stock the place till we're approved."

He nodded in understanding.

It was a backward arrangement, accepting a loan from a laborer in his employ. But that had also been a little insurance. It would be in Billy's best interest that the pub get up and running.

Denny set his hands on his thighs. "Seriously, man, I can't thank you enough for your patience with all this."

"No worries. Fuck those inspectors."

"Yeah, maybe I should have listened to my dad, taken them out for beers and slipped them a few dollars."

Billy grinned and cocked an eyebrow. "Is that how he did it back in the day?"

"So he says. But he likes to tell tales."

"Don't all Irish fathers."

Denny laughed. "So, I just wanted to tell you in person. The inspectors will be signing off in two weeks. We open next month."

Billy pointed at Denny. "That there is good news."

Time to test the waters. "I know I missed three payments and you've been understanding. You know better than anyone it just took longer than expected to repair the foundation issue."

"Strange, that. Every time we thought we had the damage fixed, there turned out to be more." Billy tossed a hand. "Goes to show. You never know with old construction, like."

Denny lowered his voice even though no one else was there. "You got a look at the damage. Did it seem to you like old pipes really caused all that? My dad thinks someone made it happen."

Billy blinked in surprise. "He said that?" He thought for a moment, then shook his head. "Dunno. I was there when we dug it all up. Can't say I saw any sign of foul play."

Denny had heard that several times now. Maybe his dad was just wrong.

"You need more time, I take it?" Billy asked.

"One more month would do it. New pub opens, some capital starts rolling in." He waved toward Billy. "I start paying interest again. Within two months I'll be working on the principal. Worst-case scenario, you walk away with your sixty grand, plus at least twenty-five percent by the end of the year."

Billy seemed to study Denny for a moment. Then he smiled wide. "Sounds good to me."

Now would be the time to specifically mention the three-month default clause, the one that gave Billy the option to put a lien on the pub in West Manor. Denny would have liked reassurance that Billy had no intention of invoking it.

But then Billy reached across and clapped Denny on the shoulder. "No worries, mate. Just make sure to invite me to opening night, yeah?"

This guy had no intention of taking legal action, there was no reason to even bring it up. He probably hadn't even read the damn contract. All he wanted was to make some money and be part of the action, get some free beers for a while. "Of course, man," Denny said. "You're at the top of the guest list."

Billy laughed and pounded the table with his hand, the fingernails chewed to painful-looking nubs.

"So you're good with all this?" Denny asked.

"Sure if I can't help out a fellow Irishman with my money, what good is it? Besides"—he hoisted his shoulders up—"amn't I making a pile of money on this venture?"

They talked for a few more minutes, and when they finished up and Denny saw Billy out, it was with the reassurance he needed.

When Denny walked into the pub a few mornings later to find Kale's family there, his first thought was to text Sunday. She wasn't far behind him, and he could give her a heads-up. But he decided against it. They'd all managed to avoid this uncomfortable meeting for the last week, but the Band-Aid had to be ripped off at some point.

Vivienne was sitting in a booth flipping through a magazine, and Luke was up at the bar spinning slowly on a stool. Denny could hear Kale talking on the phone in the office.

He gave Luke a quick tickle. "What's this? A minor up at the bar?"

"Uncle Denny," Luke said, "is Molly wiff you?"

"With," Vivienne called over.

"Sorry, small fry," Denny said. "She's at school." He lifted a tray of clean mugs onto the bar. "Okay, buddy. You slide the mugs down to me and I'll load them in the cooler."

Vivienne watched them for a moment before going back to the magazine, her bracelets bangling against the table as she turned pages.

When Kale first started seeing Vivienne, it had been a relief. Six months after Sunday left Kale was still steeped in depression and looking for relief at the bottom of a bottle. When he began hanging out with someone, Denny thought it was a step toward recovery, not the fast track to marriage and a kid. He had always harbored a strong suspicion that the unplanned pregnancy may not have been so unplanned.

He and the family had accepted Vivienne the best they could, but there was no way around it: Kale had married outside the tribe. No doubt she was hot. Long blond hair and pouty lips, great body—Kale wouldn't confirm she'd had a boob job, though he wouldn't deny it either. But there was a touch of cheap that her uptight posture and knockoff designer clothing couldn't hide. And when she was around, the atmosphere was slightly disturbed. His dad and Jackie never went beyond polite conversation with her. Theresa tried, but they had little in common. Vivienne never got their jokes and hers fell flat. It was a lost cause really, because none of them ever forgave her for being so uncomfortable around Shane from day one.

As soon as Sunday walked in the front door Denny doubted his decision not to forewarn her. She was still looking pretty ragtag, her face a dark patchwork of magenta and yellow. She wore a black laptop bag strapped across her body, and a baseball cap. Tired of gawkers, she'd taken to wearing one of Shane's Yankees hats in public. Initially she headed toward the office, but then she glanced about and stopped in her tracks. Denny understood why. She had spotted the spitting image of Kale sitting up at the bar.

She stared at Luke for a long moment before turning to the booth where Vivienne sat, and Denny kicked himself once more. His sister stood frozen in the middle of the room, looking like she wanted nothing more than to turn and run back out the door.

He walked around the bar to make introductions. "Sunday, this is Kale's wife, Vivienne."

A cloud of distress passed over her face before she regained some composure and walked over to the booth with an uncertain smile. "It's nice to meet you."

Vivienne slid out to shake hands, her eyes touching on Sunday's injuries. "You too. Welcome back."

"Thank you." Even in the shadow of her hat, Denny could see a subtle startled expression on his sister's face as she really looked at Vivienne.

Kale came out from the office and stopped next to Denny to watch with wide eyes.

"Sorry to hear about your accident," Vivienne said. She winced and tilted her head. "Looks like it was pretty bad."

"Yeah." Sunday touched the brim of her cap. "I'm afraid this isn't very effective."

Vivienne shrugged. "Some quality makeup would help cover it up."

Sunday pressed her lips together and nodded. "I should look into that."

The contrasts were striking. Vivienne's silky hair and clear skin to Sunday's cap and beat-up face, the clingy dress and tall boots to the baggy T-shirt—that fit over the cast—and slip-on sneakers. Denny had the sudden urge to move his sister away from Vivienne. "This is Luke," he said, waving an arm toward the bar.

"So you're Luke," Sunday said, stepping away from Vivienne. "Molly told me all about you. I'm her aunt Sunday."

Luke stared at her face and arm. "What happened to you?"

"Luke!" Vivienne said.

"That's okay." Sunday stood next to him and her eyes roamed over Luke's face like she was trying to soak up every inch. "I was in a pretty bad car accident, but I'll be all better soon."

"Did Molly draw that?" he asked, pointing to a glowing orange flower on her cast.

"Yep. She used her uncle Jackie's paint." She laid her arm on the bar in front of him. "This is her ladybug too, and that caterpillar."

Luke started tracing them with a finger, his head leaning toward Sunday's.

Something was just wrong with this picture. Denny looked away, which is when he noticed Vivienne staring hard at Kale.

Kale was wholly absorbed by Sunday and Luke.

"Does it hurt?" Luke asked her.

She grinned. "Only when I look in the mirror."

He put a finger in his mouth and giggled.

Vivienne pulled her bag from the booth and walked past Sunday to pick Luke up from the stool. She placed him on the floor and took his hand. "We should get going. Ready, Kale?"

He nodded.

"It was nice to meet you, Sunday," Vivienne said.

"You too. Bye, Luke."

His little splayed hand waved as Vivienne led him to the door. Kale followed them out without looking back.

Denny rested his hands on his hips. "Well, that wasn't awkward or anything."

Sunday slumped on the stool Luke had occupied and put her hand on the edge of the bar like she needed to hang on to something. She'd made her own bed, but his heart went out to her. He walked behind the bar.

"The little boy," she said. "He looks . . ." She stopped and swallowed.

"Yep." He reached down for the bottle of Jameson and a couple short glasses.

"She's gorgeous."

"Yep." He poured two small whiskies.

She looked over her shoulder, out the front window, to the little family loading up in the Honda. "She seems nice."

"She's okay." He stood the bottle on the bar. "But she doesn't hold a candle."

She blinked against watery eyes and gave him a sad smile.

He picked up one of the glasses and held it up to her.

After a brief hesitation she picked up the other one, tapped it against his, and allowed herself the first taste of alcohol since her accident.

"Daddy?"

"Yeah, Molls?"

"When are you gonna pull your head out?"

He stalled at the stop sign and looked at her in the rearview mirror. *"What?"*

She was staring out her window. "I asked Aunt Angie when Mommy and me are going back home, and she said when your daddy pulls his head out."

Nice. His sister-in-law had always been a real ballbuster.

"What does she mean, Daddy?"

He drove on. "Nothing, baby. Don't listen to Angie." He would have to talk to Theresa about that.

"Don't forget to pick me up after school because Mommy works late."

"Are you kidding? I would never forget that."

"I told Sunday I would play dollhouse, and Shane said I could help with his LEGOs. But you have to take me back before bed so Mommy's not alone. I don't want her to be sad."

Denny pulled into a parking space in front of the school and turned to face Molly.

Her little brow was wrinkled and the corners of her mouth drooped. She looked way too concerned for a four-year-old.

"Hey, it's all going to be okay." He reached back and squeezed her knee. "I promise. Things are just a little crazy now. But Mom and I are figuring it out."

Though they weren't really. And it had been almost a month.

He walked Molly up to the front door, reassuring her he would be there to pick her up after school. Then he headed to the pub, where he was scheduled to meet with his lawyer to finalize the business license application for the new location. But maybe asking some questions about his domestic situation would be a good idea too.

Things had been tense with Theresa for a long time. There were the usual pressures—demanding jobs, raising a kid, trying to manage the house and everyone in it. Stuff they complained about at times . . . just part of the full life they'd built together. But there'd been a new kind of stress in the last year, one that didn't ebb and flow like the others, only seemed to solidify. While Denny was busting his ass to keep control of the financial mess, Theresa wanted to have another kid and she was tired of waiting.

That had always been the plan, at least two kids. But they had enough going on right now. It was terrible timing. And for some reason she decided to draw the line in the sand one morning last month. He'd come home from dropping Molly at school to find her packing a suitcase.

"I can't do this anymore," she'd said, pulling clothes from a dresser. "I've talked to you until I'm blue in the face and it doesn't help."

This was so not what he needed right now. "I told you we can talk about the baby after the opening."

"That's only part of it. I don't even know if we should have another baby now." She stopped packing then, straightened up to look at him, and he could tell she'd been crying that morning. Her face was puffy, pale against her dark hair. And when he walked around the bed to put his hands on her arms, she stiffened. He couldn't remember the last time he'd seen the smart-aleck spark in those brown eyes, or the teasing grin she liked to lay on him.

She told him things he'd already heard—he'd been distant for a long time, she didn't know why, he wasn't talking to her. There was too much chaos in the house and he was checked out. They were two people who lived together but had different lives.

He reminded her the grand opening was so close now, but she told him he'd been saying that for half a year. He guilt-tripped her about the family needing her, and she reminded him that this was his family, not hers, and she'd been helping him take care of them every day for years. He said it wouldn't be good for Molly and she told him it would be better than her worrying about two very stressed-out parents all the time. When Theresa closed the lid on her suitcase and zipped it shut, when it was clear she was serious about leaving, he asked her what the hell she wanted.

"I love you, Denny. But I am not another family member you have to manage. I'm your wife." She waited for a response, her eyes digging into his.

But what was he supposed to do—tell her he'd brought them to the brink of financial ruin? She thought she was pissed off and disappointed in him now, that would really do it.

So he said nothing, and she had taken her and Molly's cases and left.

Four weeks later he didn't know what to think. It was possible she was considering divorce, especially with Angie whispering in her ear. And if she was thinking about going for custody of Molly what recourse would he have?

By the time he arrived at the pub he'd decided to talk to his lawyer, get some information about what he might be facing.

Sunday walked in a few minutes later, while he was doing paperwork up at the bar. She stayed by the front door and glanced around the pub.

"He's not here," Denny said.

"I wasn't looking for anybody."

"Mm-hmm."

She walked over beside him. "I want to check the inventory in the cellar. There are a lot of blank vendors on the accounts payable. You've been paying some of the bills, I just can't tell which ones. Maybe I can match up order numbers from delivery slips."

"Just ask Kale. He knows most of those codes by heart."

She puckered her lips to the side. "I think I'll try this first."

The front door opened again and Sunday did a double take when the tall blond guy walked in. Michael Eaton was Denny's lawyer, but he'd also been a friend in high school.

Denny waved him over and made reintroductions, though they were probably unnecessary. At least for Michael. He'd had a thing for Sunday back then. He used to ask Denny regularly if she and Kale had split yet, no matter how many times Denny told him he was barking up the wrong tree.

"Don't mind her face," Denny said.

Sunday's eyebrows went up. "Thanks, Denny."

"What?" He flicked a thumb at Michael. "He knows about your accident. He's the one who recommended your DUI lawyer."

"Oh." She adjusted her hat. "Thanks for that."

"Sure," Michael said. "It's the least I could do. You used to come to all our soccer games, rain or shine."

"I did. And you used to brighten my day when you scored more goals than Denny. He was much more tolerable after those games."

"Good thing it didn't happen often," Denny said, gathering his paperwork.

"You still hang around with him?" she asked Michael.

"He pays me to."

"He's my lawyer," Denny said.

Michael clapped his hands together. "Ready to finally file the new business license?"

"Yep. I also want to talk to you about what's going on with Theresa."

"Why?" Sunday asked.

"It's been a month and I don't know what she's planning. I just want to be ready."

She lowered her voice. "For what?"

Michael ducked his head and stepped back.

"In case she's thinking of . . . next steps."

She put her hand on his arm. "Denny, you have to fix this."

He didn't want to tell her he had no idea how to do that, so he ended the conversation by heading back to the office.

CHAPTER SEVEN

Sunday

D enny, you have to fix this."

Talking to a lawyer? He had to be overreacting.

But he didn't answer her, just headed for the back.

Michael stepped in front of her. "Don't worry. I won't let him do anything stupid." He had smiling eyes and dark blond hair that was just the right degree of messy. The suit was quality and he wore it well, but the whole *GQ* look was softened by a long nose that was slightly off-center. Maybe an old soccer injury. And he rocked from heel to toe while standing there, like he had nervous energy. He threw his chin after Denny. "He just has a lot on his plate right now."

She nodded. Maybe Michael knew more about what was going on with Denny than she did.

He slid his hands in his pockets. "But I heard you'd gone out to LA to do some writing. How did it go?"

"It didn't" came to mind, but she couldn't quite say it. She knew what he must be thinking about her. Sad woman with failed Hollywood dreams forced to come home after getting trashed and totaling her car. Scraping for some dignity, she surprised herself by admitting something to him that she hadn't told anyone else. "I published a couple short stories."

His eyebrows shot up. "Good for you."

"Well"—she waved a hand—"it was in a very low-budget LA Arts Council magazine that no one's heard of."

"Still, that's great."

She tugged her hat down a bit on her head, wanting to end the subject. It had been a mistake to say anything. Hopefully he wouldn't mention it to Denny.

"I better get in there." Michael gestured toward the office with an elbow. "It was good to see you again."

After he followed Denny she dropped into the nearest chair. When she first heard about her sister-in-law leaving, she assumed it was temporary, that Theresa just needed a little break. There were still signs of her everywhere—clothes in the laundry, shoes in the mudroom, corkscrew hairs attached to bands left on random surfaces. And Theresa and Denny had been rock solid from the get-go.

She pulled out her phone and flipped back through years of photos, swiping fast enough to keep most of them blurry, until she found what she was looking for. The picture of Denny and Theresa taken the night he proposed to her. He had scooped her up high in his arms while she pushed the back of her left hand toward the camera, a bright shiny solitaire on her third finger. Sunday had taken that photo, captured them both in a moment of unblemished happiness.

Denny had never wanted for girlfriends. As an adolescent he somehow managed a free pass on the painful phase everyone else endured—acne breakouts, voice wobbles, awkward growth spurts. He was always so comfortable in his body and his surroundings. Girls were drawn to his confidence, and he ate up the attention. But one night when he was a junior in college and bartending at a restaurant near campus, Theresa walked in and ordered banana daiquiris.

Sunday and Kale were sitting at the bar that Saturday night, sipping free drinks Denny was passing them, when a long-legged girl in short shorts and spaghetti straps came in with a friend and grabbed the last two open seats at the busy bar. Her untamed black hair, high cheekbones, and flawless skin caught Denny's eye immediately. It was obvious, because as slammed as he was between the bar crowd and waitstaff drink orders, he made a beeline for her. But his winning smile hesitated when Theresa asked for two frozen banana daiquiris.

Sunday understood Denny's reaction. A banana daiquiri was a huge pain in the ass to make. It meant pulling out the blender, squeezing copious fruits, and tracking down obscure ingredients, like coconut milk. So, Denny told them he didn't have any bananas, to consider something else and he'd be back.

With great amusement Sunday and Kale watched Theresa look over to the fruit bowl behind the bar, which held limes, lemons, oranges. And two bananas.

Denny stopped back a few minutes later. "What did you guys decide on?"

Theresa leaned forward on the bar, chin in hand, big eyes on his. "We'd still like two banana daiquiris." She pointed to the fruit bowl behind him. Sunday was sure Denny would just make the drinks then. He'd been totally busted.

Instead, he grabbed the bananas and threw them in the trash with gusto. "Sorry, those were bad. I don't have any bananas."

If Theresa had thrown the nearest drink in his face or demanded to talk to the manager, Sunday wouldn't have blamed her. But she didn't. A slow smile spread across her face. "Okay," she said. "Thanks, anyway." Then she turned and left, taking her bewildered friend with her. Denny's eyes followed them all the way to the door, his expression one of mild remorse, as if realizing he may have won the battle, but he'd paid a high price.

Sunday wasn't present the second time they met but it had been etched into Brennan family lore. Theresa returned to the bar alone the next night and settled on a stool.

"What can I get you?" Denny asked, with a big smile.

"I'd like a frozen banana daiquiri."

He made a show of checking the fruit bowl, where no one had restocked the bananas. His hands went up in helplessness. "Sorry. No bananas."

"That's okay. I brought these." Her hands lifted from under the bar and placed two fresh bananas in front of him.

The story went that Denny crossed his arms and considered the bananas for a moment. At this point Theresa always said she had no idea what he was going to do, but if he didn't make the drink she planned to leave and never come back. But Denny shook his head with a grin and reached for the bananas. "All right." And then, according to both of them, he'd concocted one of the best banana daiquiris ever made. Denny and Theresa had been together ever since.

The sound of Paul and one of the lunch cooks coming through the door drew Sunday's attention from her phone. They headed toward the back to prep for their shifts. When she looked down she realized she'd flipped through several more pictures, ones she had deliberately avoided for a long time. The photo she'd ended on was her and Kale at the engagement party her parents had thrown for Denny and Theresa. They stood close together, his arm around her. How perfectly she had fit there, snug under his shoulder.

They had been engaged that night as well, though no one knew it. He'd told her he was going to marry her several times by then, the first on her eighteenth birthday. It always went the same way.

"I'm going to marry you, Sunday."

"Are you asking me or telling me?"

"Telling, so you can't say no."

"You have to ask, but I won't say no."

"Promise?"

"Promise."

It was such a given in their minds they felt no need to rush it or make it official with a drawn-out engagement, which would only give her mother the chance to barge into the planning. They even knew where they wanted to elope: Magens Bay in St. Thomas. Beautiful, tranquil, secluded. She'd tracked down a postcard, an overhead shot of a serene stretch of coastline, gentle waves lapping white sand, a few tall palm trees swaying in the breeze. She'd given it to Kale, after drawing two smiling stick figures in the bottom corner. They were holding hands, "Kale" above the male figure, "Sunday" above the female.

They'd just been waiting for the right time. Waiting for her mother to finish her cancer treatment and her dad to recover from his heart attack, for the pub to get off the ground, and for Shane's meds to stabilize again so he was a little more self-sufficient. Waiting to save enough money so they could pay for the trip themselves. Then they decided to wait because they didn't want to upstage Denny and Theresa.

But the night that photo was taken, just before they went to the party, Kale had led her to the fridge in his apartment, where the postcard was magnetted to the door. Without looking at her phone she would have remembered the light blue button-down that lit up his eyes, how he had given his face the rare close shave for the occasion. "This is the last delay," he'd said. "After their wedding next year, it's our turn. I'm taking you there"—he tapped the postcard—"and we're getting married." And Sunday knew they wouldn't wait long after that to start a family. It was important to Kale to have kids while they were relatively young, a product of growing up with an older father who always seemed to be sick and frail.

That postcard had floated around the apartment for a couple of years, moving from the fridge to a bedside table to the dresser mirror. They played hide-and-seek with it sometimes, left it somewhere the other would come across it, a desk drawer or between pages of a book. Or they'd grab it and burrow back between the sheets on weekend mornings to get lost in their plans and each other.

Now he was married to someone else, and he had a son. Meeting his family had been brutal. When Sunday had first laid eyes on Vivienne, she wanted nothing more than for the floor to open up and swallow her whole. Bruises, cast, frumpy clothes, and all. No one had mentioned Kale's wife was so beautiful, like, model beautiful, and several years younger. Sunday couldn't help feeling disappointed in Kale though. She just wasn't sure whether it was because he'd been sucked in by the superficial, or because he sought out someone so different from her.

Then there was Luke. Nothing could have prepared her for Luke. Kale's son. Who wasn't much younger than Kale had been when she first met him. With his youthful purity and his dad's sweet smile, the little boy symbolized everything she'd lost.

The phone screen became blurry and her eyes were in danger of spilling over. How had she and Denny both made such a mess of things since the night of that party? She couldn't let what happened to her and Kale happen to Denny and Theresa. She had to find a way to get them talking.

After jabbing the Sleep button on her cell she slid out of the booth and went to work. But first she made sure to close the photo app so the picture wouldn't be sitting there, waiting for her, next time she used the phone.

On Saturday morning Jackie and Sunday drove over to get Molly for the day because Theresa had a shift at the hospital. The truth was Sunday had been avoiding her sister-in-law because, frankly, she was a little pissed off. Every time Denny had to take Molly across town at night or go a day without seeing her, the question of how Theresa could put her family through that presented itself.

Though Jackie had come to Theresa's defense when Sunday talked to him about it—*Don't be so quick to judge. You don't know what it's been like to live with Denny the last few months.*

Theresa and Molly met them at the curb, Theresa in pink scrubs and Molly in a "Kick Like a Girl" T-shirt and her Strikers jacket.

Sunday smiled at her. "You know, your dad was a soccer star in high school."

"I know. I'm gonna be one too. Right, Mommy?"

Theresa ran a hand down Molly's long hair. "You can be anything you want to be, baby."

While Jackie loaded Molly and her car seat into his truck, Sunday turned to Theresa and lowered her voice. "When are you and Denny going to figure this out?"

"You need to ask your brother that."

"Whatever is going on between you"—Sunday waved toward Angie's condo—"this can't be the solution."

Theresa crossed her arms. "Did Denny tell you Molly was home when your dad had the accident in the garage? She saw him right after, when he was disoriented and bleeding. And then Shane started banging his head against the wall."

Sunday winced. When Shane felt his most out of control he resorted to that behavior. And watching it happen had to be traumatic for a four-year-old.

"She started having nightmares about both of them dying," Theresa said. "She'd come to our room in tears. She was afraid to go to school unless she knew someone would be home with your dad."

Denny hadn't mentioned any of this. Sunday looked at Molly in the back seat of the truck. Jackie had climbed in beside her so she could show off her sticker book. It made Sunday's chest hurt to picture her spitfire of a niece crying because she was afraid something might happen to her family.

"I didn't want to leave," Theresa said. "But I need to take care of her. It's calm here. Denny and I aren't bickering all the time. Her nightmares have stopped."

"What's Denny saying about all this?"

"Nothing." She shrugged. "He just keeps saying the grand opening will fix everything. Whatever's going on with him, he won't talk to me about it."

As soon as the thought occurred to Sunday, she knew it was true: Denny's financial situation was worse than anyone realized. It made sense. The short-lived bookkeepers, the discrepancies in the bank account, his cagey answers about the ledger. He didn't want anyone to know how bad he'd let things get because they'd lose faith in him. His desperation to hide his mistakes from Theresa was only driving her away.

And Sunday knew a thing or two about that: the terrible fallout that came with hiding shameful secrets from the people who mattered most.

She walked alone to meet Shane after his shift that evening because Jackie had signed up for an art class in Purchase. No one else in the family had ever encouraged his painting much, but she loved his work, how he captured movement and light in his portraits and landscapes. Soft visible brushstrokes, atmospheric touches. She sensed so much going on beneath the surface, just like Jackie.

Shane was perfectly capable of walking home by himself, but it meant so much to him when she showed up. He'd rush out to greet her with excitement. And relief, which made the guilt rain down. She'd been the person he counted on most in the world for a long time, and then one day she was gone.

Theresa was right, it wasn't healthy for Molly to fret so much about everybody. Sunday had done too much of that growing up. She understood now that Theresa had made the tough choice to leave because her first concern was her daughter. She encouraged Molly, wanted to protect her from taking on worries and burdens that didn't belong to her. If Molly ever went to her mother at her most desperate moment for help, Theresa would hold her, tell her it would be okay.

Sunday's mother had been so different. She'd always been frail, and growing up there'd been lots of watching the noise level lest they bring on one of her "splitting headaches." She suffered from insomnia, her joints ached, and when they didn't, it was her back. She ventured outdoors less and less, preferring to sit on the couch and watch TV. On one occasion when Sunday suggested therapy, her mother had said she'd sooner run naked through the streets of West Manor—*Have you gone soft in the head? What bloody good would that do my achin' joints?* When the breast cancer was first diagnosed, a small part of her mother seemed to take warped pleasure in it, like it served them all right for ever doubting her.

She had borne the brunt of her mother's health issues. Her father and brothers bulldozed their way through colds and viruses, sprained limbs and broken bones, determined to recover and get back at it as soon as possible. When they realized her mother seemed to seek illness out, they scratched their heads and became useless. So by default Sunday took the lead, helped her mother through these bouts, put everyone's mind at ease.

When she made a right turn onto Saw Mill Road, people were still making their way to and from restaurants or the frozen yogurt shop or

the one-screen indie movie theater. She headed toward Newman's Market
at the far end of the strip.

The steepest price she ever paid for her mother's health problems was
giving up a trip to Ireland with Kale, Denny, and Theresa. It had been
planned for months. They were taking her dad and Clare to see their family south of Belfast, and then visiting Kale's extended family near Dublin.
Jackie had a good handle on operations at the pub and would be left in
charge, and Grail had offered to check on Maura, who was, by then, in
remission from the cancer but not up to traveling.

Three days before they were supposed to leave, her mother informed
them she was experiencing back and chest pains, shortness of breath, and
weird spasms in her abdomen. Her doctor had scheduled a battery of
tests over the next two weeks. When her dad asked her if they should be
canceling their plans, she said heavens no, she wouldn't dream of it . . .

"But I don't know that I could do without you, Sunday," she'd said.
"Especially if they tell me the cancer's back. My biggest concern is for
Shane. If I take sick or they want me in the hospital overnight for tests?
Well, you know how he gets. And you're so good with him."

They had all looked at Sunday then, her parents and Denny, and she
offered to stay home and take care of things because that's what she always did.

She could hear the music coming from Brennan's before she stopped
by the window and looked inside. It was hopping, the tables and barstools
full, most people turned toward the far corner where a local guy played
guitar. Kale was behind the bar, chatting and laughing with a customer.
Super casual as ever, he wore jeans and a T-shirt. Denny had nagged him
about stepping up his wardrobe a notch when they opened the business.
But it was to no avail, and that had been just fine with Sunday.

He looked so at ease in the cozy pub, she had a hard time imagin-
ing him in the large restaurant in Mamaroneck. The song ended and he
raised his hands to join the crowd clapping for the guitarist. The light
caught his wedding ring and she figured it was time to move along.

When she decided to skip the trip to Ireland, Kale had been the only
one to fight her on it. His reaction had surprised her. As a rule, he avoided

conflict. He was easygoing, a natural mediator, whether it was between two hotheads in the pub or Denny and Sunday. He was happiest when everybody was getting along—especially the family—even if it came at the cost of what he wanted. But he'd been good and mad when she told him she was staying home.

"No way," he'd said, pacing his small apartment. "You're not staying home."

"We'll take a trip to Ireland later, just us. Besides, they paid for my ticket."

He squeezed his eyes shut.

They hadn't been able to afford two tickets. Her parents had paid for hers, just like they were paying her college tuition. On top of the loan for the pub. It was a point of pride. He itched for the day he could take care of her without her family's help.

"Kale, I've been worrying about leaving Shane alone anyway. And I don't want to upset everything now, with the wedding in a couple of months—"

"No! You're coming."

She rocked back a bit on her heels, startled by his vehemence. Startled, but also something else. Hopeful, maybe. Perhaps he wouldn't just go with the family flow this time.

"We just need to get her through the wedding next month," Sunday said. "That's what this is really about for her, Denny's leaving."

His face, normally so relaxed, was unyielding. Not a side of him she often saw.

Maybe he was going to take a stand against her. Or, really, for her. If he did, if he insisted she go with him, she would do it. If Kale was willing to risk drama with her family, so was she.

But then he flopped in a chair and hung his head. And Sunday had told him how grateful she was, while she told herself the relief at his acquiescence outweighed the disappointment.

She arrived at Newman's and waved through the window at Shane, who was wiping down conveyer belts at the registers. A few minutes later the glass front doors slid open and he came outside, waving over his shoulder to his coworkers. He gave her a warm hug and gripped the straps of his backpack as they headed home.

While they walked he told her stories about his day. She laughed and responded in the right places, but only half listened. Her mind was stuck in an alternate universe, one where she had gone on that trip to Ireland with Kale.

But when she really started playing out that scenario, thinking about how different her life would be now, she shut it down.

That was just too damn painful.

Kale was working on his laptop in a back corner booth when she arrived for their meeting a few days later. She wanted to help Denny get the financial chaos under control, and her convoluted method of trying to fill in gaps in the ledger was taking too long. So she'd asked Kale for help.

It was early. The pub was empty except for a prep guy working in the kitchen. Kale didn't notice her right away so it gave her a second to get past the uncontrollable reaction that still kicked in when she saw him. What tugged at her most in that moment was his feet. He rested one sneaker across the instep of the other. He'd been sitting like that as long as she'd known him and for some reason it had always struck her as a little vulnerable.

She headed behind the bar and asked if he'd like some coffee. When she sat across from him and placed two mugs on the table, he reached for the sugar caddy.

"I already put two sugars in," she said.

The way his hand froze midair made her feel like she'd done something wrong by remembering how he preferred his coffee.

He pulled his hand back. "Thanks."

She slid a page of accounts payable from her bag and laid it on the table. "I'm hoping you can identify some of these vendor codes or charges so I know how to classify them."

Before studying the page he reached into his own bag and slipped on a pair of eyeglasses.

"When did you get the glasses?" she asked.

He gave her a sheepish smile. "Two years ago. But I only need them for fine print."

"Right." She allowed a teasing grin to seep through.

"Shut up."

"No, they look good." And they did. The narrow black frames accentuated his eyes, lent an intensity to his open face, which had rounded out a bit over the years but still lived in a constant state of low-grade scruff. "Seriously, not at all nerdy."

They both laughed then, and their eyes met and held. The rush that started in her chest and rippled through her body was unexpected. And intoxicating. For just a second the whole of the last five years fell away. He must have felt something too because his smile faded and she saw a spark of alarm in his expression before he straightened up and focused on the paper. She played with her pen, reaching for something to say. But anything that came to mind seemed either too forced or too familiar. She wasn't sure how to find the middle ground with Kale now.

He trailed a hand through his hair. "Look, I think I'll just take this home and go through it, let you know what I figure out." He closed his laptop and started to gather his things, like he couldn't get away fast enough.

"Well, that's just part of it. There's more."

"How much more?"

This was not going according to plan. She'd hoped to ease into it because she was pretty sure he had no idea how bad Denny had let things get. "Never mind. Why don't you just start with those and I'll take it from there."

"Do you want my help or not?" His tone and overall mood had decidedly changed.

She pulled out several more pages.

He flipped through them. "Jesus."

"Let's just go one line at a time. And we don't have to figure it all out today."

He got right down to business, starting with the first line item. Half an hour later they'd made their way through two pages. He used his memory and old order forms to help her translate codes and match payments. It was much easier than doing it on her own.

"Is there more I should know?" he asked, scanning the pages they hadn't got to yet.

"What do you mean?"

Kale looked at her and narrowed his eyes. "What aren't you telling me?"

How the hell could he still read her so well? But all she had were unsubstantiated suspicions at this point. And she didn't want to create trouble between him and Denny. "I'm just trying to clean up the ledger," she said.

"Why didn't he tell me how bad it was?"

She shrugged. "Because he's Denny."

"Well, he's had a lot on his plate the last few years." The accusatory note was unmistakable.

"Then maybe you should have asked him if he needed help."

He pulled back in surprise at her sharp tone.

"When's the last time you even looked at your own books, Kale?"

"Denny said he had it under control."

She shook her head and started gathering her notes. Typical Kale. Would rather bury his head in the sand than rock the boat.

They both looked over at the sound of Denny coming through the front door. He walked over and pulled a chair up to the end of the booth to join them.

"Why didn't you tell me this was such a mess?" Kale asked him, holding up the pages in his hand. "You said you were behind, but this is ridiculous."

"It's not that bad."

"It goes back months. What the hell happened?"

Denny held up his hands. "Look, I've been paying the bills, I just didn't track the details. It's not a big fucking deal, okay? I'm sorry I didn't say anything, but I know how you worry about this stuff. Sunday's getting a handle on everything now—it'll be fine. Right, Sun?"

She could feel both of them looking at her, waiting for an answer. Kale wanted the truth and Denny wanted her to cover for him. "I think I'm making good progress," she said.

"See?" Denny said.

Kale just stared at her. He knew she was hedging.

"And listen," Denny said. "I have good news. Michael officially filed the new business license with the city."

"Great." Kale's tone was flat.

"Christ, don't get so excited."

Kale just shook his head and packed his bag.

"That reminds me," Denny said, turning to Sunday. "You have any interest in going out with Michael?"

It was so out of the blue she looked to see if she'd heard him correctly. "What? No."

"He's a good guy. And he's interested." He jerked his eyebrows up and down.

Kale concentrated on his bag.

Her cheeks started to burn. "I said no, Denny."

"I'm gonna give him your number—"

"Don't do that!"

Kale's head came up. "Guys . . ."

"Why not?" Denny asked. "You got a guy back in Cali?"

What a dick. He was just doing this to deflect attention. "You know, Denny, instead of worrying about my personal life, why don't you work on yours?" she asked. "I saw Theresa over the weekend. She said you won't talk to her."

"She knew how much I had on my plate and she still left." He shook his head. "That's something I just can't understand. But I guess maybe you can, huh?"

If he had slapped her across the face the sting could not have been worse. Her entire body recoiled.

Kale shifted in his seat. "Come on, Denny."

But Denny jabbed the table with a finger. "Maybe I wouldn't be in this situation if you'd been here helping the last few years, Sunday, instead of"—fling of the arm—"finding yourself in California."

That produced an image in her mind. A picture of her apartment. Like the apartment, her life in LA had been small and quiet, but it had been hers. No tiptoeing around old fiancés or resentful brothers.

Then she thought about her dad, Jackie, and Shane. And Theresa and Molly. How she was finally becoming part of their lives again.

"You want an award for taking care of things the last five years, Denny? Because I did it for a lot longer than that." She leaned toward him. "I was always the one who had to take care of everything, and you let me do it. If it wasn't for you, I would have been on that trip to Ireland."

His face twisted in confusion. "What the hell are you talking about?"

Kale was also looking at her like he couldn't understand the turn this conversation had taken.

She started stuffing papers in her bag. "Nothing. Never mind."

"Fine," Denny said. He stood, shoved his chair under the neighboring table. Then he pulled a hand down his face. "You know what I really don't get, Sunday? If I was so awful to you back then, why was I your emergency contact?" He didn't wait for an answer, just stalked back to the office.

She stared after him, feeling shaky with emotion, and swallowed a threatening lump in her throat.

Kale sat a few feet away, eyes nailed to the table. She could sense his debate about what to do next. It was in his nature to throw her a bone, offer some sort of support—*He's just stressed. Don't let him get to you.* Pathetic how hungry she was for it.

But in the end all he said was, "I better get going," right before he grabbed his bag and left, heading for the front door.

CHAPTER EIGHT

Kale

I better get going."

That's all he said because he was afraid to say more. He couldn't afford any more shared moments with Sunday. When she remembered how he took his coffee, he remembered how she took hers—splash of cream. When she teased him about his glasses and they laughed together, he'd been transported back in time. He had to keep his guard up around her.

He jumped in his car and headed toward Luke's school, where Vivienne worked part-time as an administrative assistant. They were having an early lunch. He'd been making an effort to see her a little more the last few weeks. And, if he was being honest with himself, to keep her away from the pub. Introducing Sunday to his family had been disturbing. Watching her talk with Vivienne was unnerving, but when she interacted with Luke there'd been some deeper emotional component he didn't care to explore.

Viv had been on high alert since that day. He thought she might be encouraged, seeing Sunday's bruises and her cast, the offhand wardrobe. Appearance was a measuring stick for his wife, how she sized up other women. But seeing Sunday back in her natural element, with Denny in the pub, a place Vivienne never felt at home, only seemed to amp up her anxiety. She was more watchful, asked lots of questions about work. But the dead giveaway was how often she came on to him. Not that he was complaining exactly. It's just that sex meant different things to Viv. There were times it felt less about connecting than a way for her to get some kind of reassurance, like she could check it off the list of things to do to keep a happy marriage.

The drive calmed him only so much. Sunday was appropriating too much real estate in his brain. She'd always been there, but he'd managed to relegate her to a quiet back corner for a long time. Kind of like the Magens Bay postcard. He could never bring himself to throw it away, but he'd slipped it into the bottom of a drawer long ago. Now he saw her almost every day. And as her bruises faded and she looked more like her old self, it was getting difficult to ignore the things that had always stopped him short. Her smile. Soft shirts and jeans that molded to her shape but still left a little to the imagination. The way she talked with her hands and often sat with one leg folded under her.

Yet he'd noticed changes too. He saw a wariness in her eyes, even in the way she carried herself—head down a lot, one hand gripping the bag strap across her chest while the other was still encased in that dark cast. There was an edge to her now that made him curious about her time in LA. He saw it in how she dodged his questions, in her veiled answer about the books, her willingness to call Denny out so directly. It was as if the gentle side of her personality had been sharpened against the reality of life the last five years.

And, Kale had to admit, he'd enjoyed watching her put her brother back in his place.

While he was manning the pub the next day, Sunday brought Mickey in for a midday shift. Denny was in Mamaroneck doing a final walk-through before the inspection. Sunday went straight to work in the office and he didn't see her until he stopped in there to grab his jacket before he left for the afternoon lull.

"Do you have a minute before you go?" she asked. "I have a few follow-up questions from yesterday." She stood and gestured to her laptop on the desk.

He glanced at the screen. "I'll make you a deal. I'll help with that if you tell me what's going on with Denny."

"What do you mean?"

He tilted his head.

"I'm just trying to clean up your ledger, Kale."

"I know he's keeping something from me."

"I guess you should ask him about that."

"I'm asking you."

She shook her head. "You know what, I'll figure it out myself." She pulled her hat off and tossed it on the desk, ran a hand through her hair. "I'm having a hard time keeping up with your mood swings anyway."

"What?"

"I just never know what I'm going to get from you day to day." The look in her eye, the flash of green. She was pissed off.

"Are you mad at me for some reason?" He regretted asking the question before he finished asking it. He was stepping down a risky road.

"I just wish I knew when you'll be done punishing me." She blinked and her eyes grew bigger, as if she couldn't believe what she'd just said.

Neither could he.

"Look, just forget it." She turned to the file cabinet, started searching for something.

He stared at the back of her head. The safe, smart bet was to leave right now.

Instead he reached over and swung the door shut. "I'm not punishing you."

"It feels that way sometimes."

A determined swell started to rise in his chest. A lid was lifting off the jar of anger he had stored up in there for years. "I would think you could understand this has been difficult for me and my family—"

"Oh, I know." She gave up her search and slammed the drawer shut. "It must be so hard for you and your wife that I'm here."

The nerve. The absolute gall. "What the hell did you expect? To come strolling back after all this time, and what?" He jerked his shoulders up. "We'd all be besties?"

Her eyes drifted to the floor. "No, of course not."

The fight had left her, but he was just getting started. "You walked away five years ago." He was having trouble controlling the emotion now that it had leaked out. "You have *no* idea what I went through after you left."

"Really? You seemed to get over it awfully quickly."

He couldn't remember the last time he'd been so angry. It took real effort to keep his voice down. "Do you know how long I waited for you to come back?"

"Probably as long as I waited for you to come after me."

The middle of his body contracted, like she'd punched him in the stomach.

"That thought never even crossed your mind, did it?" she asked.

"Don't give me that *bullshit*. You. Left. Me."

Her expression softened. "You're right. I did."

He waited because he thought she might say more. It was the way she was looking at him, with such sadness. Or regret.

But when she spoke the edge was back. "So you just hold on to that righteous anger, Kale. You seem pretty comfortable with it at this point." Then she walked past him, yanked open the door, and left.

His afternoon breaks were typically dedicated to running errands, but instead he drove to a quiet bar in Ossining, about fifteen minutes away. It was much easier to remain anonymous among the town of 25,000 where the largest employer was the Sing Sing Correctional Facility located right along the Hudson. He didn't want to talk to anyone, nothing would distract him. He sat on a stool and ordered a tall beer. Then he let it all hit him, the black hole of memories he'd been playing hide-and-seek with since the night he found her in the office.

Kale couldn't remember a time when he didn't love Sunday Brennan, though for many years he thought it was much the same way he loved

Jackie and Shane, as a quasi–big brother. He'd been unofficially adopted by the Brennans, blending seamlessly into the mix from the beginning. Though it wasn't by accident. He'd chosen them, and, in hindsight, it had a lot to do with Shane. Even at a young age he sensed something special about a family that would rally around the most vulnerable of the bunch so strenuously.

He'd always appreciated Sunday's good nature. She was smart, a good sport, unafraid to scold her brothers. A welcoming presence, cheering at his and Denny's games, encouraging her brothers, helping her mother through various illnesses. When Shane had rough days at school, it was Sunday—not Maura—the teachers called to come help him calm down. The first time Kale's father went into the hospital due to the wheezing and crackling in his lungs, the beginnings of the emphysema that would take his life when Kale was in college, it was Sunday who brought comfort food to the house. There was a maturity and selflessness about her that was a little intimidating.

As she moved into high school he noticed the changes. The leaner face that needed none of the makeup other girls wore, the longer legs in her cross-country shorts, how she began to fill out T-shirts—he would have had to be blind not to notice. But it was so fleeting he didn't even experience much guilt. She was Denny's little sister, so that's where that ended. It wasn't until he was a junior and she was a sophomore that his feelings betrayed him. If he'd realized what was happening, he might have had a chance to get ahead of it. But it had snuck up on him literally overnight. She took him by surprise and he'd never been the same since.

One morning midway through that year, as he sat in homeroom ignoring announcements like everybody else, a familiar name over the loudspeaker grabbed his attention: ". . . our own sophomore Sunday Brennan took first place in the short story contest hosted by the State University of New York literary magazine! This is quite an honor, so make sure to offer Sunday congrats when you see her in the halls." Kale was used to hearing Denny's name during announcements—heroic soccer performance, nominated for homecoming court, parked in a restricted spot again—but he'd never heard Sunday's before.

He was halfway through dinner at the Brennans' that evening, post-practice, sitting in his usual seat at the table—between Jackie and Denny, across from Sunday and Shane—before he thought of it again. As usual Denny and his mother were dominating the dinner conversation with the topic of Denny.

"This spring is critical." Denny was speaking around a large quantity of food in his mouth. "Coach said college recruiters start coming to the Olympic Development practices and take video." Bent over his plate with elbows on the table, he dug into his chicken and pasta, using his fork to stab and shovel his food.

His mother sat next to him, at one end of the table, across from Mr. Brennan at the other. She'd hardly touched her own dinner, as usual, and sat with chin in hand. "Wouldn't that be something. A college scholarship for soccer. Can you imagine, Mickey?"

"What's that?" Mr. Brennan looked up from *The Irish Echo* newspaper that was folded by his plate. "Aye, that would be something."

Mrs. Brennan waved him off and turned back to Denny. "Now, you've to make sure you take care of yourself. You can't be risking illness nor injury."

"I know, Mom. I know."

Kale tuned out as she asked another question. He'd heard all this before and none of it applied to him. He was a mediocre player, second stringer, hadn't even tried out for the Olympic Development team. Glancing around the table at Jackie to his left, and Shane and his sister across the way, he wondered if they resented the spotlight Denny garnered or were relieved by it. When his eyes came to rest on Sunday, he recalled the announcement. After waiting for a break in conversation he said, "Congrats on the contest, Sunday."

Her head snapped up, like the rest of the family. As he'd suspected, they had no idea what he was talking about.

"Thank you," she said.

"What contest?" Denny asked.

"She won a writing contest," Kale said. "Didn't you hear the announcements today?" He stole a glance at Mrs. Brennan, who watched her daughter with a stiff expression.

"I never listen to those. What's up?" Denny asked.

All eyes were on Sunday. She shrugged. "It was a short story contest for high school students."

"Oh boy," Shane said. "You won a contest?"

Her fingers fiddled with her knife. "Yeah."

"Nice," Jackie said.

"Hah. That's great," Denny said.

Her dad reached over and patted her arm. "Nice job, Sunday. And you only a sophomore."

Mrs. Brennan's voice cut across the enthusiasm. "What, exactly, did you win?"

"They're going to print it in a SUNY journal. And I won a scholarship to a writing workshop this summer on the Purchase campus."

"We'll have to see about that."

"It'll just be good to put on college applications," Sunday said.

"Hmph. Can't imagine there's much scholarship money for that sort of thing." She turned back to her eldest. "Speaking of scholarships, I wonder if we shouldn't consult one of those college counselors, make sure we find the best place for you . . ."

And just like that Sunday's limelight was redirected. Mrs. Brennan was the closest thing Kale had to a mother, but that night, for the first time, he believed she was jealous of Sunday. Jealous of her talent, or her connection with Shane, or her wide-open future. Why else would a parent steal one child's moment and hand it to another.

He watched Sunday's eyes and spirits sink. She stood and began gathering dishes. On her second trip to the table for more cleanup, Mrs. Brennan stopped talking to Denny long enough to ask her to put on the kettle. Jackie and Shane had already taken their dishes to the kitchen and headed upstairs where Jackie would make sure Shane showered and got ready for bed. Mr. Brennan had gotten a call on his cell and stepped outside to answer it. A brief but profound spark of disappointment shot through Kale, similar to when he'd learned that Mark McGwire and Sammy Sosa had been using steroids during the Great Home Run Chase. It was painful to recognize failings in the people you idolized.

He stood, grabbed his own plate and silverware, as well as Denny's, and took them into the kitchen. He paused in the doorway to watch Sunday as she turned from the kettle on the stove to sigh at the massive pile of pots, pans, and dishes it took to feed a family of six—seven, including himself.

He moved forward. "Why don't you load the dishwasher and I'll work on pots and pans."

"No, that's okay. I got it."

"Come on, it'll go a lot faster with two of us." He added the plates he was carrying to the pile, then stepped back next to her, surveying the damage.

"At least let me do the pots," she said. "It's the worse of the two jobs."

He put his hands up in front of him, as if trying to grasp the scope of the task. "No, really, I think I can do it."

She grinned. "Suit yourself."

They worked alongside each other at the double sink for a few minutes. Sunday had the dishwasher loaded before he finished scraping the second pan. He wiped his forehead with his sleeve. "Your mom ever hear of nonstick?"

"She thinks Teflon is lazy. And she likes to use as many pots as possible when she cooks." She grabbed the large pasta pot and went to work on it.

"We should get Denny in here to help."

"Nah. He's too busy hanging the sun, the moon, and the stars." But there was no trace of bitterness in her voice or in the smile she flashed him.

The job was winding down when Denny yelled for Kale, and Sunday told him to go. Before he rounded the corner she called his name. He turned and her eyes met his head-on. "Thank you."

"You're welcome."

Ten minutes later, after giving Denny some homework assignments to copy, he gathered his jacket and backpack to walk home—where, no doubt, his father was waiting for help getting himself and his oxygen tank moved from an armchair in front of the TV up to his bedroom. He called a general goodbye to Denny and his parents and headed for the door as Sunday appeared from the kitchen, teapot in hand. "Sunday?" he said.

She looked up from where she was pouring her father a cup.

"Can I read the story?"

The other three faces swiveled up and over to him.

"Sure. If you want to."

Kale noticed Denny's eyebrows go up a touch and tried to keep a casual tone. "Okay. I'll catch you after school tomorrow." He left somewhat satisfied that he'd managed to mention it again. Even if no one else in the room had asked to read her work.

When he found her at her locker the next afternoon she seemed surprised that he had followed through. "Are you sure you want to read it?" she asked.

"Yeah." He shoved his hands in his pockets and moved closer to her locker to avoid the surge of bodies rushing for the exit. "Unless you'd rather I didn't . . ."

"No, that's okay." She fished out a couple books and a folder. "Where should we go?"

He had assumed she would just give it to him to peruse when he had time but realized now she planned to hang around while he read it. Looking about he suggested they go to the commons, which would be clearing out by then. She followed him, and they were saved from making conversation while navigating the flow of traffic. Despite the fact that he practically lived at her house and saw her every day, they were rarely alone together and he had no idea what they'd talk about. He led her outside to the large courtyard area and chose an empty picnic table still bathed in the sun because she wasn't wearing a jacket. They flung off their packs and sat across from each other.

He waited while she dug in her bag, rifling through books and papers, zipping and unzipping pockets, and he suspected she was stalling. At last she placed a red folder on the table in front of her, laid her hands on top of it. "You know, you really don't have to read this." Her wavy hair lifted around her face and shoulders with the breeze, and a pink flush had slid up her cheeks.

"I wouldn't have asked if I didn't want to read it."

She nodded and pulled out a few pages stapled together. "I just didn't want you to feel obligated." Laying it in front of him she said, "I haven't edited it since I submitted it. And if you get bored or have to go, that's fine. You can finish it later . . ." Her hands swirled, gestured the rest of the trailing thought.

He'd never seen her like this before, so apprehensive. He'd meant to call her family's attention to her accomplishment, not make her feel so self-conscious. But he was afraid to repeat his offer to not read it in case she took it the wrong way. Besides, now he was curious. "Got it. Are you going to just sit there and watch me read?"

She laughed, her face lighting up with some relief. "Sorry, no. I'll work on my Spanish." She reached for a textbook.

He picked up the story, which was typed and double-spaced, and titled "Dream Walking." Sunday was looking down at her book, but he could tell she wasn't actually studying. Right before he started reading he worried her anxious presence would prevent him from focusing, but by the third or fourth sentence he was engrossed.

The story was about a guy his own age named Henry, who was weighed down by the pressures of school and caring for a chronically sick mother. Henry was a good student and a dutiful son but dreamed of freedom. At night, when he could get away, he took walks and thought about what it would be like if he never turned back, but kept going instead. Walking to the next city, the next state, over bridges and through tunnels, across the country. A fresh start, no obligations. Each walk produced a different scenario: climbing mountains in Alaska, attending classes at a foreign university, sailing across an ocean. Henry's dreams were boundless. However, by the time his walk ended each night he was always glad to be back home. The fleeting escapes helped him appreciate what he had, the people in his life, and while the future remained wide open, for now it was enough just to know it was there.

He delayed looking up when he finished the last page. Her writing was smooth, descriptive, bits of humor mixed in. But what gave him such pause and caused an unsettling internal reaction was the sense that she'd seen right into his own soul.

In the periphery her fingers flipped the corners of her textbook pages.

He looked up to find her staring at him, chewing the tip of a pen. Her eyes bolted down to her book.

"Uh, it's . . ." He cleared a hitch in his throat. "It's really good."

She continued to work the page corners, lifted a shoulder. "Thanks."

"I mean it. Seriously." He wanted to say more, offer specific feedback, but he was finding it hard to pinpoint a coherent thought.

"I should tell you something." She did that thing where she pulled her sleeves over her hands, something he'd watched her do since she was a little girl. "You gave me the idea."

"What?"

"I know you walk sometimes. At night." She rushed to explain. "I just happened to see you go by a few times. In the alley behind our house."

He sat up a little straighter, feeling caught out for some reason. "Yeah, lately things are tough at home. Dad's in and out of the hospital, there's always someone at the house to help take care of him, people from church or one of his sisters from Ireland. Sometimes I go for a walk after he's in bed. You know, to take a breath."

She nodded. "When I need to take a breath I sit on the back porch at night. That's how I saw you."

It didn't answer how she had gleaned what he was thinking about on his walks. Not the detailed scenarios, but his conflict between wanting to be a good son yet needing to make sure he ended up nothing like his father, his vacillation between wanting to explore the world some days and never leave West Manor others. His uncertainty about what he wanted for the future.

He stared at her longer than he should have. Long enough to take note of the faint scattering of freckles on her upper cheeks. She played with her pen and blinked several times, looking off to one side and the other. His attention made her uncomfortable, which was no shock. She lived with three brothers in a house where the boys, one in particular, reigned supreme in their mother's heart and mind, and her checked-out father was along for the ride. She hadn't been reading his mind, just thinking some of the same thoughts, and he wondered when she realized they had so much in common. He had known Sunday for ten years as Denny's little sister, known her to be sweet and smart, but the well ran much deeper than that.

"You're not saying much," she said.

"Sorry. It's just because . . ." He scratched his head. "I'm just having trouble finding the words right now. But I'd like to read it again. Can I have a copy?" He was doing a piss-poor job of responding after all she'd been brave enough to share with him. Not just her writing, but the fact that she'd written about him. But he needed time to digest what was going on here. Some fundamental shift seemed to be taking place between them.

"Sure. You can keep that one." Worry shadowed her features. "I hope you're not mad. Maybe I should have talked to you about it first, but I never thought I would win or anything."

"I'm not mad."

"Promise?"

"Promise."

She blew out a sigh of relief.

"But when they publish your first book you have to dedicate it to me."

The wide smile reached her sunlit eyes and stayed put, a pure and singular smile he would, over time, come to think of as only for him. In that moment a small but powerful adjustment had taken place as Sunday moved into first Brennan position in his heart.

"You're distracted tonight," Vivienne said.

It was a couple of hours later and they were eating dinner at home. He had asked Paul to stay on for the evening. After nursing a beer for two hours, steeped in disconcerting memories, he wasn't up to going back to the pub. Guilt was at work too. Spending that much time thinking about Sunday felt like a betrayal of his marriage. The least he could do was go home and have dinner with his family.

"Sorry. Just a busy day. How was school, buddy?"

"Good. Miss Maggie read a story about a giving tree." Luke was trying—and failing—to shovel spaghetti into his mouth.

Kale took the small plastic fork from him. "This is how you do it. You twirl smaller bits and scoop up. Here, you try it."

"Daddy, when can I play wiff Molly again?" His soft round cheeks were smeared with butter and parmesan cheese.

"Luke," Vivienne said, "it's wi*th*. And you know Molly's in school all day now."

"Yeah, but I didn't see her for a long time."

It was true. Molly and Luke had always spent a lot of time together, at each other's house or at the pub during quiet hours, while their dads were working. They hadn't seen each other since Sunday returned. And Kale hadn't been in the Brennan house for almost a month.

"I'll talk to Denny," he said. "We'll get you guys together soon."

After helping Luke with his bath, Kale tucked him in—"Tight like a burrito, Daddy"—wrapped an arm around him, and read a story. It was the most peaceful he felt all day and they were both out halfway through the book. He woke to Vivienne shaking him.

"You should come to bed." She didn't like when he fell asleep with Luke, said it wasn't a good idea.

He followed her into their room, doing his best not to wake fully while he pulled off his jeans and shirt and fell into bed on his stomach, deciding against brushing his teeth in hopes he could drift back to sleep.

She climbed in beside him. "What happened at work today?"

"Nothing."

"You seemed preoccupied. Upset, even."

The numbing edge of sleepiness was slipping away. "No, I'm just tired."

"Was Sunday there?"

His eyes shot open as the attempt to sleep officially failed. "Briefly."

She rolled toward him and put her hand on his back, scratched lightly with her nails. Which felt more grating than relaxing. "I just want to know what's going on with you," she said.

For the tiniest moment, he considered telling her what happened, how Sunday had accused him of making her pay, had the audacity to suggest he'd done something wrong five years ago. That moment passed though. The last thing she needed to know was that Sunday was causing him this kind of turmoil, and once he said it there would be no unringing that bell.

He turned over and looked at Vivienne's insistent eyes. She was not going to let this go. "It's just the new place," he said. "We're getting close to opening and it's stressful lately. That's all."

She studied him, trying to decide whether that was, in fact, all.

He opened his arm so she could snuggle up. "Let's get some sleep."

She put her head on his shoulder but then started kissing his neck and reaching under the blanket. He let her make the move, but it was somewhat mechanical for him. There was no other way when his head was filled with another woman. Afterward, as much as he tried to steer his mind in other directions, it drifted to the old apartment he'd shared with Sunday. His apartment, technically. She never officially lived there. Her parents needed a lot of help at home, and Maura didn't approve of living together before marriage. But Sunday spent half her nights there with him. He remembered how she wore his T-shirts to bed. The way they talked and laughed for hours in the dark. And weekend mornings when they could take their time with each other before the family and the pub demanded their attention.

Vivienne didn't seem to notice, or if she sensed it she ignored it. She was a little like Denny that way. If it didn't fit her narrative she stiff-armed it aside. While he lay there, his mind running like a hamster on a wheel, she fell right to sleep.

The next morning he decided to take a very rare day off work. He needed more time before he saw Sunday again, and sinking into a day with his family would bolster him. Denny told him to enjoy it, days off would be hard to come by once the new place opened.

They had breakfast out and drove to the park where Viv watched him and Luke kick the ball around. While she had her nails done, a standing Saturday-afternoon appointment, they went for a bike ride and had ice cream. Spending time with Luke brought the calm he was yearning for. It also reminded him that as much as Sunday pulled at him, he couldn't wander down the what-if-she-never-left road. If she'd never left, there'd be no Luke.

When they returned home, Vivienne suggested they take a walk before dinner. "We can stop by the pub and drop off the list of bookkeepers I put together," she said.

In an effort to put Viv's mind at ease Kale had mentioned that Sunday was looking for someone to take over the books. Vivienne had done some research and generated a list of possibilities in a pretty transparent effort to help.

"She won't be there this late," he said.

"That's fine. We'll just leave it in the office."

Since he needed to pick up deposits anyway, he agreed to go. The pub was steady with late-afternoon weekend patrons, high energy but not yet the rambunctious crowd that would be overflowing the tables and barstools later that night. Paul was behind the bar and Denny would be in to help. Kale was momentarily waylaid by the kitchen staff, then hurried after Vivienne and Luke to the office. If they didn't make this quick his night off would cease to exist.

He opened the office door to see Vivienne standing there talking to Sunday. He was surprised Sunday was there, though Denny had probably told her Kale was off for the night. It was painfully uncomfortable, being in the same space where they'd argued yesterday, watching an oblivious Vivienne show off her list of potential bookkeepers.

Sunday's eyes met his for a second, then dropped to Luke before she focused on the pages again. "Vivienne, this is great. I'll check these people out."

Luke pulled on his hand. "Daddy, can we play with the cars?"

Grateful for something to do, Kale knelt down and opened the bottom drawer of the file cabinet, where they kept a few toys for the kids. He focused on keeping Luke occupied with Matchbox cars, listening while Vivienne described reviews she'd read or heard about the various candidates.

"I'll show you the two I would start with," Vivienne said. "Let me find a highlighter . . ." She sat at the desk and started digging through drawers.

Kale gave Luke the two-minute warning so they could get the hell out of there ASAP without a fuss.

"Thanks again," Sunday said. "I'll start making calls . . ."

Luke held up two cars. "Should I put these away, Daddy?"

"Yep. Let's park them back in the drawer."

It took a moment to realize the silence behind him had gone on for too long. When he looked back over his shoulder, he saw Sunday staring down at the desk. Vivienne, sitting in the chair, appeared to be looking up at her, but he couldn't see Vivienne's face.

Sunday swallowed. "It's just . . . a silly keepsake," she said to Vivienne, with a dismissive shake of the head.

"Daddy, should I close the drawer?"

"Yep." Kale stood, trying to see what it was they were talking about.

Vivienne rose. "Well, maybe you shouldn't *keep* it here."

The way Sunday froze, eyes wide, mouth open but nothing coming out. It was like she'd been busted with something she shouldn't have.

Then Kale knew.

He stepped near them for a closer look at what was sitting on the desk, clinging to the hope he was wrong. But he wasn't. It was the postcard. He'd slid it in a desk drawer years ago, wanting it somewhere nearby but safe, where it would cause no harm. Sunday hadn't been busted, he had.

"It's not appropriate," Vivienne said.

He drew in breath. "Vivienne—"

"No, she's right," Sunday said. "I'm sorry. It must have gotten mixed in with papers I brought from home." She reached for the postcard with the Kale and Sunday stick figures drawn on the beach, the one they used to find ways to surprise each other with, and slid it into her laptop bag on the floor.

She was taking the fall for him. Was he going to let her do it?

Her cheeks were flaming when she straightened back up, but she met Vivienne's eye. "I'm really sorry about that."

Vivienne, slight lift to her chin and pucker to her mouth, nodded. Then she turned to Luke. "C'mon, sweetie. Time to go." She took his hand and led him past Sunday and out of the office, shooting Kale arched eyebrows on the way.

Sunday remained, staring at the space where Vivienne's face had been seconds before.

He had, indeed, let her take the fall.

She closed her eyes, turned away from him.

What was he supposed to say—Thanks? I'm sorry? Oh, and yes, I kept our postcard all this time.

If the situation with Sunday had become more complicated the day before, it was a hot mess now. But he couldn't fix anything in that moment, while his wife and son waited on the other side of the open door.

So he turned and followed them out without saying a word.

After dinner they popped in a Pixar movie, but Luke was out in ten minutes. When Kale picked him up, Luke's little arms wrapped around his neck. He carried him up to his room but didn't put him down right away. Instead Kale held him and gently swayed for a bit, grounding himself in his life. In his son's bedroom surrounded by all his toys, in the house he'd shared with Viv for almost four years now. She had asked him about the postcard when they got home, if he and Sunday had gone to that beach, and he said no, it had been a "maybe someday" thing. He officially moved from lying by omission to lying by commission when he agreed with her that it was irresponsible for Sunday to leave it in the office where anyone could find it.

He'd assumed the postcard would be safe in that drawer; he was normally the only person who used the damned desk. Maybe Sunday had already come across it, but based on her reaction in the office he doubted it. She had taken the blame, and now they were complicit in this lie.

And it wouldn't be long before she noticed the note he added to that postcard just a few months before she left New York.

Maybe she covered for him as a peace offering after their argument. He still had trouble believing the things she'd said. *Probably as long as I waited for you to come after me.* That just didn't make sense. She was the one who changed back then, the one who accepted a job three thousand miles away and left him wondering what he did wrong for years. Just like his mother had.

You seemed to get over it awfully quickly. The truth in that one stung a bit. Viv had gotten pregnant less than a year after Sunday left. They'd been dating—casually, in his mind—for a few months when she told him. Initially they'd used condoms, but she was also on the pill so he went with that after a while. The cold truth was he hadn't been paying much attention.

As the weight of a decision pressed upon him, there'd been a moment when he considered going after Sunday, or at least calling her. But what would he have said—Hey, I got another woman pregnant so I just want to make sure it's really over between us? Besides, she'd been gone ten months, and from everything he heard she was doing well out there. And he couldn't just walk away from his responsibilities. Planned or unplanned, he was going to be a father.

So he decided to embrace it, despite Denny's response—*I forbid you to marry her*. He saw it as his chance at a family. He cut way back on his drinking and made plans with Viv: moved into the empty house his father had left him, attended doctor's appointments and Lamaze classes, had a small wedding ceremony, which the Brennans had attended.

He laid Luke down in his bed and tucked him in tight like a burrito. Once Luke had come along the doubts had quieted. He loved his son to an impossible degree. So much so it eclipsed uncertainty about Vivienne, those moments when it felt like something was missing or he was married to someone he would never quite know, not all the way.

As he headed back downstairs to his wife, he admitted to himself that he wanted answers from Sunday to questions that had plagued him for years, and she had added more to the list since coming back. But asking those questions would lead nowhere good, and no matter what her answers were, they would never justify what she did to him. The only solution was to focus on his family, keep his distance, and seal up the crack in the box that held their history.

And he would hold on to a little of that righteous anger she had mentioned. It was straight-up self-preservation.

When he arrived at work the next morning he was greeted by an enthusiastic Shane, who was helping Jackie stock the bar.

"Where have you been, Kale? We didn't work on our GT model in forever."

That triggered a twinge of shame. Kale hadn't talked to Shane in weeks. "Sorry about that, Shane. What're you guys doing here?"

"I offered to open," Jackie said. "Don't worry, I got permission from my probation officer. Denny wasn't sure when you'd be in and he had to go out to Mamaroneck."

"What for?"

"The foreman's there today and Denny wanted to ask more questions about what the hell happened with that pipe." Jackie shrugged. "He can't let it go."

Shane picked up two empty crates. "I'll take these out back and break them down, okay, Jackie?"

"Thanks, dude."

Shane headed out the back door.

"He doing okay?" Kale asked.

"He had a rough night at work yesterday, started head-banging after one of the asshole cashiers yelled at him for not getting the carts in from the parking lot fast enough."

"Shit," Kale said. "Do we need to talk to that cashier?"

"I had a chat with him. I don't think it'll happen again." Jackie pulled his hands through his long hair. "It's no wonder though. Things are just tense lately. Theresa's still gone, Denny's in a shit mood." He checked over his shoulder and lowered his voice. "And Shane's afraid Sunday will leave again. He follows her around like a puppy."

Shane had always been the family barometer. Things in the Brennan house were out of whack.

Jackie started playing with a bar towel. "It's not easy for her, being back here."

Maybe she'd told Jackie about their argument. "Is she here?" Kale asked.

"She's down in the cellar with Molly."

Kale headed for the stairs.

"What happened between you two?" Jackie asked.

"Why? What'd she say?"

"She didn't say anything, but I know when she's upset."

"It was nothing."

"Maybe to you." Jackie leaned on the bar. "We just got her back, man, you know?"

Kale didn't respond, the message was clear. He went downstairs where he heard Sunday and Molly talking.

". . . it go here, Sunday?"

"Yep. That's right."

When he got to the cellar he leaned against the doorjamb and watched.

Molly was taking her time placing a bottle on a low shelf just right, label facing front. She stepped back from her work. "Did I do it okay?"

Sunday was crouched down next to her with a clipboard. "That's perfect. But just wait until I tell Auntie Clare you were carrying around a bottle of scotch."

"*Nooo*, Sunday. You won't do that."

"I will."

"You better not!"

"Oh yes, I will." She started tickling her, but Molly broke away in a bubble of high-pitched giggles and ran out the door, stopping to return Kale's high five on her way past.

Sunday stood and spun. When she saw him standing there her smile didn't fade exactly, just became sort of rueful. The bruises were almost gone, though there was still a shadowy tinge to the skin around her eyes. The scar on her left temple was less obvious; her hair covered most of it. She flipped the clipboard up against her chest, crossed her arms over it.

"I'm sorry about yesterday," he said. "I didn't think about the postcard. It's been in there for years." Just a silly keepsake. But had she taken it out of her bag and flipped it over yet? "I should have told Vivienne the truth."

"That wouldn't have made anyone feel better. Especially her."

He shoved his hands in his pockets and stepped farther into the room. "Listen, about the other day . . . I think it's best we stay away from the past, you know. Just keep it all in the rearview."

She nodded. "I'm sorry I'm complicating your life. But I don't think I can leave just now—"

"Leave? I don't want you to leave." He'd said it without any thought.

He was about to follow up with a lame platitude about how they'd all get through it, but Jackie appeared.

He raised his arms up against the sides of the doorframe and eyed them both. "Everything okay in here?"

"Yeah," Sunday said. "We're fine."

But Jackie didn't look convinced. "Since you're both here," he said, "I think it's time for a come-to-Jesus with Denny."

Kale was about to ask whether Jackie was referring to a come-to-Jesus about Theresa, the money, or the family. But it was probably all three.

CHAPTER NINE

Jackie

I think it's time for a come-to-Jesus with Denny."

It had been brewing for weeks. The tension at home was thick and Denny had to pull his head out of his ass before he fubar'd everything and Theresa never came back, or Shane ended up in a hospital, or Sunday left again—which had caused Shane's first and only trip to the psych ward. Jackie was used to riding out Denny's storms, maybe because he caused a lot of them. But this was getting out of hand.

"Okay," Sunday said. "When?"

"He closes tonight," Kale said. "Let's catch him when he gets home. He'll be tired, maybe it'll be less of a fight."

Jackie cocked an eyebrow. "Have you met Denny?"

"No, that's a good idea," Sunday said. "Let's do it." She turned back to inventorying shelves. There was a weary quality about her, flat tone, wilted shoulders. That's what worried Jackie. She'd been beaten down physically when she first got home, but her spirits had been good. Over the last five weeks it had reversed.

· · ·

He made sure his dad and Shane were in bed by ten, doors closed in the event things got loud, a distinct possibility with Denny. Kale walked over around ten thirty.

Jackie opened the door for him. "Since when do you knock?"

Kale just shrugged, like he no longer knew what the rules were.

A wave of nostalgia hit Jackie when he led Kale back to the kitchen where Sunday waited. The kitchen table had been the center of their universe for many years. Everything else—school, friends, jobs—had revolved around this space, where they all started and ended so many of their days together. Where they celebrated and commiserated, argued and laughed, planted themselves until the late hours. Watching Kale choose the seat across from Sunday, rather than his old one next to her, felt unnatural.

They made nervous chitchat for a few minutes, but before long Denny blew in the back door, along with the strong odor of cigarette smoke. His eyebrows shot up when he saw Kale. "What're you doing here?"

"Waiting for you."

Denny looked around the table, from one to the next, and let out a long sigh that ended in "Shit." Then he reached up to the cabinet above the fridge.

"We want to talk to you about a few things," Sunday said.

"I think I'm going to need some sustenance for this discussion." He pulled down the Jameson bottle with one hand and four shot glasses with the other, placed it all on the table, and sat across from Jackie. Then he started to pour. "And I'm not participating in this little intervention unless you all have a drink with me."

Everyone reached for a glass and Denny tapped his on the table twice. "Sláinte." They all drank to their health.

He did his arms-crossed, hands-in-pits pose. "Well?"

Jackie kicked it off since this had been his idea. "You're a mess, Denny."

"Pot, kettle."

"He's right," Kale said. "Just tell us what's going on."

"If this is about Theresa, first I'll just say it's none of your fucking business. But once she sees how things calm down after the opening, it'll be fine."

"So you haven't talked to your lawyer again?" Sunday asked.

One side of his mouth pulled up. "Only when he called me to ask about you."

She rolled her eyes and went red.

Classic Denny, turning the tables. "What about your foul moods lately?" Jackie asked. "They're upsetting everyone."

Denny turned to him with narrowed eyes. He was the one used to demanding answers, not the other way around. "You have enough of your own problems without worrying about mine, Jackie. You know, taking care of this family isn't easy."

"Oh, is that what you've been doing?"

"Think you could do a better job? Why don't you give it a shot. You can support us all with your painting—*after* you finish paying off your lawyer fees from two years ago."

"Fuck off, Denny."

"Stop it," Sunday said.

But Jackie had swallowed enough of Denny's shit; he was tired of being his scapegoat. "Your wife left, you're lying to everybody. Time to grow a pair and tell us what's going on before you torpedo everything and it's too late."

They all gaped at Jackie. No one was used to him jumping into the conflict. He usually avoided it, or nodded and smiled his way through. Even Denny seemed at a loss for words.

Kale seized the opportunity. "What about the money, Denny?"

His response was to glare at Sunday.

"What did you think was going to happen?" she asked. "Your books are a disaster, there's no rhyme or reason to the cash flow. I can't make sense of it."

"Sorry I asked for your help."

"It's not her fault," Kale said. "I know you're hiding stuff from me. I'm your goddamn partner. What the hell is going on?" His tone was insistent, with a pinch of pleading.

Denny poured himself another shot and threw it back, shifted around and grunted. He ran his hands down his face, and Jackie could hear his palms scraping stubble. "I was going to tell you in a couple of weeks, after the pub opened." He held his hands up. "Just know before I start that it's all worked out, everything's taken care of." Which, to Jackie, sounded way more ominous than reassuring.

Once Denny decided to talk, he didn't stop for a while. His voice was the only sound in the house, and it grew coarser as he went on. He stared at the table and told them how it all went down, how he drained his personal account and then the business account to stay afloat and pay for his share of the new place. Then he'd resorted to a home equity loan and credit cards. He talked them through the darkest hour, when the city threatened condemnation, and the possibility of bankruptcy became very real.

The cabin pressure in the kitchen changed with the weight of shock and anger coming from Sunday and Kale. Sunday more shocked, Kale more angry. Curiously, Jackie didn't feel much anger toward Denny. For the first time, his older brother was the one having to answer for a significant fuckup and, it could be argued, this particular fuckup was worse than any of Jackie's. But rather than relish Denny's reckoning, he felt an alien sympathy for him. Denny might be a controlling asshole much of the time, but there was no denying they all relied on him. It was an unspoken agreement; they let him figure everything out so they didn't have to. Just like they'd let him claim the family spotlight when they were younger. Better to let him be responsible for making their mother happy, maybe even healthy. Let her pin all her unrequited hopes on him.

The more Denny explained, the more his whole demeanor sagged. Jackie had only seen him like this one other time. When he lost his place on the Olympic Development team senior year after wrenching his knee in the wrong direction during a slide tackle.

When he explained that he'd taken a loan from a private investor secured by Brennan's in West Manor, an ear-piercing silence descended on the room.

"My God," Kale said. "How much do we owe?"

There was trepidation on Denny's face when he met Kale's eye. "With interest, close to seventy grand."

Sunday gasped. "You could lose the house *and* Brennan's?"

Denny didn't answer.

Kale pulled back from the table, clenched the sides of it, and hung his head. Even though Jackie loved Kale like a brother, there'd always been a thin layer of jealousy wrapped up in it because he and Denny were so tight. It seemed a given they'd be best friends and partners their whole lives. But maybe this would be the wedge that drove them apart.

"I have a plan for paying it back," Denny said. But it sounded hollow. As if he'd said it to himself so many times the words no longer had any substance.

Visions of his family packing boxes and crowding into some row house or having to split up materialized in Jackie's mind. If that didn't propel Shane over the limit of his anxiety capacity, nothing would.

Kale was still stiff-arming the table with his head down. Sunday held hers in her hands. But they couldn't give up; there had to be a way to fix this.

Jackie laced his fingers on the table. "What do you need, Denny?"

There was gratitude in Denny's eyes when he turned to Jackie. "I just need the new place to open on time. Everything's riding on it now. The inspectors come day after tomorrow. We're in good shape, but they're going to give us a to-do list. I need to be out there twenty-four-seven, getting the place ready."

"All right." Jackie patted the table with his hand. "I'll get some time off so I can work at the pub. It'll free you guys and Paul up to prep the new place. Would that help?"

"Yeah, but what about your probation officer?"

"The two-year limit is about up. I can get him to go for it."

Sunday spoke next. "You give me access to everything—everything, Denny—and I'll try to get it under control." She stood and walked over to the counter while she spoke, flicked on the electric kettle to start water, like she needed to fortify herself with tea. "I can prioritize bills, make some payment plans with vendors."

Denny gave her a weary nod.

Kale lifted his head. "Why the hell didn't you tell me?"

"Because you didn't want to go to Mamaroneck in the first place."

"That's not true—"

"Come on." He daggered Kale with a look of disdain. "You wouldn't say no but you fought me every step of the way."

"I asked questions—"

"You were just waiting for it to fail—"

"Stop!" Jackie tried out his newfound credibility and stood up. "You two can argue later. Now that we know, we can deal with it."

They both shut up but didn't look at each other.

Sunday collected the Jameson bottle and glasses, put them on the counter. "We'll figure it out. It'll be okay." She turned to the whistling kettle.

Kale shoved back from the table to stand up. "I'll look into an expedited home equity loan. But I want to know one other thing. Who'd you borrow the money from?"

Denny shrugged. "Just some guy in Katonah that sold his mom's house and didn't know what to do with the cash. You might remember him." His voice perked up a bit like that would make everyone feel better. "He went to school with us. Billy Walsh. Everyone called him Belfast Billy back then. He lived—"

Sunday's cry cut him off.

Jackie had just grabbed on to that name mentally—*Walsh*—when he turned to see that she had jerked the kettle while pouring. Scalding water had flowed over her good hand, which was resting on the counter, and then run onto the floor. She uprighted the kettle and her eyes met Jackie's. *Walsh.* It couldn't be. Her hand was already turning bright red.

Kale stepped toward her, but Jackie moved in and turned her to the sink, pushed her hand under cold running water. Billy Walsh. No fucking way. Jackie had confirmed that Billy was still gone from West Manor. But he'd never thought to check a small town up the road.

"Would you grab the first aid kit from the laundry room?" Jackie asked Kale.

He headed down the stairs off the kitchen.

Denny pushed up out of his chair for a better look. "Are you all right?"

"She's fine," Jackie said.

"I'll go find some rags for the floor." He started down the hall.

Jackie lowered his voice. "Sunday, look at me."

She shook her head, trying to ward off what she'd heard. Or maybe what he was going to say.

"We have to tell them," he said.

Kale jogged back up from the basement. "Found it." He unzipped the medical kit on the counter, started rifling through.

"No," Sunday said, pulling her arm away from Jackie.

"Yes," Kale said. "You need to bandage that. But I can't find any aloe vera . . ."

"There's some in the downstairs bathroom," Jackie said. When Kale left again he turned back to her. "We have to tell them."

"No, Jackie. Not now."

"But they—"

"*Please*. I can't now." She squeezed her eyes shut and her burnt hand gripped the counter.

Kale reappeared with a bottle in his hand. "What's wrong?"

"Nothing," Jackie said.

"That's not nothing."

Sunday pulled herself up straight. "I'm fine. Just a headache."

Jackie needed to get her, and himself, away from Kale and Denny for now. "I just have to get her to bed."

"Go ahead. I'll bring up the first aid stuff."

Jackie helped her up to her room. Kale followed them in and placed the kit on the foot of her bed.

"I think it's a migraine," she said. "I've gotten a couple since the accident." She reached over and shook two pills out from a bottle on her side table, downed them with water. "I'll be fine, really." Then she lay down and pulled a pillow over her head.

Kale seemed to realize where he was. His eyes started to wander around the room.

"Thanks for your help, dude," Jackie said.

"Yeah, sure." Kale took a last look at Sunday and left the room.

Jackie sank into Sunday's desk chair and let his head roll back. He'd felt so good about the talk with Denny, the most hopeful he'd been in a while.

Then Denny had mentioned Billy Walsh.

He picked his head back up and looked at his sister, buried under the pillow. It reminded him of another time he'd sat in that chair, watching until she fell into fitful sleep while he wondered what the hell to do about the dark secret they shared. After smearing some aloe vera on a large bandage he did a clumsy wrap around her hand with gauze. The steady breathing meant she was on her way to deep sleep, which was good. She'd feel better tomorrow, and they had a serious talk in their future. They had to decide what to do with this information, what it even meant.

He started to head to his own room but stopped at the door to check on her once more.

She still lay there, in pain and hidden away. Kind of like the last five years of her life.

When Sunday appeared at the breakfast table the next morning she looked like a "before" picture. Puffy face, narrow eyes, hand still wrapped in his haphazard gauze job.

"Wow," Denny said. "You look like shit."

Dad swatted the back of his head. "Don't be saying that to your sister."

"Don't say bad words, Denny," Shane said. "You shouldn't say bad words."

"Sorry, Shane."

"What happened to your other hand?" Shane asked her.

Sunday looked down at it. "Nothing. It's fine." She poured herself some coffee and headed back upstairs. Not once did she look Jackie's way.

He let her be for a few hours, until Theresa dropped Molly off with him on her way to a Saturday shift. He took Molly up to knock on her door around noon.

"Hey," Jackie called through the door. "Hot-Ta-Molly and I are headed to Hollis Park. You should come."

"Please come?" Molly asked. No way Sunday would turn down a voice that sweet.

But she did. Without opening her door she said sorry, she wasn't feeling well.

So Jackie had taken Molly to the park alone. She kicked the ball and he played goalie for a while, he pushed her on the swings and watched her boss a couple of other kids around on the climbing structure because they weren't doing it right. They headed home a couple of hours later and, as they approached the house, there was a flutter of anxiety in his stomach. It was there until he brought lunch up to Sunday a little later. Some small part of him had actually been afraid she might have left, packed a bag and headed back to California.

But she answered and said he could come in. She was sitting at her desk, working on her laptop, or, more like, just staring at it. She didn't look at him when he came in and put a plate down on her desk. He'd thrown together a turkey sandwich.

"Thanks," she said. Her legs were pulled up on the chair.

He took a seat on the edge of her bed, behind her. "Sunday, we need to talk about this."

She spoke to her screen. "I can't right now."

"When?"

"Later."

"Jesus." He lifted his hands and let them drop on his legs. "At some point you have to deal with it."

She turned her face to him, and if looks could kill he would have been a goner. "You have no fucking clue what you're talking about."

He didn't have the heart to push it. Or maybe he was too scared. "Fine. But do you think it could be a coincidence?" Dealing with Billy Walsh being back in town was one thing—and they would absolutely be dealing with that fucker one way or the other. But if he had a specific agenda behind the loan to Denny . . .

Her forehead fell down against her knees. "No," she said. "I don't think it's a coincidence."

Early the next morning he went to the pub to help Kale with deliveries. It was a two-man job and Denny had some function at Molly's school. But Jackie forced Sunday to come with him. She hadn't come out of her room since their talk, not even for dinner. He covered for her, told everyone she was sick—déjà vu from when he made excuses for her five years ago. With his typical warmth Denny had said, "Tell her to stay in there, for Christ's sake, so the rest of us don't get it."

The clock was ticking. It had been a day and a half since Denny told them about Billy Walsh and she still refused to talk about it. As soon as they got to the pub she mumbled hello to Kale and disappeared into the office.

"She all right?" Kale asked.

"Yeah, she's fine."

But Kale stared after her like he could see through the door. He wasn't buying it. Apparently even now he and Sunday were tuned to each other to an obnoxious degree.

They'd always been that way, like they lived in their own little world and the rest of them just visited from time to time. When they started dating in high school, Jackie had been angry with both of them. Not only was Kale best friends with Denny, now he was taking Sunday too. And she was breaking an unspoken pact. She was the one person he could count on to be in his corner, to drop everything and take his side without fail when the rest of them were coming down on him for shitty grades or being lazy. And he was that person for her, unswerving support when she had an argument with Denny or needed something from their parents. Kale was usurping his role and Jackie wished he would get his own damn family. He even tried some minor sabotage, like being a third wheel or needling Kale—*Don't you have your own home, Collins? My parents should charge you rent.* He gave up before long though, because it became obvious they were going the distance, and alienating Kale would mean alienating Sunday.

They were in the middle of unpacking and breaking down boxes when a familiar blond guy wearing a high-end suit walked in. He stopped by the bar and cocked his head. "Jackie?"

"Yeah?" It was starting to come back. Jock-type friend of Denny's from high school, had gone somewhere Ivy for college.

"Michael Eaton." He walked over and extended a hand, then turned to Kale. "Hey, Collins. Good to see you."

Kale answered from behind a tall pile of cardboard. "You too, Michael. You looking for Denny?"

"Yeah, we have a meeting."

"He won't be here for another ten minutes or so," Jackie said. "But you can have a seat and wait for him."

"Thanks." Michael hesitated by the bar. "Is Sunday here by any chance?"

Kale's head picked up at that question.

Jackie yelled toward the office for her and went back to flattening boxes.

"Wow," Michael said when she stepped out. "You're all healed up."

She shrugged a shoulder. "Getting there."

"No, really. You look great."

"You meeting Denny?" she asked. "You want some coffee while you wait?"

"Sure, thanks." Michael turned to Kale again. "Excited about the new place?"

"Yep." But Kale didn't sound very excited at the moment. He turned away and went to work with a box cutter.

Sunday grabbed the coffeepot from behind the bar and led Michael to a booth. He had a bouncy walk, like he had trouble containing his enthusiasm.

"I wanted to thank you for recommending that DUI lawyer in LA," Sunday said, pouring coffee. "He's trying to wrap it up quickly."

She sat across from Michael and explained the details. She was pleading no contest to a wet reckless, which would mean a three-month driving suspension and one to two years of probation, but she wouldn't have
to go back to California for a court date. Jackie focused on binding cardboard stacks for recycling while he listened, but he stopped when Michael
said something about finding her stories.

"Sorry?" she asked.

"The ones you published in the LA Arts Council magazine. All their
back issues are online."

"Oh," Sunday said. "I didn't know that." Her glance drifted in Jackie's
direction but didn't quite reach him.

"Yeah. I thought they were really good," Michael said.

"That's nice, but I went through years of 'No thanks' before anyone
bit."

Jackie listened to her play it down, but apparently her time in LA hadn't
been a total washout.

Kale was clearly taking all this in as well. He stood very still, box cutter
in one hand and ball of twine in the other, his head half-turned toward
the booth behind him so he didn't miss a word.

Michael folded his arms on the table. "You changed the names and
details, but the one story was about Denny, right? How hard it was on
him when he had to give up on soccer senior year, refigure his whole
future." He shook his head at the memory. "I bet it meant a lot to him."

Sunday offered some noncommittal mumble in response. What else
could she do—Jackie knew damn well Denny had never read the story.
None of them had.

Michael kept going, oblivious he was outing her. "And the other one,
about Shane . . ." He considered his words. "You wrote about his strug-
gles, but it was more about his strengths. That was unexpected."

Sunday flashed a small smile, the first Jackie had seen since she heard
Billy Walsh's name the other night.

"You working on the next one?" Michael asked.

"I am," she said.

Was it about him? The other brother? Probably not. The tightest bond they shared would have been too painful for her to write about.

"Well, if you're ever looking for a test reader . . ." Michael flipped his hands toward his chest.

"Thanks. I'll keep that in mind."

Kale finally moved then. He laid his box cutter and twine on a nearby table, walked back into the office, and closed the door.

Jackie would have bet all the cash in the safe that Kale was already on his laptop, pulling up those stories.

Midafternoon on a Tuesday was pretty dead. Jackie's only customers were two old-timers nursing their Buds while they watched a baseball game.

He had always loved working the bar. Having a regular's drink ready before they took their seat, laughing with strangers, lively action on a busy night. Being the hero for waitstaff by making their customers' drinks fast and strong. He had worked evenings and weekends at Brennan's for years, which was good money, enough to afford his own apartment and stay supplied in canvases, paints, and brushes. It also left his days free. It had been a perfect setup. But Jackie's probation officer had forbidden it for two years following his sentencing. That's when his dad had to get him a job as a laborer, and Denny and Kale had to hire Paul.

Not only had his arrest and conviction cost him the best job he ever had, it had also been a major setback for his painting. At the time he'd been taking classes, spending hours at galleries, even selling small pieces at local craft fairs. Mostly touristy stuff—a tranquil Hudson River, peaceful Catskill Mountains. But he'd been making progress with the work he was more passionate about. Scenes or portraits that were more complex, challenged a little bit, and evoked emotion.

Then one night he'd accepted a last-minute invite for an evening out with a few loose acquaintances, amped-up-bro types that called him "Jackie Boy." Guys he'd always been able to get along with but normally avoided. They'd ended up at some nameless person's raging house party. Jackie had stayed sober that night because he was the designated driver, which was by design. He didn't want to get stuck somewhere, waiting around for people.

He had dropped them all off a little after 1 A.M. and was less than five minutes from his apartment when he pulled up to a Memorial Day weekend sobriety checkpoint after getting off the Taconic. He wasn't surprised when the officer asked him to submit to a field sobriety test. His pickup smelled offensively of beer because someone had spilled half a can in the back seat on the way home. He also granted approval for a vehicle check with a "Be my guest." He passed the sobriety test, but the cops found a large Ziploc crammed full of marijuana under one of the seats. One of those dickheads had left his stash in the truck and, since it was Jackie's vehicle, he'd literally been left holding a bag that weighed enough to bump the possession charge up to a felony. Not long after that, Jackie was out of a job and moving back home so he could start helping with his lawyer bills as much as possible.

He had just brought the two baseball fans another round when his father walked through the door and headed for the bar.

"Hiya, Mick," called one of the guys with a wave.

"Boys." His dad chatted with them for a couple minutes. They all probably knew each other from construction days.

As long as Jackie could remember, his dad had been well known in town. Whenever the family went anywhere—church, a restaurant, July 4th parade—there was a lot of "Hey, Boss" and "How's it going, Mickey," men stopping them on the street to shake his father's big calloused hand. He'd been a project manager with a contracting company that started riding the construction boom in 1990s New York and kept growing. He'd loved his job and his crew, usually spending more time at work than home.

His dad had always been a hard worker. Before leaving Ireland, he'd helped support his family of twelve by working the farm and driving trucks. During visits with Irish relatives over the years, when lips were loosened by whiskey, Jackie had caught references to his father "being a friend" to the IRA and having to make a hasty departure from home. It was hard to know what to believe. The Irish had a flair for the dramatic, but at the same time they lived by a rigid don't-ask-don't-tell code.

Though Jackie was pretty sure there were a few buried secrets. When he was a kid, during a game of hide-and-seek, he had found a stellar hiding spot in his parents' closet. The downside had been how long he sat there, waiting for someone to find him. Out of boredom he discovered the loose carpet in the back corner, and then a small compartment under a floorboard, the size of a shoebox. He was briefly celebrated by his older siblings for finding it. There were some official papers to do with the house, and his dad's green card. But what had always stayed with Jackie were the photos. A few worn black-and-whites of menacing-looking men and women, including his father, dressed in '70s garb and posed against what looked like one of the walls in Belfast that separated Catholic neighborhoods from Protestant ones. They stood shoulder to shoulder, arms crossed, grim expressions on their faces. Each of them had a gun slung over an arm.

None of them had ever asked their dad about those pictures, and, as far as Jackie knew, none of them had ever invaded his hiding place again.

Dad finished up his conversation with the men, clapped them on the back, and headed down to a stool at the other end of the bar.

"I didn't know you were coming in today," Jackie said, pouring him a Harp.

"I had to get out of that house for a while."

"Something going on?"

"Why don't you tell me? Unless you're as in the dark as I am."

Jackie brought him his beer. "What do you mean?"

"Thanks." He took a sip. "Your brother's in rare form, and he's after having a lawyer at the house this afternoon. Theresa's been gone over a month. Your sister's like the walking dead lately—Shane asked me if she's going to leave again. And Kale's fallen off the face of the earth."

For a man with a slippery memory, he'd summed it up nicely.

"What the hell's going on, Jackie?" The piercing eyes and furrowed brow demanded answers.

Jackie wondered when they had all relegated him to the feeble old guy who read newspapers all day and didn't know what was happening in his own house.

"Tell me, son. I'd like to help."

Jackie's chest constricted at the commanding yet pleading tone. His dad wanted to be of use, but there was nothing he could do here. "I think everybody's just stressed about the new place, Dad. There was that leak and the opening was pushed back. It all got expensive . . ."

His dad slapped the bar. "I knew it had to do with money. That damn pipe." He pointed at Jackie. "Mark my words, someone caused that damage. I don't care what those inspectors say."

His dad had made this declaration before, but Jackie had always dismissed it because who the hell would want to hurt Denny or their family that way. But right then, for the first time, he could think of someone.

"Listen," his dad said, "I could take out a small loan on the house. Sure there's loads of equity in it and I could give the cash to Denny and Kale until they get past the worst of it." His expression was so hopeful Jackie had to look away. "What do you think? It would take the pressure off."

This was the first time his father had consulted him about a significant family matter. He just wished he didn't have to lie to him. "I think they have it under control, Dad."

"Even if they do, a little money could offer a lot of breathing room."

Jackie had to kill this idea before his dad decided to act on it. He didn't know if his father would be more furious or humiliated to find out Denny had already obtained that home equity loan behind his back. "Let me talk to them, feel it out. They'll be honest with me. If it sounds like a good idea, I'll let you know."

His dad narrowed his eyes. "Don't think I haven't noticed, you around the house more, helping out here. It's been good to see." He raised his glass with a wink.

Jackie settled into a time-out from his worries while they shot the shit for the next fifteen minutes, touching on the new restaurant, politics, Gaelic football. But in the back of his mind he was making a decision.

He had to help Sunday confront this whole situation, and he had to do it that night.

His family was being crushed under the weight of secrets and, one way or another, all of it had to finally come out.

"Hey, can I show you something?" Jackie asked. He and Sunday were finishing up the dinner dishes.

"What is it?"

"Something in my studio." He air-quoted that last word. His studio was his bedroom.

He led her upstairs to his room at the end of the hall. Giving up his apartment two years ago had been a blow, but he'd always loved his room in the house. It was tucked under a long eave, with sloped ceilings and a large skylight. He watched Sunday's eyes breeze past his bed and dresser along the one wall to the studio portion of the room. Canvases of all sizes were piled on his desk or leaned against walls or sat up on a couple of easels. A drop cloth occupied the floor in that part of the room. A stack of palettes sat on a shelf, splattered in rainbows of mixed paints, and several jars crammed with brushes were scattered about. She smiled as she soaked up the colorful chaos, like a proud parent; she was the one who had championed his painting from the beginning. The rest of the family had humored it when he was a kid, but later treated it as the self-indulgent hobby they thought it should be.

He waved her over to his desk. "Remember 'The Little Fireman'? The story you used to tell Shane all the time and I would pretend I wasn't listening?" He opened a large folder and spread out several small sketches.

"Oh my God. When did you do these?"

"I've been working on them for a few weeks." He'd started as soon as he heard she was coming home.

She leaned close to study his vision of the little fireman and his world. "They're perfect."

"I had Shane help. He remembered some details that were really distinctive." No wonder. Shane had demanded that story every night for years when he was little, and even beyond, because he tired of bedtime stories far later than most kids. And Sunday never refused. "I thought maybe we could collaborate on a children's book," he said. "It's your story. You could write it and I could do the illustrations. We could get Shane's name on it as a coauthor or something. What do you think?"

"I would love that," she said, her eyes lighting up from within.

"Okay. I mean, I know children's books aren't your thing. Apparently short stories are." He gave her a pointed look.

Her shoulders slumped. "Sorry I didn't tell you. It was such a small thing, just two stories. And I didn't want to get into all of it . . ."

"It's okay. As long as I can read them."

"Sure. As long as I can take a look." She nodded toward the canvases resting against the walls behind him.

Stepping back from his desk, he opened up her view to the rest of the room and gestured toward the rectangular area where he kept his work, in all its varying degrees of completion. Some of it in a very early, experimental stage, many abandoned partway through. A few closer to finished. Although he rarely felt like one of his paintings was finished.

She moved to the largest one first. "You're still working on this one?" He'd sent her pictures of it before. It was a painting of the exterior of the house that he'd been "finishing" for years, long enough that he'd had to change Molly and Luke from babies to little kids. They played on the tire swing while Mickey looked on from the front porch rocker.

"Yeah, I don't know. I just keep finding things wrong."

She rolled her eyes and moved on to the next one. "Wow, Jackie." It was a portrait of Shane from the chest up, caught mid-laugh, shoulders pulled up and head bowed. "You totally captured him, his spirit."

"I'm not happy with his chin and mouth. Something's not right. Do you see it?"

She studied it. "Maybe just a little too angular?"

"Yep." He sat in his desk chair, steepled his hands, and waited.

She moved down one side of the room and up the other, making observations, showering praise. "I'm glad you're getting more into people."

"They're a lot harder than landscapes. Less room for interpretation."

She stepped up to a twenty-by-twenty-four-inch canvas vertically oriented on a tall easel, hidden under a light sheet. "Oooo. Can I?"

He swiveled his chair toward her. "Sure."

With a theatrical flair she whipped the sheet off with her good hand. He heard no sounds in the house other than the slip of fabric and his own heartbeat. The sheet swooshed to the ground and she took a step back, staring at the painting while her face morphed from open curiosity to stunned realization.

He stood and moved near her, his whole body tense, not knowing what to expect. Her eyes were riveted and he was pretty sure she was holding her breath. It was hard to just let it hit her, to not say something to soften the blow, but this was the only way.

"When did you do this?" she asked. It was almost a whisper.

"I started it like six months after you left. There were nights I couldn't sleep, couldn't shake certain images. I thought it would help."

Without taking her eyes off the painting, she asked, "Did it?" There was a note of longing, like she had failed to find her own remedy for the same problem.

"Yeah. Did you ever try writing about it?"

She pulled her eyes to his. "No."

"I worked on it for a while, till things got better. I just pulled it out again a few weeks ago."

"Since I came home?"

He stalled because he didn't want her to feel guilty—she had enough of that going on to sink a ship—but this was all about ripping off the Band-Aids. "Yeah."

She backed up and dropped onto his bed. "I'm so sorry, Jackie. For making my secret yours all these years." He saw deep regret in her watery eyes when she turned her face up to him. "That wasn't right."

"Don't do that. We both did the best we could."

She looked up at the painting and quiet tears started to roll. He'd gotten through the fog of fear and denial she'd wrapped around herself since Denny told them about Billy Walsh.

"Sunday, we need to tell them. I can do it, or I can do it with you. But they have to know who they're dealing with."

She wiped heavy drops from her chin and nodded. "I'll tell them tonight."

Jackie sat back down in his chair. Fingers crossed, this would be the first step in healing a secret wound that had been festering for the last five years.

CHAPTER TEN

Sunday

I'll tell them tonight."

As soon as she said it panic blossomed in her chest until it threatened to choke her.

But down below that, in the bottom of her stomach, there was something resembling relief. She'd known for at least the last two days, since hearing Billy Walsh's name, that she had no choice but to tell them the truth. And there was a slight lifting of pressure, mentally and physically, in accepting it. Now the thing just had to be done.

When she turned to Jackie again, his hair tucked behind his ears, eyes full of compassion, a tidal wave of shame slammed into her. By making him the guardian of her secret, he was one of the people she'd hurt the most in all this. And she'd hurt a lot of people. She lifted the sheet off the floor and took time positioning it just right over the painting, straight and centered. Never again would she look at that image of herself, so scared and ruined.

But more than that, she refused to be that version of herself ever again.

Jackie stood and slid his hands in his pockets, watching and waiting, likely wondering if she would zombie-out again or change her mind.

"I'll head to the pub now," she said. "They'll be closing up. It should be empty."

"It's going to be okay, Sun."

If she looked at him she would lose it, so she walked toward the door. In the hall she stopped but didn't turn around. "Thank you, Jackie." She left before he could say anything else.

The walk to Brennan's was quiet and chilly. She'd headed down the stairs and directly out the front door, not even stopping for a jacket. Like she was trying to outrun the part of herself that wanted to find a reason to put this off. She crossed her arms against the cold and focused on breathing the night air in and out. As she walked past houses lit up by cozy lamps or shifting screen lights, a few scenarios dashed across her mind. Maybe Denny and Kale closed up early and left. She could get a taxi to the airport and disappear. Perhaps an act of God would intervene. But they were fleeting. She was resolved.

She gripped the cold bronze door handle for a moment before going in, letting it ground her. One more deep breath and she swung it open.

They were both behind the bar, Kale washing and stacking glasses, Denny doing math at the register. Their backs were to each other and she had the distinct impression the silence had gone uninterrupted for a while. Kale would get over Denny's deceit in time, but it had taken a toll. Off to the right corner the kitchen lights were off. No one else was here.

Denny turned, cash and receipts in his hands. "Hey."

Kale nodded from the sink.

She stayed by the door.

"What's up?" Denny went back to counting.

"I need to talk to you."

He looked up at the tone of her voice.

Kale turned off the faucet. "That's fine. I can finish this tomorrow."

"You too, Kale."

Denny's arms fell by his sides. "Listen, Sun, if this is about the books, we're not up for it tonight."

"It's not about the books."

"Okay. What is it?"

She watched them both for a moment, Kale drying his hands on a towel, Denny clutching money and paper, and wondered how this was going to change everything. This was the before. She had no idea what the after would look like.

Denny's eyebrows went up. "Sunday?"

She didn't answer, just walked across the room, behind the bar, feeling their curious eyes on her. After reaching for the Jameson bottle with one hand and two glasses with the other, she came back around and sat at a small table in the middle of the restaurant. Then she unscrewed the top, poured a finger of whiskey in each glass, sat back, and waited for them.

They exchanged a puzzled look, came around opposite sides of the bar, and joined her.

"Are we really going to need that?" Denny asked, nodding toward the whiskey.

"I would advise it."

"Wait. Are you leaving again?"

Kale's attention snapped from Denny to her.

"No," she said.

Denny relaxed a bit, picked up his glass, and held it toward Kale. "Cheers."

They clinked and drank. Denny crossed his arms and settled back in his seat. Kale waited, hands resting on his thighs.

She stared at her lap for one more moment, stunned this was about to happen. After everything she'd done to keep this secret. Leaving the people she loved, living a shell of a life in LA. The whole of the last five years had been about avoiding this moment.

She filled her lungs with air and stepped across the point of no return. "You remember when you all took that trip to Ireland . . ."

They both nodded.

"And when you got home I was sick in bed for days with the flu."

More nodding.

The pub was impossibly silent. She sat back against her chair, rested her cast in her lap, and settled her breathing. When she started, she made sure her voice was calm and steady.

"I didn't have the flu."

Kale, Denny, and Theresa had been gone for a week. She had exchanged several emails with Kale, and talked with them all a few times, often catching them in the middle of some noisy celebration that involved drunk Irishmen standing on chairs and belting out ballads. Which was hard to listen to considering she should have been on that trip. Instead she'd spent the last seven days shuttling her mother to various clinics for X-rays, lab work, and doctor's appointments, and listening to a litany of complaints—even though all the tests had come back negative. Half the family was gone, Jackie had his own place, and Shane had taken a second job on a snow removal crew. With Clare away as well there was no buffer. And it was taking a toll. Sunday had been tense and exhausted lately. When Grail asked her to come out for a drink she was quick to say yes.

She had half-heartedly protested the proposed location, the Penny Whistle Pub. It was in Ossining, and a lower-end bar. With its cheap drinks and no-frills ambience it was kind of the antithesis of Brennan's. But Grail insisted. It was quiet, and she wouldn't run into fellow cops. Kale wouldn't have been thrilled about her going there, but he was living it up in Ireland without her for ten days. So she and Grail headed out in a taxi so they wouldn't have to worry about driving home.

The Penny Whistle was fairly empty, a few people scattered around the small, dimly lit room. They grabbed two stools up at the bar and looked over a drink menu.

"Wow," Grail said, keeping her voice low. "Check out the bartender."

When Sunday followed her gaze to a tall guy carrying a couple cases of beer from a back room, it only took her a moment to recognize him. Billy Walsh had been a year ahead of her in school. She hadn't known him, but she'd known *of* him. Most girls did. The unruly strawberry-blond hair, long lashes, and penetrating eyes had been hard to overlook.

"Damn," Grail said, her stare glued to his biceps while he lifted the cases onto the bar.

Sunday covered her mouth with a hand. "Wait until you hear his accent."

She didn't have to wait long. After unloading the boxes he spotted them and strolled over.

"Ladies." He spread his arms wide, leaned on the bar, and offered a boyish smile that hinted at mischief. "Howyas doing tonight?"

"Good," Grail said, nudging Sunday's leg under the bar to acknowledge the soft but potent brogue. "How about you?"

"I'm grand, thanks. Girls' night out, is it?"

"That's right," Grail said. "Can we get two gin and tonics?"

"Sure thing." His eyes lingered on Sunday for a moment before he moved away. Maybe he was recognizing her too, but she doubted it. It's not like their paths had crossed much. He'd been older, and his extracurricular activities had seemed to be all about girls and partying.

Grail set her chin in her hand and watched him while he made their drinks. She had no shame; her eyes boldly slid up the slim jeans that sat low on his hips.

"Jesus, Grail. You remember you have a boyfriend at the moment, right?"

"I can still look."

Her cousin had never been shy. Or very monogamous. She often lamented the fact that Sunday hadn't lived a little more before settling down with Kale.

He came back with the sparkling drinks, slices of lime floating on top, and set them down. "Cheers." He watched while they both took generous sips. "You're Sunday Brennan, yeah?" he asked.

"I am."

He folded his arms across his fitted black T-shirt. "Don't suppose you remember me?"

"Of course I do. Billy Walsh." She felt Grail's eyes on her and wondered if she'd answered a little too quickly. "Everyone called you Belfast Billy." She introduced him to Grail. "Billy was a year ahead of me, in Denny's grade."

"That's right," Billy said. "And my dad worked for yours for a long time."

"I didn't realize that," Sunday said.

"No? Well, I suppose loads of men around here worked for Mickey Brennan."

Sunday wasn't sure how to respond to that so she just shrugged a shoulder.

"Saw an announcement in the paper that Denny's getting married soon," he said. "How's that pub a'his doing?"

"Okay," Sunday said. "But, you know, the pub business is unpredictable."

"He still partners with your man? What's his name?"

"You mean her boyfriend, Kale," Grail said, leaning sideways like she wanted in on the conversation. "Yeah, they're still partners. Let's get two shots of tequila."

"Wait," Sunday said, turning to her cousin.

"Come on. You deserve it after the week you've had." Grail nodded at Billy. "One for you too."

He grinned and said he'd be right back.

Sunday would have been happy enough to just sip her drink. She could already feel the gin going to work, loosening her muscles, softening the angst she'd been feeling the past couple weeks.

But Billy returned with three shot glasses, the rims partially dipped in salt and adorned with a lime wedge. "That there is top-shelf tequila—or as top-shelf as I've got here." He winked at Grail. "But I'll only charge you for the well."

She smiled wide and picked up her shot, and Billy followed suit. They both turned to Sunday.

Kale's frowning face materialized in her mind, and she heard his voice— *You're going to regret that.* But Billy and Grail cheered her on, so they all licked their salt and downed the shots.

As she sucked on the lime wedge she felt the heat from the tequila light up her throat and esophagus as it descended to her stomach, which she just realized was empty. "We should get some food."

"Sorry," Billy said, collecting the shot glasses. "Kitchen closes early midweek. Not many people come in here for the food, like." He left to check on a group of guys at a table in the back corner.

"How well did you know him growing up?" Grail asked, tilting her head Billy's way. He was chatting with his customers, arms raised above him so his hands rested on a low ceiling beam that ran across the room.

"I didn't," Sunday said. "I was surprised he knew who I was."

Her cousin snorted. "Everybody knew who you guys were, Sunday."

"That's not true."

"Whatever you say."

Grail loved to do that, talk to Sunday like she was naïve or in denial or something. But Sunday knew that as tough-girl as Grail played it, she'd always wished she'd had a father and siblings of her own, other voices to warm up the small, lonely house she'd grown up in. So Sunday let it go and updated Grail on their extended family in Ireland, then got her complaining about her workload for a while.

Billy checked on them a few times, brought them another round, hopped into their conversation when he was in the vicinity.

They'd been there about forty-five minutes when Grail asked him for another round of shots.

Sunday held up a hand. "No, thanks."

"Don't be such an old married woman," Grail said.

"You're just right, Sunday," Billy said, leaning his folded arms on the bar. "Don't give in to peer pressure. Sure isn't that what I remember most about you? You were always a good girl." There was a teasing twinkle in his eye as he lifted a beer from behind the counter and took a pull.

Grail chuckled. "She's just in a bad mood because her family and boyfriend went to Ireland without her."

Sunday's face began to burn so she finished off her drink to provide coverage.

"Is that right?" Billy asked. "They're all back in my neck of the woods then. My father didn't grow up far from yours."

She didn't want to admit that she didn't know that; he seemed to know so much about her family. So she asked when he'd last been back to Ireland.

"Four years ago," he said. "When we took my dad home to bury him."

Sunday hadn't known that either. "I'm so sorry," she said.

He lifted his lightly freckled face to hers and pressed his lips together. "Thanks."

"That's it," Grail said, slapping the bar. "Now we definitely need another round of drinks and shots."

Billy pulled his eyes from Sunday's and grinned at Grail. "Good idea." He pushed up from the bar and went to get it.

Grail arched her eyebrows. "Don't forget you have a boyfriend at the moment too."

"Funny."

No question another shot was going to make for a rough morning. But her mother had no appointments the next day, so she could sleep in. And this was the most relaxed she'd felt in a while. Even before Kale left on the trip she'd been on edge, more emotional than usual.

Grail's cell phone dinged and she pulled it from her pocket. "It's Brad." Her fingers flew around the keyboard. Brad was the latest in a long line of infatuations. Grail's romantic relationships were like supernovas, they burned bright but died young. The phone sounded again, and whatever Brad sent caused Grail to break out in a provocative smile that was kind of gross. "He's back from his conference early and hoped he could swing by and pick me up."

"Seriously?" Sunday checked her phone. "We've only been here like an hour. And you just ordered another round."

"I know. That's shitty." She brought the palms of her hands together. "But he travels so much. He's gone again the day after tomorrow."

Sunday shook her head even though she wasn't terribly disappointed. "Fine," she said.

"Thank you. Because he's on his way."

Billy was back, setting drinks down before them.

"To Billy's dad," Grail said. After they all threw back the shots she started rooting around in her bag. "We actually need to close out—"

"Just go," Sunday said. "I'll get this one."

Her cousin's brow furrowed. "What are you talking about? We'll drop you home."

Sunday was over Grail's extra-prickly teasing for the night. And the last thing she wanted was to bear witness to Grail and Brad's reunion. "That's okay," Sunday said. "Brad lives close to here. I'll just call Jackie."

Grail slumped on her stool, like she didn't know what to do.

"I can make sure she gets home safely," Billy said, whisking away the empty glasses.

"I'm not a child," Sunday said. "I'll get home just fine."

He held his hands up in surrender, backing away. "Have to check on the lads in the corner."

"You sure you want to stay?" Grail asked.

Sunday looked down at the full drink in front of her, which she didn't need. She should just go with Grail, avoid bothering Jackie or paying for a cab.

But her mother would still be up watching some crime show on TV, and undoubtedly kill the nice buzz Sunday had going.

She turned to Grail. "I'm just going to have this last one. Hopefully Mom will be asleep by then."

"Okay, I get it." Grail hopped off her stool. "Call me tomorrow." Then she fast-walked across the room and out the door to meet Brad.

Sunday pulled out her phone to check messages. Nothing new from Kale, but it was the middle of the night over there. She read over a few of his previous messages and longing hit hard. Despite the upcharge for international messages she sent him a text: *I really miss you.*

"Poor Sunday." Billy stood across the bar, hands behind his back, bottom lip stuck out in exaggerated sympathy. "Everyone abandoned you."

She smiled, put her phone down, and picked up her drink, her third gin and tonic. God, she'd done a shot as well. No. Two shots.

He placed a small fluted glass in front of her. "On me," he said. "That's a lemon fizz. It's lovely. Go on, try it."

She nodded toward the full drink that still sat in front of Grail's stool. "Only if you drink that. Otherwise it'll go to waste."

He leaned forward on the bar so they were eye level, sliding the glass in front of him.

She sipped the tart lemony concoction he'd made. "That's really good," she said. Reaching for something else to say, she glanced around, feeling her head wobble a bit. Only a couple of tables were occupied. "It's pretty quiet in here tonight."

"Usually is. Not like your place, I'm sure. Probably full to the gills most nights."

"Sometimes."

"Well, suits me since the owner lets me stay up there." He rolled his eyes up toward the second story.

"That's handy."

"Actually, it's a shithole." When he laughed, faint wrinkles fanned out from his eyes. "You know, I didn't think you'd remember me," he said. "It's not like we traveled in the same circles in school."

"It was hard to miss the accent." She winced. "And I'm pretty sure you were called to the principal's office a lot."

He laughed again and nodded. "Fair enough."

They sipped their drinks and chatted about old teachers and classmates for a bit before he left again to check on his other customers.

She pulled Kale's soft blue hoodie tighter around her—she'd worn it because it smelled so much like him—and took another healthy sip to soften the sting. Four more days and he'd be home. And she meant everything she had promised him. The benefit to spending the week with her mother had been how much it bolstered her resolve. As soon as Denny and Theresa were married they would get to that beach and elope. Charge it to credit cards, whatever. She wanted to make some kind of note on the postcard, like *ASAP!* or *Can't wait xoxo,* leave it on his pillow the day he came home. But he must have found a hell of a hiding place this time because she hadn't been able to find it since he left.

When she checked her phone again there was no response from him, not even the promise of three blinking dots.

"Expecting a call?" Billy asked. He was unloading glasses from a tray into the sink behind the bar.

"Not really." She picked up the gin and tonic because at some point she had finished off the lemon drink. Denny would call her an idiot for mixing her alcohols. "I should probably get going."

"Right," he said. "Let me just cash out those guys."

She checked the time, 10:35 P.M. She could call an Uber. But if Jackie picked her up she could make him come in the house with her, head off their mother's questions. Besides, he owed her. She'd covered for him plenty of times over the years.

"Here's the damage." Billy laid the bill in front of her and drained Grail's drink.

She fumbled pulling her credit card out of her back pocket and it dropped to the floor. "Whoops." When she slid off the stool to pick it up her legs felt unsteady. One side of Billy's mouth curled up when she grabbed the edge of the bar for balance. Great, now he thought she couldn't handle her liquor. She carefully retrieved the card, laid it on the bill, hoping her movements looked smoother than they felt. She reached for her phone to call Jackie.

Billy brought the receipt and settled down across from her again. "Hey, did you know our dads played Gaelic football together after coming to the States?"

"No way."

He nodded. "Sure they used to play down in Van Cortlandt Park at the weekends, back before any of us were born."

Sunday smiled. "My dad still talks about those games."

Billy's eyebrows shot up. "Have you not seen photos?"

"No."

"My dad saved pictures from back then. I've got them upstairs." He straightened up and started wiping down the bar nearby. "Dunno if your dad's in any of them, but there's a good chance. They were on the same team once or twice."

If that was true, if her dad was in any of those photos, he would have been about twenty-five years old. She'd seen precious few pictures of him as a young man, before her parents were married. He always said his own parents were too busy looking after so many kids to worry about taking photos of them.

Billy collected a few glasses off the bar, brought them to the sink. "You're welcome to take a look if you like."

He meant right now? But he was still working. She looked around the room and realized everyone had gone.

Wait, she still hadn't called Jackie. Had she?

"If we find one, you could take it to get copied." He shrugged, shaking water from his hands. "Or take pics with your phone . . ." He walked toward the far end of the bar to grab a towel.

She'd be a hero to her brothers if she got her hands on such a photo of their dad—not only at that age, but possibly playing football, or, at the least, in uniform. But it would mean going up to Billy's room with him, which was weird. Maybe. Or maybe it was just that, outside of her brothers, she was never alone with a man other than Kale.

Kale. Without a doubt he would not want her going up there, spending time alone with a known ladies' man. But Billy knew she had a serious boyfriend. And God knows he didn't need to hit on drunk girls with boyfriends.

"We'd have to get on with it," Billy said, walking her way. "Otherwise I'll be at it all night." He threw his chin around the room, at the cleanup he still had left to do.

"Are you sure you don't mind?"

"Not at all. It's nice to have someone interested. I'm the only one who looks at them anymore." He gave her a sad smile. "Since my dad died."

She could see pain in his eyes when he mentioned his dad. They'd probably been close.

"Well, I'd love to take a quick look," she said.

"Right." He tossed the towel on the counter. "Follow me." He headed down the bar, toward a door in the corner of the room.

Sunday checked her phone once more as she slid off the stool. No response from Kale yet. He must not have seen her text.

She slipped the phone into her back pocket and followed Billy.

. . .

The short, narrow staircase on the other side of the door had little light and no railing. Billy reached behind him to offer a hand, which was welcome because the shots caught up to her in a wave of dizziness. Idiot. She'd had too much to drink, and on an empty stomach. She focused on his black boots, followed his steps so she didn't trip.

They walked down a dingy hallway at the top of the stairs to the only door up there. He opened it to an efficiency apartment and "bachelor living" came to mind. An unmade bed with no headboard was pushed up against one corner, a tattered blanket was tacked up to cover the window, clothes were thrown all over.

"Sorry for the mess," he said. "Wasn't expecting company."

Sunday stayed by the door. "No worries."

He opened a closet and reached up to a high shelf. "Here they are." He pulled down a beat-up shoebox and sat on a more beat-up love seat. "Let's see," he said, flipping through old-looking photos. "There's some family ones mixed in here as well . . ."

Sunday took a closer look around. Dishes were piled high in the sink, empty beer bottles littered the tiny countertop, and what looked to be a weed pipe sat on a bedside table. She'd grown up in a house full of boys, but his personal space smelled different from her brothers' or Kale's mix of laundry detergent and deodorant. Billy's apartment was more cheap cologne layered over something darker. Maybe mildew, or mold.

"Is this your dad, no?" he asked, holding up a photo.

She stepped closer so she could see. He was pointing to one of several men standing together in cleats, shorts, and jerseys, shaggy early '80s hair. "Nope. That's not him."

"Shoot." He handed her a small stack. "Take a look through those and I'll check the rest of the box."

She sat beside him because there was nowhere else to sit, and flipped through the photos, none of which contained her father. While he searched the rest of the box she waited quietly, though she really just wanted to go home now. The pleasant fuzziness was wearing off and her head was swimming again.

That's when she remembered she still hadn't called Jackie. She pulled her cell out and sent him a text: *Please pick me up at the penny whistle asap*

Billy showed her another photo and she shook her head.

Her phone vibrated with Jackie's reply: *Seriously?*

Yes

"Haven't seen this one in a long time," Billy said, holding up a photo and staring at it.

The phone buzzed again: *Be there in 10.*

Knowing her brother was on the way instantly made her feel better.

Billy was still focused on the picture in his hand. "This is my dad," he said.

She leaned in to see if she recognized the man who had apparently played football with her father when they were young, and later worked for him. But the photo was decades old. "You look a lot like him," she said.

"Yeah, he was about my age here." He shook his head. "That was long before everything went to shit." He turned to her with a hangdog expression. "Sorry. It's just he had a hard time later in life, you see. Drank himself to death."

She drew in a sharp breath. "That's awful. I'm so sorry."

"Thanks." He held her gaze while he lowered the photo to his lap. "I just don't understand it," he said, his voice low and soft.

She couldn't understand it either, a father doing such a thing.

"I can't understand how your boyfriend left you home alone."

It took a moment to process that they were no longer talking about his father. "Oh, well. His family was expecting him." She shrugged. "He didn't really have any choice."

"Of course he did, Sunday." His eyes went back and forth between hers. "He could have demanded you go with him. And if that didn't work he could have stayed here with you. That's sure as hell what I would have done."

For a second she considered telling him Kale had tried those things, that they'd argued about it. But she didn't. Because in the end Kale had backed down and gone without her. "He just doesn't like to create conflict," she said.

"Neither do I," Billy said. "But some things are worth it."

It's not that she didn't see his face moving toward hers, his gaze dropping down to her mouth. It was just her brain was trying to catch up to the sudden turn this conversation had taken and find an appropriate response. But when his unfamiliar lips brushed hers she jolted to attention.

She pulled her face back. "Whoa."

"I mean it," he said. "What kind of fella would do that to you?" He leaned in again, his arm sliding around her waist.

She put a hand against his chest. "Stop."

His head tilted. "Come on now, Sunday. It's just us here." His hand skated up to her shoulder, pulling her toward him.

"That's enough." She moved to the edge of the love seat, scraping her fingers through her hair.

Behind her he sighed. "Christ. What did you come up here for then?"

"For the pictures."

He laughed. "That's it? Really?"

She looked back at him over her shoulder, at his snide smile and raised eyebrows. "Look," she said, "I'm sorry if you misread the situation . . ."

"Exactly what did I misread?" He scooted forward next to her. "The way you flirted downstairs, and stayed behind after your cousin and everyone else left? Or was it the hand-holding on the stairs I misread?"

What the hell—they'd only been talking. She opened her mouth to say just that, but in a split second of clarity she saw herself. Drinking with him. Taking his hand. Alone with him in his room. Sitting this close. Everything he said was true.

But she'd only come up here because he mentioned the photos.

"You never thought you had a picture of my father up here, did you?" she asked.

He lifted his shoulders in an exaggerated shrug.

She bolted out of her seat and her phone dropped from her lap to the floor.

They both reached for it but he got there first. He pulled it away from her and a cold grin spread across his face.

For the first time that evening alarm crept in. How long ago had she texted Jackie? No way he was here yet.

"Give me my phone," she said, hoping he'd assume the shake in her voice was anger and not fear.

He stood, holding the phone close to his chest. "You too good for a Walsh, is that it?"

She put out her hand. "Give it to me."

"I will," he said. "But not until I tell you something about your family."

"You don't know anything about my family."

"I know the whole lot of you think you're better than the rest of us. I know Denny walked around like he owned that fuckin' school."

She took a couple steps backward, toward the door, away from his bitter words. It was like he'd become a different person.

He followed her. "And I know Mickey Brennan's a selfish bastard who doesn't give a shit about anyone but himself. He fired my father after a decade of hard work because it suited him. And that's not all." He paused and his mouth twisted into a smug sneer, like he couldn't wait to say whatever was next.

"Fuck you," Sunday said. "Keep the phone." She turned and her stomach lurched because the room kept spinning even when she'd stopped. After touching a hand to the doorframe for momentary support she headed out into the hall.

He hurried after her and pulled her around by the arm, his fingers digging into her flesh. "We're not done here."

She tugged her arm up and down, tried to wrench it from his grip.

But he held tight. "Where are you going?" he asked. "To cry to your daddy and brothers?"

She thrust her face toward his. "You better hope I don't."

Then she saw it. A spark of panic in his eyes while he considered his next move. When he spoke his tone was venomous. "Get out of my sight, you stuck-up bitch!"

He pushed her arm away at the same time she pulled it. The force of it all twirled her round and she found herself staring down the dark, tight staircase directly in front of her.

She lifted a leg forward to stop her momentum, but something caught and held her foot. Then she was groping—for him, a railing that wasn't there, anything. But her hands skidded uselessly along the wall and she pitched forward.

She was aware of falling, of parts of her body slamming against stairs—a shoulder, her back, a hip. Aware enough that she conjured up an image of herself as a rag doll and wondered what would hit next. At some point it was her head, and the world faded.

"Hello?"

That was what she remembered next, the uncertain voice pulling her up from the depths. She had been semiconscious for some time, maybe the whole time, aware that she landed on her side, the hard floor beneath her. But she didn't open her eyes right away, just lay motionless, mentally assessing her body, waiting to see if any part of it started screaming in pain.

"Sunday?"

She couldn't tell where Billy's voice was coming from, she just knew she had to get up, get away from him.

"Sunday?" His tone was more urgent now, moving around, like he was looking for her.

Only it wasn't Billy's voice. It was Jackie's.

She slowly rolled onto her back. So far her limbs seemed to be in working order. There was a scrambling noise and she opened her eyes to see Jackie kneeling above her. "Jesus, Sunday. Are you all right?"

"I'm fine." Her voice was coarse so she cleared her throat. "Just help me up."

He got an arm under her. When he lifted her to a sitting position the head rush was powerful.

"What the hell happened?" he asked.

"I fell down the stairs."

"What . . ." He scanned the room, spotted the staircase through the open door behind him. "Is anyone else here?"

That's when she experienced vague recollections of Billy after she fell, hearing him run down the stairs and call her name. The sound of his boots rushing around the room, swish of the front door opening.

"No," she said. "No one's here." When she tried to push off the floor, her wrist gave way and she cried out.

"Let me see," Jackie said. He took her arm and gently eased her hand side to side. "I don't think you broke it . . ."

She brought her other hand to her head, which was pounding. And now her stomach was hurting as well. But not like she was going to be sick. More like cramping.

"We need to get you checked out," Jackie said.

"No, it's fine." She pulled her arm away. "I just want to go home—"

"Sunday. You're bleeding."

She turned to see him looking down, but not at her arm. She followed his gaze to see bright red blood staining her jeans. On top of everything else she'd finally gotten her period, which was like weeks late. That tended to happen when she was stressed out, or if she was inconsistent taking her pill. And lately she'd been both.

"Shit," she said. "I don't have anything with me." And it was doubtful this place had a tampon machine in the restroom.

Jackie swallowed. "Are you sure that's all . . . ?"

She looked down again, and understood his question. There was a lot of blood.

Too much blood.

When her eyes raised to Jackie's she saw her own fear mirrored there.

"We need to get you to the hospital," he said.

She pulled her legs up to her chest as another wave of sharp cramps rippled through her abdomen. Something was wrong. "No."

He looked at her like she'd lost her mind. "Yes. You might have some kind of internal bleeding going on."

She wrapped her arms around her knees and started rocking. There was so much blood. Way more than even her heaviest days.

Jackie glanced back at the staircase. "What the hell were you doing up there?"

Phrases started presenting themselves like bullet points: Period weeks late. Exhausted and emotional lately. Appetite all over the place. Even a couple bouts of nausea.

Oh my God. No, no, no, no . . .

"Sunday, did someone hurt you?" Jackie studied her with narrowed eyes. "If so, we need to call the police—"

"No, Jackie." Though Billy did hurt her. He had pushed her . . . and tripped her? There was nothing else she could have stumbled over other than his foot. But had he meant for her to fall down the stairs? Even if he did, she wasn't reporting this to the police, or anyone else. She'd been drunk, held his hand, gone up to his room. *Exactly what did I misread?* he'd asked.

She stood up and backed away from Jackie. "We're not calling the police."

"Okay, okay. Calm down." His tone was cautious, like he was talking her off the ledge. "We'll take this one step at a time." He retrieved her phone from the floor—where Billy must have dropped it—and handed it to her. She looked at the screen to see that Kale had responded six minutes ago: *Miss you like crazy too. Never leaving you again. Promise!*

She felt her face crumple, and her legs almost did too.

"Sunday, I need to take you to the hospital." Her brother sounded afraid, of the blood, of her crying, of the question of what had happened that night.

How could she possibly explain it to him, or to her family?

How could she possibly tell Kale what she'd done? Panic moved in with that last thought, a sense that she had irrevocably changed her life.

"I'll make you a deal," she said, hearing her voice get a bit stronger. "You can take me to the hospital. But you have to *promise* not to tell anyone about this."

"I don't know—"

"I mean it, Jackie! Otherwise I'm not going."

He dug his hands into his hair—almost as short as Denny's at the time—and weighed her proposal. Despite her pain and fear she had some inkling of what she was asking of him, that it was too much.

"Okay. You let me take you to the ER . . ." He shook his head. ". . . and it's up to you from there."

She just stared at him.

"I promise we won't tell anyone until you're ready."

Even as Jackie made that promise she knew he was assuming she'd change her mind, that she'd calm down, decide to tell their family. Or maybe he thought he'd be able to talk her into it; God knows he tried. But whatever he was thinking in that moment, Jackie had kept that impossible promise for five years.

Sunday stopped talking but continued to stare at the Jameson bottle on the table in front of her. She'd taken deliberate note of it several times while telling her story, a beacon of safety that reminded her she was sitting in Brennan's whenever the memories threatened to overwhelm her. Never before had she spoken about this. She was almost finished.

"I should have known I was pregnant, but I didn't." She could feel Kale's eyes on her, sense his shock, but she didn't dare look at him. "The doctor confirmed I had a miscarriage. I was almost two months along."

She'd been aware of their reactions while she talked. Denny shifting in his seat while he gripped his arms tighter and tighter until his knuckles were white. Ragged breathing from Kale, who had leaned forward on the table at some point, his hands curling into fists while he listened. She almost wished there was more to say, so she could delay the moment when she'd have to look at them and they'd have to respond in some way. But there was no more, she was at the end. She'd told the story as she recalled it, except for one thing. She hadn't yet mentioned Billy Walsh's name. They knew him as The Bartender.

She pulled her head up to face Denny. His eyes were wide and shiny and angry. He said only one word. "Who."

"I'm going to tell you. You need to know."

"Who was it?"

"But I want a promise first—" She jumped when his fist hit the table.

"God damn it, Sunday."

She raised her voice. "I need your word you won't do anything stupid."

He lifted his brow and tilted his head, putting together that whoever it was, he must be within reach.

"You need to think about Theresa and Molly," she said. "You can't go off the deep end and hurt someone—"

He sprang from his chair, sending it flying behind him. Then he leaned forward and placed his hands on the table, hung his head.

Still hoping to de-escalate the situation, she stayed in her seat and checked to see if Kale might help, but he still looked stunned, like he was trying to catch up.

Denny lifted his head. "Okay. Just tell me."

That was as close to a promise as she would get, and he needed to know. That's why she'd put them all through this. "It was Billy Walsh."

Denny stared at her while he pulled up off the table. He'd get over the initial shock quickly so she had to work fast.

"Listen to me, Denny." She stood and moved next to him. "We have to be smart about this. It's not a coincidence he loaned you money. He has it in for our family. I think he's trying to hurt you."

Denny nodded, but then his brow furrowed. "Why didn't you tell us?" There was a tinge of accusation in his question, but mostly just a true lack of understanding.

"I couldn't." It was the only answer she had.

"I have to go."

"No, wait," she said, following him as he grabbed his keys off the bar and headed for the door. "Denny, please." She reached for his arm, but he pulled it away.

"I have to go," he said again. Seconds later he was out the door.

CHAPTER ELEVEN

Denny

I have to go."

And he meant it. He had to get out of there, away from Sunday, away from the things she was saying and the images they were creating in his mind. That fucking guy preying on her, hurting her, and then leaving her there, alone. He shook his head to dispel thoughts that would not be dispelled and jumped behind the wheel of his Jeep. He was going to Katonah. He was going to find Billy Walsh. And he was going to beat the shit out of him.

He slammed on the gas and peeled out. No one was going to stop him. He headed toward the parkway and moved into the northbound lane. He'd be there in less than thirty minutes. He didn't know Billy's address, but he'd get it. And if he wasn't home, Denny would search every shithole bar in Westchester County until he found him. Within minutes Kale called his phone, then Sunday. He declined both calls, silenced the phone, and concentrated on the road.

Something had fallen into place when Sunday said Billy was out to get him. It explained what Michael told him earlier that day, that he'd been contacted by Billy's lawyer.

"That guy has a lawyer?" Denny had asked. "What did he want?" They'd been sitting at the kitchen table in the Brennan house.

Michael lowered his voice. "He said he filed for a lien because you defaulted on the loan. Is that true?"

"I missed a few payments, but Billy was cool about it. I talked to him." Still, a thin slice of panic cut through his chest.

Michael, who had warned Denny this loan was a terrible idea, slumped back in his chair. No need for him to say anything; it only would have amounted to "I told you so."

Denny had assured Michael it was a mistake, that he would clear it up. Maybe Billy got nervous and this was a shot across the bow, but once he knew opening was a week away and he would be the guest of honor, all would be good.

But if Sunday was right, Billy was after Brennan's. He could cost Denny and Kale everything. He'd already cost them Sunday. That's the colossal missing link that had been discovered tonight. Denny finally knew why she left. A fissure of guilt penetrated his anger. He'd become fairly holier-than-thou with her for leaving him holding the Brennan bag of needs. In his darkest moments he had blamed her for many things, including his financial troubles and shaky marriage, believing if she'd stayed to help him, none of it would have happened.

He passed the exit for Mount Kisco. Ten minutes to go.

The question of why she left had been answered, but now a new one took its place. Why the hell didn't she tell them what happened? He could only imagine how difficult it was to talk about it—he'd just watched her do it. He'd watched his sister, small and alone in that chair, share her most traumatic experience, and do it with composure. The whole time he just kept grabbing his arms tighter, holding himself in place, making himself listen because he understood she needed to say it as much as they needed to hear it. But she could have done it so long ago. Saved them all, especially herself, so much pain.

A car on his left was trying to get over to make the off-ramp. The driver leaned forward, gave a friendly wave, and sped up, assuming Denny would let him in. But he didn't. Fuck that guy.

Instead he hit the gas and pulled up alongside him. The driver looked at him with confusion and signaled with his hand but Denny ignored it. When the guy laid on the horn and sped up again, Denny tried to keep pace but the other driver swung over, forcing him onto the shoulder. He had to slam on the brakes so he didn't hit a guardrail.

"Fuck!" He grabbed the steering wheel and yanked on it, like he was trying to shake it loose. Then he threw a solid punch at the roof of the Jeep. His fist made contact with the interior light, and the cover and bulb shattered. That dissolved the last of the anger and he let his head fall back against the headrest.

He didn't know what to do. He knew what he wanted to do. Find Walsh and make him pay. But Sunday had begged him not to do anything stupid—*Think about Theresa and Molly*. Theresa and Molly.

Feeling depleted, he straightened up and checked around him before he pulled his car into the off-ramp lane. He exited, crossed over the highway, and got back on going south. He knew where he needed to go, and it wasn't Katonah.

Angie answered the door in a long robe when he knocked, all pursed lips and disapproving eyes. "Molly's asleep, Denny."

"I want to talk to my wife."

Her brows pulled up. "Well, that's a change. Wait here." She closed the door in his face.

When it opened again Theresa stood on the other side, mouth set, hand on the hip of her pajama shorts, ready for battle. He let out a gentle groan, hit hard by how good she looked and how much he missed her. Her rigid expression melted into concern. "What's wrong?"

He didn't know where to start.

She reached for his hand, pulled him inside, and extended her arms. He let himself sink into them.

When he said he needed to see Molly—just look at her—Theresa led him upstairs, opened the door to the bedroom she was sharing with their daughter, and stepped aside to let him in.

Molly was on one half of the queen bed, her arms flung up by her head. Her hairline was damp. Like her dad, she was a hot sleeper. She was totally out, asleep to that deepest level only kids seem capable of achieving. He watched her little chest rise and fall, listened to her steady breathing, and realized with a heavy heart that if Sunday and Kale's baby had been born, he or she would be just a little older than Molly.

Then he felt a stab of fear so sharp it almost brought him to his knees. There was evil in the world. How was he going to protect her from it? He wanted to pick her up and hold her, but if she woke and saw him like this, unsteady and emotional, she'd be scared. So he gently kissed her forehead and left, closing the door quietly behind him.

Theresa led him downstairs to the couch in the softly lit living room and sat close. Maybe it was the example Sunday had set earlier that night, the fact that she'd been so honest with him, but he decided to do the same with Theresa. He stayed calm, held her hand, and told her everything. No excuses, no prettying it up.

He got a few head shakes when he explained how the financial problems started, but he could tell she was working hard to not react. She interrupted with calm questions—*How did you get the mortgage without your dad knowing? How much do we owe on the credit cards?* He loved her for using the word "we" and keeping her voice neutral, like she was gathering info so she could help attack the problem. The way her eyes moved around without focusing on anything, he could tell her mind was churning, thinking through how they would get out of the hole.

"Okay," she said. "We just start cutting expenses, get on a tight budget. I'll take on extra shifts and overtime, cancel my gym membership. We can sell one of the cars if we have to." Her eyes and hands held on to his, like she was trying to transfer hope. He was ashamed for ever thinking she would give up on him. He didn't know when he'd stopped having faith in his own wife.

There was a moment when he considered leaving it right there, keeping the worst of it to himself. She was still with him, on his side. Maybe he could shield her from the rest. But he'd been so relieved to hear the truth from Sunday. As painful as it had been, it was better than being in the dark.

"Theresa, there's more."

It wasn't until he mentioned the hard money loan and using Brennan's as collateral that she began to look frightened. Even then she stayed composed, but he could see the tension in her shoulders, feel it in her hands.

"Is this guy going to work with you? Give you some time?"

He told her about Billy Walsh and what he'd done to Sunday.

She sat with her hand to her mouth for a long time. "Poor Sunday. But it makes so much sense now."

"What does?"

"Why she left. What else could have driven her away from all of you? From Kale?"

"But she could have told us. We would have helped her deal with it."

"Denny, can you imagine what it was like for her? The shame she must have felt?"

Sunday had referred to stupid mistakes she made that night: going to that bar, drinking too much, being nice to that fucking guy. Going up to his room had been straight-up stupid, but he'd tricked her. "It wasn't her fault," he said.

"No, but part of her will always believe it was." She spoke with the authority of a nurse who'd worked with her fair share of trauma victims.

"She could have told me. I would have done anything to help her."

She offered a sad smile. "I know. But, knowing Sunday, she was afraid none of you would look at her the same again. Especially you and Kale."

He thought back to the weeks between the trip to Ireland and Sunday's departure for LA, tried, in hindsight, to look for the signs. She had seemed off after they got back, a little distant. However, she'd also just spent almost two weeks alone with their mother. And she was supposedly getting over the flu. But he remembered now how spaced-out she seemed, to the point where he was annoyed with her. He and Theresa were trying to get ready for the wedding and the move to a new house half a mile away, and Sunday had been less than helpful. She forgot to bring Shane and Mom to appointments, tried to get out of attending Theresa's bachelorette party. There were times no one could find her and it turned out she was sleeping in her room. He remembered Kale complaining about how little time she was spending with him.

Had he asked her what was wrong? Doubtful. He assumed she was throwing herself a little pity party. She'd missed Ireland, had to put in extra family time, Denny was moving out. He remembered sitting her down one morning and accusing her of being passive-aggressive.

No wonder she hadn't told him.

He turned to Theresa. "I have to talk to her."

She nodded. "Go."

He drove home, assuming Sunday would be there by now, and thought about that morning he laid into her, not long before his wedding. She hadn't argued with him, only apologized, which should have been a dead giveaway. Sunday had never been afraid to put him in his place. She was a peacemaker, but only to a point with him. When he lost his temper or his sarcasm was too searing, she'd tell him to knock it off. And she had subtle but effective ways of getting what she wanted.

One of the more memorable battles of their wills had been over none other than Kale. When he asked Sunday if he could read her story that night so long ago, Denny had feared something was afoot. He spotted them in the commons the next afternoon and recognized the signs: how engrossed they were, the way he looked at her, how she fidgeted and smiled at him. The last thing Denny wanted was for his best friend to start dating his sister. It would inevitably lead to high drama. He threw a few hints at each of them and figured that was the end of it.

So he was decidedly perturbed to learn they were often seen taking walks together through the neighborhood at night. Some guys on the team had spotted them on a bench at Hollis Park and reported back. Instead of confronting Kale, he waited around one night and watched it happen. Sunday sat on the back porch after everyone went to bed. When Kale came walking down the alley, she jogged across the yard to meet him. He took her hand and off they went. Denny had to nip this in the bud before it went to the next level.

His solution was to set Kale up with Katie Hall, a nice mix of hot and easy, and, coincidentally, friends with Michelle, Denny's girlfriend at the time. They would all go somewhere Sunday would see them and that would be that. She'd be disappointed, but it was for her own good.

To be on the safe side, he pulled a fast one on Kale. They planned to meet up at the West Manor Summer Festival one night, and Denny showed up with Michelle and Katie. Pure dread was written on Kale's face when he walked up to them, and of course he was too well-mannered to just leave. Several times he tried to talk to Denny, but Denny blocked him at every turn. Kale looked miserable while trying to be distantly polite to Katie, but it served him right for messing with his best friend's little sister.

The plan culminated with a visit to the Ferris wheel, where Sunday was working as a ticket collector. As the four of them approached, Denny called to her and she turned with a wide smile.

"Hey, Denny. Hey, Michelle." Her face fell when she looked behind them.

"Sunday, this is Katie." Denny waved in her direction. "She's Kale's date."

Her whole body seemed to shrink a bit.

Katie pointed up at the Ferris wheel. "How long is this ride?"

Sunday's eyes touched on Katie's cleavage and tight skirt, while she ran a hand down her shapeless *West Manor Summer Festival* apron. "About fifteen minutes."

"Perfect!" Katie reached for Kale's hand but he moved away.

"Sunday—" he said.

"You guys better load up." She held the gate open for them, staring at the ground.

Denny reminded himself this was for the best. "You need our tickets?" he asked, holding them out, hoping she'd look at him.

She didn't. "No, that's okay."

Kale stepped in front of her with a desperate look in his eyes. "Sunday, this isn't—"

"Step over to the line." She turned away, to the next customers.

After a fleeting moment of victory, Denny spent that entire ride feeling like shit, especially when he looked down to see Sunday leave the festival to walk home alone. He'd been a dick because he was pissed off they hid it from him. With each round of the wheel he realized that Kale and Sunday made a lot of sense together. And not another guy he could think of would treat her half as well as Kale would.

When he got back to the house a little later that night, she was putting away laundry in her room. She'd come home from the festival and done the damn laundry. She rotated between a pile of clothes and her dresser.

He crossed his arms and leaned against her doorframe. "I set him up with that girl. He didn't even know about it."

She kept working.

"And he wanted nothing to do with her. He left as soon as that ride was over. After calling me an asshole and telling us all you're his girlfriend." He had never seen Kale so angry, certainly not at him. "I thought he was going to hit me."

She shut a drawer and turned to him, arms folded across her middle.

"Look, Sun, you're my sister, and I thought he was . . ." He lifted his shoulders. ". . . just being a guy. I didn't realize . . ."

Still she just offered that blank expression. She was making him work for it. He couldn't stand it when she stayed angry with him. It upset their balance.

"I won't get in the way," he said, "if this is what you want."

Her chin tilted up. "It's what I want."

"But you need to be careful. If it goes south, it affects all of us."

"It won't go south."

"You're pretty sure of yourself."

"Not really. But I am sure of him."

In the face of such earnest conviction, Denny could only shake his head. "All right. Now would you please go put him out of his misery? It's freaking pathetic."

After that she hugged him and thanked him for watching out for her. And he told her he always would.

• • •

When he walked in the front door of the house, Jackie and Kale were pacing in the living room.

"Where the hell have you been, Denny?" Kale asked.

But he didn't answer because Sunday came rushing in from the kitchen, and she's the one he'd come to see.

CHAPTER TWELVE

Kale

W here the hell have you been, Denny?"

Kale had spent an hour and a half looking for him.

As soon as Denny stormed out of the pub, Sunday had asked Kale to go after him. He almost said no. He wanted—needed—to talk to her. Where Denny rocketed straight to anger, Kale had experienced acute distress while he listened to Sunday talk. Like a hand had reached in, wrapped around his insides, and squeezed as hard as possible. She'd been pregnant. With their baby. At one point, when she talked about the blood, he thought he was going to be sick, vomit right there at the table. And his mind started making fuzzy connections that were still too vague to pin down but had to do with why she had changed. Why she left.

She looked straight-up scared, with her wringing hands and anxious eyes, and the one thing he could do for her right then was find her brother. He couldn't erase what happened that night, or the things that followed, but he could stop Denny from making it all worse.

He drove north to Katonah, up and down the small main drag, which was only a four-block stretch. The population of Katonah was less than two thousand, and suburban streets quickly gave way to darker, more rural outskirts, eventually hitting the Muscoot Reservoir to the west and the Cross River Reservoir to the east. People had acreage out there, long driveways with houses set back from the road. There was no sign of Denny's Jeep anywhere.

He'd been conflicted about what he hoped to find. Part of him wanted nothing more than to find Denny, with Billy Walsh in hand. But that thought hitched in the pit of his stomach because his self-restraint would cease to exist, as would Denny's. It's not that Sunday was blameless. She'd been reckless that night, drinking far too much, putting herself in such a position. It was so unlike her, but Kale could see how it happened. They'd all left her home alone with Maura, she'd been under such strain, feeling alone in it. That fucking guy had taken advantage, and he must have been smooth because, drunk or not, Sunday wasn't a fool. Then he'd left her there alone after she fell. Kale could only imagine the violence that might take over if they laid their hands on Billy right then. He didn't know whether he was more disappointed or relieved when he found no sign of Denny or Billy and had to head back to West Manor.

While he drove, her story replayed in his mind and painful realizations snuck up on him—their baby would be over four years old now. His or her appearance and personality would be some combination of their genes. Luke would not be here—and he'd experience a moment of horrible vertigo as the world tilted a bit. He pushed the thoughts away, focused on finding Denny. But after cruising around town several times, he gave up and headed to the Brennan house, feeling like he had failed her. Again. Just like he did five years ago when he wasn't there to stop what happened. When he'd gone on that trip and left her home alone.

They'd argued about her staying home for her mother's bullshit health scare. He'd had a plan for that trip, one that had been in the works for months. After scrounging for the better part of a year, he'd pulled together the money and booked the trip to Magens Bay. They were going two months after Denny's wedding. He had the plane tickets, a confirmed ten-day reservation for a waterfront bungalow, and the simple ceremony had been scheduled. While they were in Ireland he would find a special

moment, hand her the postcard. Wait for her to flip it over and see what
he wrote on the back.

And it would be their secret. No upstaging Denny and Theresa, no
pressure from anyone—Maura—to plan a church wedding. He wasn't even
going to give her the ring until they got out of town. When they returned
home they'd be married, and that would be the line of demarcation. No
more half living together. Their marriage would take precedence.

So when she told him she was staying home, he fought her on it. But
he relented in the end because he didn't want the countdown to their
elopement to be marred by drama, to start off under duress. He decided
to wait until after Ireland, when things were calmed down. Like so many
other times he'd given in when it came to the family. And it had cost them
so much.

Everything.

He'd been waiting with Jackie back at the house for a few minutes when
Denny walked in wearing a haggard expression. Gone was the anger from
earlier, his face drained of its usual color and animation. Denny didn't respond when Kale asked where he'd been because the kitchen door swung
open and Sunday appeared. Her shoulders drooped in relief, and she
tilted her head, silently scolding her brother. In the taut silence that followed, Denny took slow steps across the living room until he stood in
front of her.

"I'm sorry, Sun," he said. His voice was raw, subdued.

"I'm just glad you're home."

"No. I'm sorry he hurt you. I'm sorry I wasn't there to stop it."

Sunday's eyes filled, and when Denny reached out and put his hand
on her shoulder, she drew in a sharp breath, a last attempt to shore herself
up. But then he pulled her toward him and she let her forehead fall down
against his chest. The only sound in the house was her uncontrolled
crying.

Kale looked away because he had to. He felt like he was intruding, and
at the same time he wanted to nudge Denny aside and take his place with
her. That's when his eyes landed on Jackie.

Jackie, who had known all this time, who had known years ago when she left. The urge to reach out and grab him, yank him away and demand answers, was sudden and powerful. But now was not the time.

He couldn't take being in that living room any longer. It wasn't her grief he couldn't take, it was the fact that he couldn't grieve with her. He turned and quietly left the house.

But he didn't go home. He couldn't face the volley of questions he knew Vivienne was waiting to throw at him. Not that he blamed her; he'd been cagey earlier when he called to ask if Denny had stopped by. She said no, then started asking what was going on, where he was. He just told her he'd be home soon and ended the call.

He ruled out going to the pub, couldn't bring himself to go back there that night, not with remnants of her disclosure still hanging in the air. After driving without a destination for a few minutes he ended up at Hollis Park, a large green space with a pond, walking paths, and lots of trees, near the center of town. The park he and Sunday had walked to countless high school nights. He would meet her in the alley behind her house, always a touch amazed when she was there again, waiting for him on the back porch. He'd take her hand in his, a point of contact he'd spend all day looking forward to, and they'd wander into town, sit on the park bench by the small pond, and talk for hours.

When his cell phone buzzed again, he didn't even look. It was Vivienne. But when it stopped ringing he sent her a text—*All good. Be home soon.*

He had no idea what he was going to say to her. He'd been procrastinating telling her about the financial mess until he'd secured the loan. But he couldn't tell her now because that would lead into everything else. And he didn't think he could tell her what happened to Sunday, it would feel like a betrayal. Something else he'd be keeping from his wife.

He dropped his head in his hands. He fucking hated secrets. Maybe it was because there'd been such secrecy around his mother's departure. No one ever talked about it. Maybe it was because he'd never been any good at keeping secrets, even when he was younger. The one time he tried had ended with a crushed Sunday walking home from the town festival alone. She had wanted to tell Denny about them, just lay it on the table. Kale had asked her to keep it quiet until he found the right way to talk to him about it. As usual, she'd been right.

After going off on Denny that night, he'd taken a long walk to cool off and ended up at the Brennan back porch, convinced she wouldn't be there. But she was. He remembered rushing up the stairs, stammering about it wasn't what she thought, he wasn't with that girl, but she had cut him off.

"I know. Denny told me." The way she slid her hands in her pockets and waited was disconcerting. Like the next words he chose would decide an awful lot.

"I'm sorry. I should have set everyone straight as soon as I got there—"

"We should have been honest from the start, instead of lying about it." She shook her head in frustration or disappointment, and he feared he'd blown it. In his effort to avoid making a critical mistake with her, that's exactly what he'd done.

"You're right. I was afraid Denny was going to tell me to stay away from you . . ."

Her eyes drifted toward the ground.

". . . but I don't care what he says, it doesn't matter. This is what I want." She picked her head up and studied him for a moment. "Promise?"

"Promise."

"Well, he's okay with it."

"Seriously?"

She smiled. "He said he thought you were just being a guy, that he didn't realize . . ." Despite the dark he knew she was blushing. ". . . you know, he didn't know . . ."

The space between them hummed with possibility.

"That it's a lot more than that?"

"Yes."

And then he did something he'd been dying to do for weeks, since the day they sat in the commons together. Something he refused to do until Denny knew about them. He kissed her. Not a peck on the cheek or brush of the lips, which is all he'd had the nerve to do so far. He took her face in his hands and, without any misgivings, he really kissed her. It started soft and slow, but became hot and breathless with staggering speed. The first of many nights Kale would summon his self-control when it was time to step back.

Denny cleared the air the next day. "I'm cool with it, man. But you hurt her . . ." He dragged a finger across his throat. ". . . I'll fuckin' kill ya." No more was said about it. And from that day forward Kale and Sunday became a fixed and permanent entity in everyone's mind.

He couldn't muster much concern over Vivienne being annoyed when he got home. She was waiting up, sitting stiff and straight in one of the kitchen chairs. Arms folded across her silky red robe, one bouncing leg crossed over the other.

He poured a cup of tea he didn't want and joined her at the table, told her Denny was stressed about the new pub and had a few too many after work. "I just needed to make sure he didn't do anything stupid."

"Was Sunday with you?"

"Just at the house, when I stopped by."

"She's been back six weeks now. Do you think she's going to stay?"

"I don't know, Viv." He took a sip of his lukewarm tea.

"I bet she decides to stay. Her life in LA couldn't have been too great if she was out driving drunk and getting into accidents."

He did not want to talk to her about Sunday. He stood. "I'm going up."

"I'll come with you."

When she reached for him in bed he claimed exhaustion even though his mind was racing. Her offended disappointment settled between them on the mattress, along with her silky red robe.

While he lay on his back in the dark, waiting for morning to come, he retraced the timeline between his return from Ireland and when Sunday left New York. He'd spent much of that time trying to find the right opportunity to give her the postcard, but they had trouble reconnecting after he got home. She was happy to see him, even cried when he walked through the door. But then she was sick for a while—or so he believed— and there was a blur of activity in the weeks surrounding Denny's wedding. Two days after the ceremony he and Theresa moved into their new house. Sunday was distant during that time, but he assumed it was because of everything that was going on. With Denny out of the house Maura was needier than ever. But even after all that died down Sunday was more and more on edge, snappy with everyone, even Shane.

And then, just like that, she was leaving. She told him she'd gotten a job as a content writer for some media company and had to give it a shot. Such a flimsy explanation that would have fallen apart under the barest of cross-examination. But he'd let her go because she was miserable and angry, and nothing he did helped. She'd taken him and her family wholly by surprise, been so insistent. They had no time to process it all, and the idea that she was lying never occurred to them.

Except for Jackie. He had known she was lying. He knew what happened, watched them all rack their brains wondering what was going on with her. He stayed quiet when she loaded up in a taxi with a couple of bags and left for the airport, said nothing when Shane ended up in a full-on episode at the store—yelling and beating himself about the head—when a coworker said he heard Sunday wasn't coming back.

Kale wanted answers from Jackie about how he let it all happen, when at any point along the way he could have simply raised a hand.

After Vivienne and Luke left for school the next morning he headed to the Brennan house. He walked in the back door to the kitchen, where Clare, Mickey, and Shane were eating breakfast.

"Well, who's this coming in the door?" Clare asked. "Do yous recognize him?"

"It's Kale, Auntie Clare."

"I know that, Shane. It was a little joke because we've not seen hide nor hair of him lately."

"Did you come for breakfast?" Shane asked.

Clare was out of her seat. "Now you sit and I'll get you a cup. Denny will be back any minute. He took Molly to school, like every morning, God love him." She put a hand to her chin and gave him the wide eyes. "Or is it Sunday you'd be looking for?"

"Sunday left already," Shane said. "But she said she's gonna meet me after work today."

Kale smiled at him. "I'm sure she will. Is Jackie around?"

Mickey pointed to the ceiling. "Still upstairs. He's not late, is he?"

"Not at all. He's been a huge help." Kale turned for the stairs. He had to catch Jackie alone.

As he climbed the steps he scanned the gallery of photos. There were, by far, more pictures of Kale on that wall than had ever hung in his own house. He hadn't been on the second floor since the night he helped Jackie get Sunday to her room, when he thought he was going to pass out from the flood of memories, the visceral reaction to just being in there again. He slow-walked down the hall because, from the sound of it, Jackie was in the shower, and the door to Sunday's room was open.

A wistful longing forced its way in as he approached. He'd spent a lot of happy time in there. Afternoons studying with her, wishing to hell her mother didn't have a sixth sense—*Sunday Ann Brennan, door open!* Climbing up the trellis, to the window over her desk. Spending nights on the floor under that white quilt with the purple flowers because her box spring made too much noise.

Still hanging above her desk was the award she won in high school, for the short story she'd written about him. He'd read the stories she published in that LA arts magazine, several times now. They were essentially tributes to Denny and Shane. Her style was still clear and smooth, but it had matured. The characters were complex. She found humor in shitty circumstances. Reading those stories was like getting a small glimpse into the last five years of her life.

The shower turned off so he walked down to Jackie's room and stepped inside the open door. Kale had been invited up there several times last summer, when Jackie was working on a portrait of Luke. Not for a specific reason—no birthday or holiday, just because. That was how Jackie did things. His latest project sat on the easel, a sheet draped over it. Kale raised the sheet and let it hang off a corner. Then he stepped back to take a look.

The woman in the painting was sitting on the floor with her legs pulled up to her chest.

Her head hung down, resting on her knees.

He couldn't see her face, but he knew she was crying.

She was Sunday.

It was like getting all the air knocked out of him, similar to fifth grade when a careening dodgeball had hit him squarely in the chest and he doubled over, unable to take a breath.

The background was dark and shadowy, so attention was drawn to her. Her long hair falling forward to cover her face. Her hands hooked on her knees while her pale forearms hung down. Her gray sneakers with the toes turned toward each other.

"Hey, dude."

Kale turned.

Jackie was wearing boxers and a T-shirt, hair damp, eyes wide. "You all right?"

He finally sucked in some oxygen. "Why didn't you tell me?"

"I couldn't, man. It wasn't my place."

Kale stepped toward him. "That's it? That's all you got?"

"She was desperate. She made me promise—"

"You let her *leave*." He grabbed fistfuls of Jackie's shirt and slammed him back against the wall. "You could have said something, anything!"

"What's going on?" Denny asked from the doorway.

Jackie kept his arms at his sides. "It wasn't my secret to share."

Kale yanked him forward, gave him another shove against the wall. "Fuck that. When she couldn't do it, you should have." He felt Denny's hand land on his shoulder.

Jackie stayed limp and stared at the floor.

Denny tugged at him and Kale stepped back. "Kale's right. You should have told someone before she left. I don't know what the hell you were thinking."

Jackie pushed off the wall. "You're goddamn right you don't know. I found her that night, I took care of her afterward when she was a mess. Don't you think I wanted to say something?" He brought his hands to his chest. "Do you know what it was like to watch her leave and not say something? But it was her choice."

Denny shook his head in doubt.

"What did you want me to do?" Jackie asked. "Overrule her like that fucker tried to do that night in the Penny Whistle?"

Kale shuddered. "No."

Denny ran a hand down his face. "You should have tried harder to get her to talk to someone."

"I did get her to talk to someone," Jackie said. "She told Mom."

"What?" Denny asked.

"Sunday told Mom what happened a week before she left for California."

Kale knew it with certainty before he said it. "Your mom told her to keep it quiet."

Jackie nodded.

"No, she didn't," Denny said. "That's ridiculous."

"She did." Jackie's voice was soft but clear. "Mom said no good could come from talking about it, it would just upset everyone. She told Sunday there was no point, the guy was gone. That she basically did it to herself. It would hurt the family, and things with you"—nod to Kale—"would never be the same."

Those specifics, very much statements Maura Brennan would make, seemed to wash away any doubt for Denny. He stepped back and dropped onto Jackie's bed.

Kale had no words. The tragedy of it, a daughter asking her mother for help at such a crucial time, and getting turned away. He didn't really believe in hell, but for a split second he hoped Maura Brennan was feeling the heat.

"What's that?" Denny had finally spotted the painting on the easel. No one answered him. He stood back up and stared at it. "Is that . . . ?"

Kale braced himself for the knee-jerk reaction—*What the hell are you doing painting that shit?* But Denny stayed quiet.

"I went back to the Penny Whistle later that morning," Jackie said, slumping back against the wall. "After I got her home from the hospital."

He seemed younger right then, shirt bunched up where Kale had grabbed him, touch of defensiveness in his voice. "I had this whole plan, to wait and get him alone, beat the shit out of him. I was so fucking angry. I even brought the gun from the bar, to scare him good."

Kale's eyes met Denny's for an instant. If Jackie had found Billy Walsh that day who knows what might have happened.

"But the owner said Billy had gone back to Ireland." Jackie turned his hands up. "I didn't know what to do. After she talked to Mom she told me she just needed some breathing room, time away to heal, work it out. That she'd be back in a few months. She sounded so sure."

And that made sense to Kale. Sunday had always been the voice of reason, so good at knowing what everyone needed. Why wouldn't Jackie have trusted that she once again knew best.

He and Denny walked to the pub and went about their routine prep in silence. It was like neither of them knew how to put voice to what they'd learned in the last twenty-four hours. They were on the cusp of losing the bar. Denny's whole family was facing full financial ruin. Five years ago Sunday had suffered a miscarriage and her mother shamed her into leaving.

So they were quiet while they worked. But conversation wasn't necessary anyway, it was all second nature. Wednesday was hump day, a busy one for them from opening till close. Everything needed to be fully prepped, in the back and up front, or they chanced slowing service down later in the evening by having to scramble to the cellar for supplies or wait for clean glassware or send one of the waitstaff to cut fruit for drinks.

Kale was stocking shelves behind the bar when Sunday walked in. She stood in the doorway for a moment, backlit by the morning sun while she gave him a small wave. Something was different. Her posture was a tad straighter, head up, no hat. And she wore a fitted long-sleeve T-shirt.

"Where's your cast?" he asked.

"I had Dad cut it off this morning."

"You sure you should have done that?"

"It was driving me crazy. They were going to take it off next week anyway." She made her way over to Denny, who was sitting in a booth with paperwork. "Listen, I'm glad you're both here."

"Wait," Denny said. "I need to ask you something first, and I want the whole truth."

She slid in across from him and sat back against the booth with a wary look, like she was wondering how much more truth she could possibly offer at this point. "O-kay."

"You told Mom what happened to you?"

She hesitated for only a second. "Yes."

"And she told you to keep it from all of us?"

When she glanced at Kale he offered an encouraging nod.

"Yes."

"Why would she do that?"

"She was afraid of the same things I was. That you guys would go after him, maybe get in trouble or get hurt. Or that Dad might have another heart attack." Sunday paused. "She said what happened was my own fault, and word would get out . . . That everything would be different." Her eyes briefly drifted Kale's way. "But she sent me money after I left. Every month until she died." Like maybe that made her mother's actions less repulsive.

Denny shook his head. "She had no right."

"Yeah, well, I think maybe I knew exactly what she was going to say, and that's why I went to her. It was like she gave me permission to keep my secret and run away." She gave Denny a moment and then said something that made Kale stand at attention. "I just came from Michael's office."

"Eaton?" Denny asked. "How'd you get there?"

"I drove Dad's truck."

"Jesus, Sunday, you don't have a license anymore—"

"I know, I know. I won't do it again. But look, we came up with a plan."

We? Kale moved down the bar, closer to them.

"Michael's going to talk to Billy Walsh's lawyer about making a deal."

"What kind of deal?" Kale asked.

"He's going to tell them to back off. That we'll get him his money by the end of the year, with interest. But he has to stop any kind of action against you."

"Why the hell would he do that?" Denny asked.

But Kale already knew. They were holding only one card when it came to this deal.

"If he doesn't," Sunday said, "I'll report him. And he'll be charged with assault and battery."

Denny furrowed his brow. "Michael knows everything?"

That created a troubling visual: Sunday baring her soul to tall, blond Michael with the easygoing smile. Kale picked up one of the glasses from the sink drainer and started drying it with a towel even though it was already dry.

"Yes," she said. "And we think this is our best chance to stop Billy from taking the pub. Michael found out he has a record—a domestic violence charge and some petty theft. He's not going to want to be arrested and questioned, or have police investigating him."

Denny nodded. "Okay. I trust Michael, and he can be forceful when he wants to be."

Somehow Michael got to be the fucking hero in all this. Kale dropped his hands in frustration and the glass hit the counter and fell to the floor, shattering on impact. Shards flew everywhere. Denny and Sunday looked over.

"Sorry. Dropped a glass."

"You're sure about all this?" Denny asked her.

Kale surveyed the damage. He'd have to take up the clean mat he'd just put down and empty out the ice bin.

"Michael seemed to think it could work." She sounded so optimistic.

Kale started scooping ice out of the bin, tossing it into the sink with force.

"Well," Denny said, "if it's to help you, I guarantee he'll go the extra mile."

Kale didn't hear Sunday's response because blood roared in his ears and he threw a scoop of ice so hard it clattered all over the counter behind the bar, then slid off and sprayed against his jeans.

He'd been keeping everything under control since she came back. He'd clamped it all down, tried to stay focused on Vivienne and Luke.

Chucking the ice had felt good and he wanted to cause more damage. He swept an arm along the counter, knocking four pint glasses to the floor, aware of Denny and Sunday calling to him and jumping up from their seats.

Kale hadn't been able to talk to her last night, hold her while she cried over losing their baby, tell her he was sorry for not being there. He was in no-man's-land. He wasn't a brother or a lawyer, just an ex-fiancé who'd let her go and married someone else. He had no place here.

When he felt Denny's hands on him, he whipped around and pushed him away.

"Hey!" Denny said. "You can have a breakdown if you want, man. But we gotta pay for this shit."

No one said anything while he collected himself. His breathing and heart rate slowed, the adrenaline ebbed. He checked the mirror above the register to see Sunday several feet behind him, evaluating his handiwork. Then he met Denny's eye and held it, asking a silent question.

Denny's eyes flicked to Sunday before he lowered his hands and walked into the office, shutting the door behind him.

Kale turned to Sunday, who was sliding debris to one side with her shoe, clearing a path.

He tried to infuse his words with every ounce of regret he felt. "I'm so sorry I let you go."

She raised her eyes from the floor. "I didn't give you any choice."

"I never should have let you leave. I didn't push hard enough—I didn't make you talk to me." He was stumbling over his words. "I knew something was so wrong." He put his hand to his chest. "But I thought it was me."

Her face crumbled and she started to cry.

"I just . . . I thought you were tired of all of it. Your mom, your family. Me. When you said you wanted to try it out there, that it was a chance at something, I believed you." Breaking glasses had felt good, but this was what he needed. "I shouldn't have gone on that trip . . ." He shook his head at the what-ifs, made even more painful because they were a betrayal of his wife and son.

She sniffed. "It wasn't your fault." Then she did that thing where she pulled her sleeves over her hands and wiped her face.

"But, Sunday . . ." He took a small step toward her and softened his voice. "Why didn't you tell me?"

She inhaled sharply and her eyes went wide, as if she hadn't expected the question, or had been dreading it, and wasn't prepared to respond. But his need to know the answer to that question was fierce.

"Did you think I would leave you?" he asked.

"No."

"Or that I would blame you?"

She swallowed. "I don't think so."

"Then, please. Tell me—"

"Kale." Denny's voice was loud and firm behind him. "Vivienne just parked in back. I'm sorry, but she's gonna walk through that door in ten seconds."

Everything in Kale plummeted.

Sunday spun to the mirror behind the bar, started putting herself back together.

There was no way he could pull it off, hide all this from Vivienne. "No," he said.

Sunday turned to him. "Pull it together, Kale." Then she was moving away from him, stepping over glass and waving at Denny to join her up front.

When Vivienne stepped inside, Denny and Sunday were standing by a table near the door, partially blocking him from view.

"Hey, Viv," Denny said. "How's it going?"

"Good. Hey, hon."

Kale waved from the bar, not yet trusting himself to speak.

Denny smiled and threw a thumb over his shoulder. "He's just upset because he broke a few glasses and we're going to have to dock his pay."

When Kale glanced at his reflection in the mirror, behind him he saw the three of them standing in an uneasy circle. Denny rubbed his neck.

Sunday kept her face averted. Vivienne stood very erect, her hands hanging on to her purse.

"Do you want some help cleaning up?" she asked.

"Don't worry about it," Denny said. "We'll get it."

Kale came around the bar. "What's up, Viv?"

"I just stopped by to remind you to pick up Luke today. I'm heading to my mom's."

"Yeah, I remember," he said, regretting the edge that had crept into his voice. But she knew damn well he wouldn't forget about Luke.

Her eyes darted to Denny and Sunday like she was weighing whether they had caught his tone. "Just thought I'd make sure. I know you guys have a lot going on with the grand opening coming up."

"I'm going to head home," Sunday said, walking over to grab her bag from the booth. She waved in their general direction.

"It was good to see you, Sunday," Vivienne said.

Sunday stopped and turned. "You too, Vivienne."

And then Kale watched her walk out the door, afraid they'd lost a moment they weren't going to get back.

CHAPTER THIRTEEN

Vivienne

It was good to see you, Sunday."

She was determined to be friendly, as she always was with the Brennans, but she also wanted a better look at Sunday's face before she left. It was blotchy, like she'd been crying. From the moment Vivienne walked in the door, she could tell something was going on. The air in the room was all wrong.

Denny cleared his throat and moved behind the bar. "Kale, why don't you walk your wife out and I'll get started on this mess."

"You ready to go?" Kale asked her. No offer of breakfast or coffee together.

"Yeah. Unless you want to come along?"

He started for the door. "That's okay."

She'd been joking. Kale was kind to her mother, stopped over to fix appliances and mow the lawn. But she knew her mother's icy behavior—criticizing how much he worked, hinting that he should take better care of Vivienne—made him squirm.

Once they were outside, she couldn't help herself. "Did she find another bookkeeper yet?"

"I don't think so."

They arrived at the car.

"She spending a lot of time here?"

He dragged a hand through his hair. "C'mon, Vivienne. She stops in sometimes when she needs help. She's doing us a favor, you know."

She had to be careful. If she nagged Kale he'd share even less with her. "Okay. I should go. I'm sure I'll have a to-do list for you after I see Mom." She gave him a kiss. "I love you."

"Me too."

She got in her car and drove to the west side of town, the far edge where the few West Manor have-nots lived. Though it was barely West Manor. If she'd grown up one block farther west she would have been zoned for the Ossining schools. While she drove she tried to pinpoint the weird energy she'd walked into at the pub. It had definitely felt like more than just broken glass.

Vivienne knew Kale cared about her very much, loved Luke as much as a dad could. He was what her mother called a Steady Eddy, in a distinctly ambivalent tone. Sharon Martin had encouraged her daughter to set her sights a little higher.

"You have the looks, Viv," she'd said. "Don't throw them away on any old loser, like I did."

Vivienne had never met her father, didn't even know his name. His "relationship" with her mother had been brief. All she knew was that he lived in Connecticut with his real family, and he'd sent money each month until she was eighteen. Her mother had grown up in West Manor. When she became pregnant her parents gave her and her baby a home, which her mother inherited when they died in a car accident four years later.

So with no money and no father, and a waitress/cashier mother, Vivienne had been raised in an upper-middle-class town filled with intact families and stay-at-home moms. Embarrassed by her circumstances and jealous of many girls around her.

Including Sunday Brennan.

. . .

"You couldn't bring Luke with you?" her mother asked.

"He has school this morning."

They were sipping coffee in the living room of the narrow brick row house she'd grown up in. The room was still busy as ever, filled with the infinite baubles and tchotchkes her mother liked to surround herself with. She'd never been much of a housekeeper, preferring to leave clothes lying around, let laundry and dishes pile up. Growing up Vivienne had kept her bedroom trinket-free and spick-and-span, a quiet refuge from the chaos of the rest of the house. She had already listened to the broken-record complaints about the inflamed sciatica, maintenance issues with the house, the snobby neighbors around the corner—*That one's always rushing her kids around in the SUV. She leaves the house every morning without a stitch of makeup on her face.*

Her mother lit another cigarette. "How's the secretary job going?" She sat in a worn floral armchair, feet up on a stool, puffing away in a pink tracksuit.

"Administrative assistant. Good. I have an interview today for a promotion, a full-time job with the district. It would start next year." She stood and started straightening up the small, cluttered living room and kitchen while they talked.

"Full time?" Her mom shook her head of frayed blond hair. "You shouldn't have to work full-time."

"It'll be more money and I can get on the school's health insurance plan, which will be a lot cheaper than the self-employed one we're on now. We can think about a house in Manor Hills."

"Hmmph. That's practically Pleasantville. You think he'll agree to go that far out of town, away from that family?"

"It'll make sense, for lots of reasons." But Vivienne sounded more confident than she felt. She pulled her wallet from her purse and started counting out cash.

"If you remember, I always worked full-time. Had no choice."

"I know, Mom. Here you go." Vivienne handed over a small pile of bills. "I put some extra in there to put toward the property taxes."

"Thanks, Viv." She thumbed through the cash. "Are you leaving already?"

"I have to get to that interview."

"If you interview with a man, I bet you get the job." Her mother glanced with approving over-plucked eyebrows at Vivienne's skirt and pumps. "Mickey Brennan was in the store the other day, visiting that dim-witted son of his."

Vivienne didn't point out that the "dim-witted son" and her mother currently had the same job stocking shelves and bagging groceries at a local market. "Yeah?" She tossed her bag on her shoulder.

"They were all aflutter because Sunday's home."

"I'm sure they are. I'll take this bag out to the recycling bin." All the wine bottles clanged together as she picked it up.

"You'd do well to keep an eye on that situation, Viv. She's got nothing on you in the looks department, but she had Kale's heart for a long time. First love and all that."

"That was a long time ago."

Her mother stood and reached for her arm. "I'm just saying be careful. I always thought you deserved better than him, but I don't want you to get hurt." She rubbed Vivienne's upper arm. "Maybe you should talk to Kale about the Brennan dad and the Walsh woman. Remind him the sort of people they are."

"Don't worry about it, Mom. Kale and I are good." Vivienne gave her a peck on the cheek and headed out to her car.

Her mother leaned against the front door, enveloped in a smoky haze. "Remember what I said. You know those Brennans. Think they're better than the rest of us, like they have it all coming."

The school district offices were fifteen minutes east, back through town. She headed in that direction, taking a roundabout route to avoid Kale on the road, just in case. She didn't want him to know she was interviewing for this job just yet.

She tried to relax on the drive, get in the right headspace for the interview. Her mother had always been her biggest supporter, but she had a way of creating dark doubts about Kale—*He's a decent provider, but I don't know that he appreciates you enough, Viv . . . You deserve someone who sweeps you off your feet once in a while . . . That family has far too much of a hold on him.*

Vivienne had been aware of "that family" as long as she could remember. Many of the men in her neighborhood worked for Mickey Brennan, and he was rumored to have a direct hand in everything related to construction in the area—contract bidding, union negotiations, inspection approvals. The Brennans had a big house, nice clothes, extra cars in the driveway. They were a clan unto themselves, and throughout her adolescence Vivienne had watched them all from afar, including Sunday. The lone female sibling had good grades, ran cross-country, and worked on the high school newspaper. Everything seemed to come so easy to her.

Vivienne was in middle school when her mother, who loved sharing salacious secrets, told her Mickey Brennan had taken up with one of their neighbors, Lynn Walsh. Like the Martins, the Walshes lived on the street known in town as Welfare Row. But that family had been a step lower than all the rest. Dirt poor, raging drunk of a father, wild-child son who often managed to smile his way out of trouble—*Stay away from that one, Viv,* her mother used to say. *He's too charming for his own good.* And Lynn Walsh worked at a dry cleaner's. Initially Vivienne dismissed the idea, believing there was no way the wealthy man who ran construction crews would want anything to do with the likes of Mrs. Walsh. But her mother had said a man like Mickey Brennan had needs, and if his wife wasn't meeting them Lynn Walsh was welcome to try, get something for herself out of it too.

Vivienne saw it herself many times, saw Mr. Brennan's big pickup truck drive down the street with the lights off and park in front of the Walsh place before the mom jumped out. So it was no surprise Billy Walsh knew about the affair. She'd come across him one night, very drunk on the stoop of his house, not long before he graduated from West Manor High. He'd waved a beer can around while he ranted about the Brennans.

"Not enough they have the money and the big house, that fucker Mickey Brennan is ruining my family."

The affair went on for over three years, and it was a mystery whether Maura Brennan ever found out. Certainly no one on the Row ever considered telling her. For one thing, Mickey was a boss, and generally respected. There was also a sort of Row Code. Who among them didn't have secrets? If Lynn Walsh was finding a little comfort from that failure husband of hers, so be it.

Vivienne never talked to Kale about it. She didn't want to appear petty, drudging up old gossip about his adopted family. Besides, he'd probably find some way to defend Mickey and end up resenting her for bringing it up.

A squat utilitarian building housed the school district offices. She parked in the lot, turned the car off, and waited. The interview was still over ten minutes away and she didn't want to appear overeager. She took inventory of the people who entered and exited the building. Most of the women wore slacks with flats or shapeless dresses with saggy cardigans. They had wash-and-go hairstyles and no idea how to apply makeup. She looked at her fitted button-down and knee-length skirt. The heels were sensible, not too high but still flattering.

She wanted this job. She'd be full time and Luke would start at the preschool next door. Relocating to Manor Hills would mean a shorter commute for her and Luke, and Kale would be closer to the new restaurant in Mamaroneck. Kale just had to go for it, which, she knew, was a tall order.

Vivienne had vaguely known of Kale Collins growing up, but they hadn't met until she moved back to West Manor after living in the city for a few years. The plan had been to start a modeling career—her mother sprang for headshots and breast augmentation surgery for her high school graduation—and meet a successful businessman, fall in love, get started on the life she wanted.

That plan, however, had failed. She landed a few onetime modeling contracts, but spent most of her days schlepping to castings and collecting rejections. She accepted a couple of "private" modeling sessions, which amounted to posing in lingerie for a very handsy photographer. It paid decent money, but during the third session he insisted she pose nude. When she resisted, he told her she had to return the money he'd paid her because she didn't complete the job. She didn't have the money, and she didn't like the menacing look in his eye, so she took off her clothes and let him take the shots, but that was the end of her modeling career. She didn't ask, and never found out, where the pictures ended up, just prayed it wasn't the internet. After that she resigned herself to retail work and living on credit cards.

There were lots of dates and some boyfriends; she'd even spent a few weekends out in the Hamptons with a Wall Street guy. She was good at catching men's eyes, getting them interested. It wasn't rocket science. The right makeup and clothes, lots of laughing and listening, moving her body in certain ways. But after some initial excitement and physical fun, when talking and finding common interests became a bigger part of the picture, it always fizzled. She was out of her depth, couldn't compete with the self-confident, college-educated women who filled the city. Women who wore power suits, climbed career ladders, and challenged the men around them. The city had made her feel more white trash than she ever had on the Row. So at twenty-two, after years of sharing tiny apartments with faceless roommates, she went home. She fell back in with old friends, landed a job as a receptionist. Then she spotted Kale working at Brennan's one night.

It took several visits to the pub before she had the chance to talk with him, and she had to take the lead. She was casual at first, just light conversation. Her real opening came late one night when he sat at his own bar and got hammered. He was still getting over being dumped by his fiancée, which was a real turnoff at times. But he owned half of the best pub in town. He was easy on the eyes, with his soft curls and lopsided smile. There was a solidity to him; he was a reliable guy who took his responsibilities seriously. The type that would always take care of his family. So she kept coming back, offered a supportive shoulder. They commiserated about having a parent who preferred not to be in the picture. Eventually he became more comfortable around her, appreciated how she laughed at his jokes.

She waited a little while before they had sex, wanted to make sure he was somewhat invested, but once they did she found him hungry for it, a salve for his loneliness. It all went according to plan—not that she manipulated him. She just worked hard to help him get over Sunday. And when she became a little careless about her birth control pill, she figured if she was meant to get pregnant, she would.

Things weren't perfect. Kale had little ambition. He put no thought into his appearance, wouldn't consider contacts instead of those schoolteacher glasses. He'd put on a few pounds the last couple of years and shaved randomly. And he was such a homebody, something she'd never had any luck changing. But they'd set down roots the last four years. When Sunday came back it had thrown Vivienne, but there was no way Kale could love her again. Forgive her, maybe, be friendly at some point. God knew Kale liked everyone to get along. But Vivienne had believed she was safe. Now, not two months later, she sensed a threat. Sunday was back in the fold of her family, which was also Kale's family. And now he knew Sunday had kept that damn postcard all these years. It had been a mistake to call her on it that night in the office. But she'd been so angry, coming across such a blatant reminder of their shared past—the Kale and Sunday stick figures holding hands on the beach. Her mother was right, Kale needed distance from the whole Brennan crew.

She checked her makeup in the mirror, smoothed her hair with a flat hand, and climbed out of the car. As she walked into the building, head high, back straight, she mentally firmed up her plan. Step one: get this job. Step two: talk to Sunday.

Three days later she found the opportunity she was waiting for. She had discreetly gathered intel: Denny and his father were out in Mamaroneck with Kale, all hands on deck getting the new pub ready for the grand opening next weekend. Jackie was covering Brennan's, so Sunday was likely home alone. Hopefully Shane wouldn't be there. Vivienne never knew how to respond to his gushing greetings and conversation. She took the morning off work and knocked on the red front door at eleven o'clock.

When Sunday answered, her eyes widened in surprise. They exchanged hellos and Vivienne asked if she had a few minutes.

"Sure." She stepped back and pulled the door open further. "You want to come in?"

"Thanks." Vivienne walked into the living room. There was a laptop and piles of paper on the coffee table.

"Excuse the mess. I was just getting some work done."

If Vivienne had accounting skills, maybe none of this would be happening. "Any luck hiring a bookkeeper?" she asked.

"Not yet. But I've been researching your list." Sunday waved toward the kitchen. "Can I get you something? Coffee or water?"

"Coffee would be great."

They went into the kitchen and Sunday gestured for her to have a seat at the rectangular wood table that was planted in the middle of the room. While Sunday poured coffee Vivienne looked around the large kitchen she'd only been in a handful of times. The worn white cabinets with glass doors displayed a mishmash of multicolored dishware. Worn pots and pans hung from hooks above the stove. Molly's drawings, family photos, and chaotic calendars cluttered the fridge doors. Kale had apparently always felt at home in this disorganized hodgepodge.

Sunday placed two mugs on the table and settled in across from Vivienne. No chitchat. She just laid her hands in her lap and waited.

"You look all healed up," Vivienne said.

"Just about."

Vivienne added cream to her coffee and studied Sunday on the sly. A tank top under a plaid button-down that looked like it belonged to one of her brothers. No makeup, hair pulled back in a random pile. "You know, you could get that scar on the side of your head lasered. Would be like it was never there."

"I'll have to remember that."

Vivienne sipped her coffee. "I haven't spent much time here, in this house. Kale brings me by once in a while, but your family never really took to me."

"I don't know about that." Sunday shrugged. "They're just a tough crew sometimes."

"It's okay. I mean, no one was going to replace you."

Sunday's eyebrows ticked up.

Vivienne took another sip. "Must be nice to be back here, with everyone."

"It's great."

"I wonder, though, if any of them ever told you what it was like for Kale after you left."

Other than pulling her head back a bit, Sunday offered no reaction. But that was enough.

Vivienne folded her hands on the table. "Of course they'd want to protect you from that. But I think maybe you should know."

"Vivienne—"

"He was really lost when I met him, and that was a while after you were gone. Just so sad and checked out, drinking way too much. He would talk about you, wonder what he did wrong. Blame himself."

Sunday swallowed hard, but she stayed quiet and never dropped her eyes. Maybe she knew she had this coming, that she deserved to hear about the damage she'd caused. Maybe it would stop her from causing any more.

"But eventually I got him to laugh a little, get out and do stuff, have some fun. I found ways to make him happy."

It was subtle, but Sunday flinched.

"Denny even told me once how good I was for Kale. I helped him get over you. We got married and had Luke, and he's the best father I can imagine. But things have been different since you came home." She was tipping her hand by admitting that, but it was by design. Sunday wouldn't respond to games. Shaming would be the most effective strategy with her.

"Is there something you want to ask me, Vivienne?"

"Are you planning to stay here? In West Manor?"

"Yes." Her expression was neutral, to an infuriating degree.

"You know what Kale's mother did to him," Vivienne said, leaning forward and poking the table with a finger. "You know that he would never forgive himself if he hurt Luke that way."

"I know that."

Vivienne sat back again. "I interviewed the other day for a job on the other side of town. If I get it, I think it would make sense for us to move there. Luke would be at the school near where I work. Kale would be closer to Mamaroneck. He could focus on the new place. What do you think?" Vivienne despised this, asking for help this way. But if Sunday was on board it would only help her cause.

"I think that makes a lot of sense."

"Me too." She stood and brought her half-full cup to the sink. "Thanks for your time. I'll see myself out." She pulled her bag off a chair and started toward the living room.

"Vivienne?"

"Yes?"

"I'm glad you were there for him."

It was Vivienne's turn to be surprised, but she didn't let it show. She nodded and left, wondering if love could really be that unselfish.

CHAPTER FOURTEEN

Sunday

I'm glad you were there for him."

She meant it. Kind of.

After Vivienne left, she sat at the table in the quiet house. The last thing she'd expected that morning was for Vivienne to knock on the door. Initially Sunday was afraid Kale might have told her the whole story and she'd come to offer moral support. It was a relief to realize she was there instead to guilt-trip Sunday into leaving town, or, at the least, leaving her husband alone. She got it though; part of her even respected Vivienne for it. She didn't want to lose Kale, and if there was one thing Sunday could understand, it was that.

Vivienne was right. No one in her family had talked to her about how Kale handled her departure, and she never asked. How was it she had never thought about how much pain she caused him? She answered her own question and it was like slamming into a glass wall she didn't see coming. She hadn't thought about it because she'd been wallowing in self-imposed exile for years, feeling betrayed because everyone carried on without her. Had she really expected Kale to somehow guess what she needed and come after her? He married someone else, but she had betrayed him before that.

One thought crystallized and she slumped back against her seat. She had done the worst possible thing to Kale. She abandoned him.

The conversation with Vivienne was a blow after the last couple of days. Since coming clean with Denny and Kale, she felt more awake, like she was shaking off a five-year winter of hibernation. For those two hours right after she told them, while Kale was out looking for Denny, she'd assumed something terrible was going to happen. But then Denny came through the door and said what he said, and even while she sobbed into his chest, she believed everything would be okay.

The next morning she'd woken up with a strong desire to *do something*, take some kind of action. First, she convinced her dad to cut off the cast and set her arm free. Then she drove his truck fifteen miles south and met with Michael Eaton at his office. He was gracious and chatty and smiled a lot while he removed his jacket and rolled up his sleeves, and she hated to pull a cloud across his sunny morning. However, eager to start solving this problem, she lost no time in getting to the point after they sat across from each other. She told him she knew about Denny's loan and they needed a way out of it. Other than coming up with seventy thousand in cash.

"I'm sorry, Sunday. This is why it was such a bad idea. It's a straightforward contract, no real wiggle room."

"What if Billy Walsh was arrested for a violent crime?"

"Well, it wouldn't negate the contract, but it could distract him for a while, tie up his resources. Especially if he was convicted." He shrugged. "Just depends on so many things. Like what crime, when it happened . . ."

"Assault and battery." Earlier that morning she'd done some research. "It was almost five years ago, but we're still within the statute of limitations."

"Is there any evidence of this crime?"

She started with the facts. "There's a hospital report that indicates I fell down a staircase one night at the bar where he was working. And I suffered a miscarriage as a result."

He blinked in surprise. "I'm sorry, Sunday."

"Thanks." In her mind this next part was a certainty as well. "I fell because I was struggling with him. I was trying to get away from him. When he wouldn't let me go, I threatened to tell my family and he pushed me toward the stairs."

"Are you saying he caused you to fall?"

That was when she began to diverge from indisputable fact in her own mind, but only by the slightest degree. In her heart she believed it was true. Something had caught hold of her foot that night. "Yes. He tripped me, and after I fell he took off and left me there alone."

He sat back in his chair and studied her, maybe trying to determine where that left them.

"Look, I know it's thin," she said. "But maybe it's enough to get him to back off the lien. He'll get his money, but we need time."

He pulled a hand down his face, reached for a pad and pen. "Okay. Let's see what we can figure out."

They spent the next half hour talking it through, developing a plan. She sensed no judgment. He attacked the problem and made her feel part of the solution. She could not adequately express her thanks to Michael when she left his office.

That whole morning had felt liberating, including admitting to Denny that their mother knew what happened. Kale's little breakdown, however, nearly destroyed her. She was wholly unprepared for both his emotional regret and his question. *But, Sunday, why didn't you tell me?* Vivienne had walked in at either the best or the worst possible moment.

She cleared the table and readied to go back to work. Vivienne had disturbed a fragile optimism that had settled in the last couple of days. An optimism that had prompted Sunday to contact her landlord in LA and sublet her apartment, then schedule an interview with a potential bookkeeper for the pub. Even begin to look into master's programs in the area. The conversation with Vivienne had shown her just how fragile that optimism was, how fast the shame would wriggle back in at the first opportunity.

She and Kale had to finish their unfinished business. They needed to let each other off the hook. After that, they could each move on with their lives.

A few days later she helped Jackie open the bar on a quiet Tuesday. The countdown until the grand opening was three days, so Denny and Kale were spending most of their time in Mamaroneck.

The busywork and excitement were good distractions while she waited for some news from Michael. But at any given moment she was aware of where she was in relation to Katonah, even catching herself leaning the opposite way at times, as if the northeasterly direction represented her own personal kryptonite. Billy would know soon, if he didn't already, that she was back in town, and he would know what she was accusing him of. So it was understood by all that she would not go anywhere alone until the situation was resolved.

She had spent the last two days calling vendors, haranguing them into working with her on grace periods and payment plans. With each success she gained a little confidence. Most of the vendors, be they beer or liquor distributors, food suppliers, even the laundry service and maintenance crew, liked and respected Denny and Kale. She made promises, there were a lot of balls in the air, but her plan was sound. As long as Billy accepted the deal Michael offered his lawyer. That was the key.

She'd also emailed her editor at the magazine because she'd made progress with her next story. It was about a guy who denied his own instincts and refused to violate his sister's trust, no matter how much guilt and pain it cost him. She was finally in a place where she could see an ending to it.

The other project she had under way was *The Little Fireman,* the children's book she was working on with Jackie and Shane. The night before, she had consulted them, taking notes while they recalled the details of the story. There were debates about finer points: Did the little fireman drive the truck or ride in the back? Did he live alone? Was the big fire at a house or building? All of which Shane won. He shot down any contrary opinions with the utmost confidence—*You guys just don't remember*—shaking his head and laughing his whole-body laugh.

Kale walked in while she was going over the story notes with Jackie at the bar. She had purposely avoided him since his meltdown, especially after Vivienne's visit. But today she planned to talk with him, find a way for them to put it all in the rearview, as he'd suggested. Which sounded really good until he walked in. As soon as she looked at him her resolve wavered. She'd seen him hurling glasses to the floor, telling her he never should have let her go.

She wasn't sure what to expect given how their last conversation ended—or didn't, more to the point. But he dropped his jacket and bag in the office, and came out next to her behind the bar to see what they were doing. "No way. The little fireman story."

"You remember it?"

"Yeah. The one you used to tell Shane all the time. And the rest of us would pretend we weren't listening." He gave Jackie a knowing smile.

"Okay, then," she said. "Maybe you can settle an argument. Did the little fireman drive the truck or ride in the back?"

"He rode in the back."

Sitting across the bar, Jackie flipped a hand up. "Dude, he drove the truck."

"*Dude,* he rode in the back. That's why he was able to jump out and grab the ladder so fast when they got to the fire."

Jackie's face pinched in consideration. "Fine. I give up." He hopped off his stool and headed for the back. "I'll get the mats."

Michael walked in the front door then, and right off Sunday lost a bit of hope because he didn't look good. His normally at-ease face seemed closed in concentration. He glanced around, loosening his tie, and headed for the bar.

"Everything okay?" she asked.

"I have some news. Is Denny here?"

"No, but I'll fill him in."

Michael glanced at Kale. "Is there somewhere we can talk?" he asked her.

"It's okay. Kale knows everything."

Michael hesitated but nodded. "I just met with Walsh's lawyer in Katonah." His mouth curled down. "What a piece of work. The good news is his client will go for the deal. With his record Walsh doesn't want to be arrested. Of course, he denies any wrongdoing on his client's part." He paused. "Can I get a beer?"

Kale made a show of checking his watch.

"I know what time it is," Michael said. "But I'd like to wash some of this away, know what I mean?"

Without a word Kale poured a draft and slid it in front of him.

"I'm sorry, Michael," Sunday said. She'd dragged him into a fairly ugly negotiation.

"It's okay. There's other good news. Walsh wants to leave the area. His lawyer doesn't think he'll go back to Ireland, sounds like maybe there are some bad guys after him over there." He shrugged. "I didn't get details. But he wants out of New York. The problem is all his money is tied up in the loan to Denny, so we'll need to come up with some cash now to help him relocate."

"How much?" she asked.

He took a healthy pull off his beer. "We went back and forth, he talked about circumstantial evidence, how much time has passed—he's a low-life, but he's not stupid. I talked about what else police might find if they start investigating. I got him down to twenty thousand. We give him the cash and you agree not to report, he leaves the state and gives you until the end of the year to repay him the rest of the loan, with interest." He leaned toward her. "It'll all go through his lawyer and me. You will never have to talk to him."

Something loosened in her chest. "That's great, Michael. Really."

"When do we need to get him the money?" Kale asked.

Michael looked at him out of the corner of his eye, like he was still unsure why Kale was in the middle of all this. "I told him I'd have it to him by the weekend."

Three days to come up with twenty thousand in cash.

"I should have talked to you first," Michael said. "But I just wanted to get him gone. And listen, I don't mind fronting the money so we can—"

"I can get the money," Kale said. "I'll have it to you by Saturday morning."

Michael didn't even turn Kale's way, just waited for her direction.

She glanced at Kale's firm expression. He wanted to do this. And truthfully, she preferred to keep it in the family. "Thanks, Michael," she said, "but I think we can figure it out."

"Okay." He finished his beer and went for his wallet.

"On the house," Kale said.

Sunday walked Michael out to his car. "I don't know how to thank you."

"I'm just happy I could help." He glanced back toward the pub. "I remember you two in high school. You and Collins. I kept waiting for you to break up, but it never happened." He gave her a sheepish grin and slid his hands in his pockets. "He's married with a kid now, right?"

"Yeah."

"Does he know that?"

She looked away.

"Sorry," he said. "Seems like he's still holding on."

Her response was a vague shake of the head. She didn't want to talk to Michael about Kale.

She reached up to give him a hug. "Thanks for everything."

Later that night she had Jackie drop her back at the pub because Kale was closing. It would be a good time to catch him and clear the air. Paul was there, wiping down the bar, and he told her Kale had run home for a bit but he'd be back to finish up the till.

After Paul left she had quiet time to consider her agenda for this discussion. Kale had a family, she needed to figure out her life. Talking about what happened that awful night, or what followed, would do no good. She believed he would be on the same page. In the past they had talked about the mother he barely remembered. Sunday used to ask him if he had any desire to find her, maybe confront her. But he always said no, he just didn't want to know a woman who would do what she did. "What could she possibly say to make it okay?" he'd ask. Kale loved his son and it wasn't in his makeup to hurt him that way.

She was in the office when she heard him come through the front door. After steadying her nerves with a deep breath, she took her rehearsed speech and headed out behind the bar. But when she looked up toward the door, it wasn't Kale standing there.

It was Billy Walsh.

For a second she wondered if this was a nightmare, but when she placed her hands on the steel counter under the bar, the cold, hard surface denied it.

He stayed close to the door. One side of his mouth curled up. "Hiya, Sunday."

The back door had already been chained up; the small silver key sat on the desk in the office. He was blocking the only exit from the building.

"You're looking good," he said.

She didn't speak, didn't trust her voice, in case she sounded half as panicked as she felt.

Billy held his hands up in a no-harm gesture. "Now I only need a minute, yeah? And I won't move from this spot." He had the same untamed ginger-blond hair, the piercing eyes. But he looked older, weathered, like he'd been through some things the last five years.

"I'm not looking to hurt you," he said.

No one would hear if she screamed. The neighboring businesses had been closed for hours. Under the bar her hands grasped for something, anything to use as a weapon. All she had ready access to was a shelf of glasses behind her and the cooler full of mugs in front of her.

The cooler. That's when she remembered.

"What do you want?" she asked.

Moving very carefully, making it look like she was just shifting her weight, she took a small step closer to the cooler. Mounted behind it, hidden from view, was a holster that contained the revolver her dad had bought. He'd insisted Denny and Kale keep it there in case of a robbery. At least, she hoped it was still there.

Billy slid his hands in the pockets of his denim jacket. "I took the deal, and I'm leaving this bloody town for good."

She slid her hand down and, with tremendous relief, laid two fingers against the butt of the gun. It was there, and, if needed, all she had to do was flick off the safety strap, grab it, and pull up.

"But before I go," he said, "there's things I need to say."

Despite the surreal nature of this encounter, or maybe because of it, she wondered what the hell he could have to say to her. Maybe, after hearing about the miscarriage, he was going to take some kind of responsibility for what happened?

"You see," he said, "I know something about your father that you don't."

She pressed the pads of her fingers against the textured grip of the gun. She wouldn't go any further unless she had to, but knowing it was there provided a measure of courage. Otherwise there's no way she could have said what she did next. "Is this when you blame my dad for your shitty life because he fired your father?"

His eyes grew and his whole body jerked. She flicked the strap with her thumb and wrapped her hand around the butt of the gun. But he didn't move otherwise, so she didn't pull it out. They stayed like that for a moment, considering each other. Long enough for her to take note of how quiet it was, how steady her breathing was. She felt calm with her hand on that gun, her senses heightened.

"No," he said. And there was the cruel smile she remembered. "Now's when I tell you that your father was fucking my mother when we were in high school."

It was like he'd spoken a foreign language and she needed time to translate.

"That's right," he said. "Wasn't enough Mickey Brennan had the big house and all that money. He couldn't take your nagging bitch of a mother anymore and came looking for comfort on Welfare Row."

Her whole body went cold except where her hand clutched the gun. What he was saying was impossible.

"They would meet at his office," he said. "Or his job sites. Even took overnight trips. She was with him for three years and then he flat dumped her."

Was this supposed to be a justification for what he did to her? She stretched her fingers, then closed them around the butt again. Her dad had taken her, Denny, Jackie, and Kale to a shooting range for a lesson when he first bought the gun for the pub—*Don't be arguing with me. It's going to be there so you all need to know how to use it safely.* One of the many rules he covered: *Grip the pistol tight, but not so tight your hand shakes.*

Billy glanced around the pub. "Not so high 'n mighty now, are yous? Having to take a loan off a lowly Walsh. Make sure you tell Denny it was me caused those problems out there in Mamaroneck." He laughed at her expression. "Sure all it took was a sledgehammer and a good hose."

More of her dad's rules came back: *Always keep the safety on and don't put your finger on the trigger until you aim at the target.* She didn't know if the gun would even work correctly after so many years. Denny used to clean it once in a while, but who knew if he still did.

Billy pointed at her. "I left my mother thanks to you. If you hadn't come to the bar that night, I wouldn't have had to go back to Belfast. But I knew your men was going to come after me. So I left, and she's gone now." He shook his head. "You fuckin' Brennans always win. I'll get my money and leave on Monday, stop you from telling your lies about that night." He sucked his teeth. "We both know what really happened, don't we? You came looking for comfort on Welfare Row too. Just like your dad."

She kept her voice low but firm. "That's not true."

"Come off it. You were looking for attention because your boyfriend left you home alone. Making eyes at me all night, coming up to my room." His mouth twisted in disgust. "Drinking like a fish even though you were pregnant."

The gun was pointed at him before she knew what she'd done.

He froze momentarily before regaining some of his composure. "Truth hurts, doesn't it. You gonna shoot me with that gun?"

"Get out." She pressed her shoulders lower and raised the gun higher. *Aim with your dominant eye,* her dad had instructed, *and align the back and front sights.* The gun felt heavy, substantial.

"I'm an unarmed man, about to walk out that there door." He pointed behind him. "You can't shoot me now." He was going for a light tone but she heard the uncertainty.

She took several steps around the bar, surprised at how steady her hands and arms were.

His smile slipped a bit and he swallowed. "I'll go. And you can keep telling yourself what happened was all my fault. But I'll always know better." He gave her a pointed look. "I didn't trip you that night. You were wasted and you fell. All on your own."

Another of her dad's rules: *Don't pull a gun on someone unless you're willing to use it.* She took two more steps forward, still well out of his reach. "Get out and don't ever come back. You fuck with one Brennan, you fuck with six Brennans." She'd included Kale without even thinking about it. When she raised the gun and lined up the sights with his forehead, she saw the sweat there.

He stared at her, his eyes pulsing with hate.

In that moment, if he made one wrong move, she believed she could shoot him.

But seconds later he spun on his black boots, threw open the door, and walked out of the pub.

After he left she stood very still, gun pointed at the door for several moments, even after she heard a car start down the street and drive off. But Kale could walk in at any time, so she lowered her arms and aimed it at the floor, adhering to yet another Dad Rule: *Always keep the muzzle pointed in a safe direction.* She waited another minute, her shoulders and arms stiff with tension, but Billy wasn't coming back. Not that night. She had scared him.

She knew she should lock the door but didn't want to go anywhere near it. So she sat at a small table by the bar, placed the gun on top after engaging the safety. Then she put her hands in her lap and waited.

Billy's words surfaced again in her mind. *Your father was fucking my mother when we were in high school . . . she was with him for three years.* Her initial reaction was flat denial, but she couldn't ignore the persistent ring of underlying truth. Her dad had been absent a lot during her high school years, claiming job demands, spending nights on building sites. Sunday had always assumed part of it was needing time away from the miserable woman her mother had become, but did that justification extend to adultery?

When she heard footsteps outside, she laid a hand next to the gun. But Denny came in the door, followed by Kale, so she lowered her hand to her lap again and took the first genuine breath she'd taken since Billy had appeared.

"Hey," Denny said. "What're you doing—What the fuck?" He stopped walking so abruptly Kale bumped into him. They both stared at the gun on the table.

She stayed very still. "He was here."

Denny ran to the door, shoved it open, and searched the street outside with his hands gripping the sides of the doorframe.

"He's gone," she said. "And he won't be back."

Kale moved closer to the table, looking her over. "Are you okay?"

"I'm fine." She nodded to the revolver. "The safety's on. Could you please put it back behind the bar?" She felt an intense need to distance herself from it, from what could have happened.

He lifted the gun, kept it pointed at the floor while he took it back to the holster behind the cooler.

Denny locked the front door. "What the hell were you doing here alone?"

"Paul went home and I didn't lock the door. Kale was coming right back. I didn't think about it."

"How could you be so careless?"

"Don't yell at me, Denny."

Kale came back around the bar. "Just tell us what happened."

"He didn't come here to hurt me," she said. "He just wanted to say some shitty things before he left town."

They both sat down and listened as she told them what happened. Denny had difficulty containing himself when she got to the part about their father, mumbling "ridiculous" and "fucking liar." But the doubt in his eyes betrayed him. He was weighing it all.

Next she told them Billy had claimed responsibility for everything that had gone wrong in Mamaroneck, and she watched as her larger-than-life brother seemed to shrink in his chair, overwhelmed by the realization that he'd been thoroughly played by such a person. Kale didn't make it any harder on Denny by reacting. He just kept his head down while he listened.

"Christ," Denny said. "He set me up? From the get-go?" He shot up out of his seat and chopped one hand with the other. "That's it. We're calling the cops. You gotta report this. All of it."

"No," Sunday said.

"Yes! He pushed you down a set of stairs, he tried to steal this place from us—he needs to go to jail."

But it wasn't that simple. She kept her voice low and steady, tried to balance out Denny's emotional state. "We have no proof he caused that damage, or that he caused me to fall down the stairs. It would just be my word against his. Besides, I pulled the gun on him."

"Why? Did he make a move?"

"No. I just wanted to scare him," she said. "And I did."

Denny threw his hands in the air, but when she met Kale's eye the corner of his mouth pulled up just a touch.

"What if he comes back?" Denny asked.

She stood. "He's leaving on Monday."

"And you trust that?" Denny turned to Kale. "Help me out here. Tell her it's time to go to the cops."

Kale rested his hands on his hips. "Sorry. This is her call."

Denny shook his head in frustration. "Get her home safely," he said to Kale, before he marched to the door and headed out into the night.

She and Kale walked to her house in a complicated silence. To Sunday it felt loaded with things they shouldn't talk about. Like how she'd been pregnant with their baby for a short time. Or his unanswered question—*Why didn't you tell me?*—which she couldn't fully explain to herself, let alone him. Or the fact that his wife had visited her the other day. No good would come from mentioning that to him.

So they focused on their feet and didn't speak. Not even about which way to walk. They were automatically following their old route, down the alley between Cedar and Poplar Streets. Maybe that's what finally made the quiet too painful.

"Thanks for having my back with Denny," she said. "About involving the police."

"I meant what I said. It should be your decision." He slid his hands into his jacket pockets. "But do you really think he won't come back?"

Billy's face materialized in her mind, the surprise that had appeared when he realized he was dealing with a different woman from five years ago. "I do. Especially after the line I laid on him at the end." She told him about threatening Billy with the retaliation of six Brennans.

Kale stopped walking. "You did not say that."

"I did."

His mouth fell open.

"I know." She put a hand over her face. "So cheesy."

He let out a stunned laugh. "No, really. Very badass."

"Shut up."

"Dirty Harriet."

"Okay." She turned and started walking.

They were silent until they got to the house. It had felt exhilarating to laugh with him, make that connection. But it was followed by such a heavy sadness that if she tried to speak she was afraid she'd cry. Her speech about moving on would have to wait for another time.

Jackie's truck wasn't in the driveway and it appeared no one was home.

"Dad and Shane had dinner at Clare's," she said. "I bet Jackie went to pick them up."

"Okay. I'll come in and take a quick look around."

She unlocked the front door and flipped on lights while he walked through the downstairs, checking the back door and windows before coming back to the foyer where she was waiting.

"Everything's locked up down here." He glanced at the staircase and ran a hand through his hair, which curled around his fingers as they trailed through. "But maybe I should take a look up there too. That old trellis is still attached to the house, right?"

That's why he was looking at the floor and not her. He meant the old trellis he used to climb to sneak into her room. "Yes," she said. "It's still there."

He nodded with a solemn expression and walked up the stairs.

She stayed by the front door and texted Jackie for his ETA. There was no way she could follow Kale to her room, where they had spent so much time together. It would have been too much.

When he came back downstairs a few minutes later he looked distracted. "It's all clear up there. I tightened the lock on that window above your desk."

"Thanks."

He nodded but didn't move.

"You can go," she said. "I texted Jackie. They're on their way back." She didn't want Kale to feel obligated to stay, but she also sensed that he was debating saying something else. And that terrified her more than being alone. She already felt shaky, like she was just keeping the emotion at bay. If they got into any of this now, she would lose it.

"I know it's been a long night," he said. "And maybe I don't have the right to bring this up now."

"Kale, I don't think we should—"

"But I need to know why—"

They both stopped when the headlights from Jackie's pickup splashed through the window and slid across the room. Then they stood facing each other, without speaking, while they listened. Car doors opened and closed, Shane's loud voice rumbled across the lawn, footsteps walked the path and climbed the porch steps. Still neither of them said anything. Kale didn't finish his question and Sunday didn't tell him she already knew what he was going to ask.

The front door opened and they all piled in, their eyebrows lifting a bit to see her and Kale standing there together. Shane gave Kale an enthusiastic hello and her dad asked him about preparations for opening night, just two days away. Sunday observed a subtle caution in Kale's demeanor while he answered her dad's questions. Like her, Kale was probably viewing her dad through a new set of eyes, unsure what to think since hearing Billy's accusation.

After catching up for a couple minutes, Kale said he needed to get home. She watched from the living room window as he walked down the street, toward his house, where his wife and son waited for him.

She filled Jackie in on Billy's visit after her dad and Shane went to bed, shooting down his self-blame about not staying with her at the pub. He reacted to the idea of her dad cheating on their mom the way she and Denny had: immediate rejection followed by the unwelcome notion that it made some sense.

Exhaustion caught up with her and she headed upstairs, though she still hoped to talk to Denny before going to sleep. She wasn't going to change her mind about the police, but she understood his frustration. He probably felt like a total chump at this point.

When she stepped into her room she pictured Kale in there earlier. Walking around, testing the window, checking her closet. She dropped onto her bed. Everywhere her gaze touched, he was present in some way. The award above her desk for the story she'd written about him. Books on the shelves they'd read together for school. The bottom drawers of her dresser, where he used to keep clothes.

She had stayed at his apartment a lot, but it never felt like living together. Not when she could be called home at any moment—*I need your help getting the house ready for the holiday dinner, Sunday. Mom's taken a bad turn and is asking for you, Sun. Shane will be alone at the house with your mother this weekend. Could you stay with them?* Denny was immersed in Theresa and getting the pub off the ground, and Jackie was attending Pace University. Rarely did she say no, lest her mother remind her once again they were paying her college tuition and had made it possible for Kale to become a business owner. It just wasn't worth it. Besides, Kale often just snuck over and stayed the night. They didn't mind the twin bed. Moving to the floor because the box spring made so much noise was a hassle. But even that wasn't so bad.

The first time they had sex had been in her room; there was nowhere else to go. His house wasn't an option, with his sick father down the hall and some relative or church member often around to take their turn watching over him.

After eight months Sunday almost didn't care where it happened. They were both nervous, having grown up in the shadow of the Catholic culture of purity, but she, at least, was ready. Kale had been the one to drag his feet. It was all about her family. Her dad loomed large in his mind. The last thing Kale wanted was to disappoint the man that had always treated him like a son. Denny's teasing didn't help—*You two better not rush it. And I'll know when it happens. I got a sixth sense about that kind of thing.* Neither did her mother's reaction to them as a couple. Maura Brennan's disapproval was evident from the start. *That's what we get for opening our home to him. And him your brother's best friend. I would have thought he'd be more honorable.* It was as if Kale had set out to defile her daughter, and her shoulder was quite a bit colder toward him after that.

So Sunday had understood Kale's desire to take it slow, but she was also frustrated. Grail had taken her to Planned Parenthood and she'd started on the pill. Kale knew that but nothing had changed. Everyone around them seemed to be doing it, and she began to wonder what was wrong with her.

It all reached a crisis point one night when they were in her room, and even though they somehow found themselves alone in the house, Kale seemed only interested in studying. She sat beside him on the floor with a textbook turned to some meaningless page and a dark suspicion bloomed. Kale was a senior, he was going to college next year, and this—him and Sunday—was just for now. He didn't want to risk his closest friendship over a high school girlfriend, didn't want to create drama with his second family, so he was riding it out until he left next fall.

By the time he stood to go home, she'd convinced herself of it. She kept it together when he kissed her goodnight, but after he left she sat on the edge of her bed and cried. He later told her he was at the bottom of the stairs when he decided to go back up, that he knew something was wrong.

He reappeared to find her in tears. Then he shut the door and knelt down before her. "What is it?"

She thought about telling him she just didn't feel well. If there was anything that would drive him away it would be a clingy emotional mess. But she decided to just tell him the truth. "I don't know what I'm doing wrong."

"What?"

Too embarrassed to say anything more, she simply looked at him.

It took a moment but then his face flushed. "Wait. You think I don't want to?"

She shrugged and shook her head.

"Sunday, it's all I think about. I just worry about everything. I don't want to upset anyone—your parents, or Denny."

"Then maybe you should date them." It came out with a sting, and his eyes widened in confusion. He thought he was doing the right thing, being considerate. Even at that age she understood the effects of his mother leaving him. He was afraid of losing people.

He took her hands. "I'm sorry."

"It's okay."

He raised himself on his knees so they were eye level, and moved his hands to her face. "I love you, Sunday."

"I love you too."

There was no self-consciousness, no feeling like she was trying out the words, wondering what meaning should be attached to them. She knew. And when they kissed, it was different. No more hesitation from him, even when they fell back on her bed and started pulling at each other's clothes.

Sitting on that same bed thirteen years later it occurred to Sunday that she had no chance of building a new life here if she stayed in this room. It suction-cupped her to the past. She needed to leave this house, find her own place. Maybe a small apartment in Purchase, close to Manhattanville College, where she was thinking about applying to graduate school.

Denny still hadn't come home, but her pillow was calling to her. The adrenaline boost that came with the confrontation at the pub had drained.

She thought about jotting a note, apologizing for their argument, providing some kind of reassurance for him.

When another idea floated into her consciousness she knew it was the right one. She dug in her desk for a copy of the LA Arts Council magazine, slipped into his room downstairs, and left it on his bed.

"No, no, no," Shane said. "That's not how they go." He took the LEGOs from her hands.

"I'm pretty sure that was right . . ." Sunday said.

But he had already pulled the tiny pieces apart, exchanged one for another from the bin of a billion pieces, and put them together. He held it up to her. "See?"

They were sitting on the carpet of his third-floor bedroom, working on one of many turrets for Hogwarts Castle. Shelves lining the walls of his room—shelves Jackie had installed—displayed dozens of finished works, including a *Millennium Falcon,* a Taj Mahal, and an Empire State Building. Shane's bed was parked against the far wall so the middle of the room was available for his projects.

He shook his head. "And you have to keep the chambers pieces separate from the tower pieces."

She watched him re-sort the LEGOs. His attention to detail when it came to this work was extraordinary. "Sorry about that," she said.

"Jeez, Sunday. You used to be better at this."

"You're good to put up with her, Shane." Denny leaned against the open door, watching them with a grin on his face.

"I know," Shane said. He stood and pointed at Sunday. "I have to get two Ziploc bags. Don't touch anything till I come back."

She watched him leave and looked at Denny. "This is way too hard."

"Yeah, give it up. No one else even tries to keep up with him." He held up the magazine. "I read your story. Why didn't you tell us you got published?"

"I guess I didn't know if you'd like it."

"Well, I did," he said, crossing his arms. "You nailed what it was like for me, when I blew out my knee." He shook his head. "I had no idea what I was going to do. One day the college offers were rolling in and the next they wouldn't take my calls."

"But you never let us see you down," Sunday said. "You just kept going, no matter what." That's what she wanted him to take from the story. It was about a guy who was strong enough to come through for everyone else, even when he was carrying around his own profound pain.

He held up the magazine. "I can keep this?"

"Yeah."

"Thanks. And"—he pushed off the door—"it's your decision, about the police. I just want that guy out of our lives." He started to leave.

"Denny?"

"Yeah?"

"You were my emergency contact because if I ever got into trouble, you're the one I wanted them to call."

He nodded. "I'm glad it was me."

Shane came in behind him then, warning her that she better not have touched anything while he was gone.

CHAPTER FIFTEEN

Denny

I'm glad it was me."

It was true. He was grateful the cops had called him the night of her accident. Asking Sunday to come home was the only thing he'd done right in a long time.

He headed back to his room with the magazine. He'd read her story a couple times now, and he would again. Understanding his sister's take on that whole time, her view of him as he lived it, was a gift.

It was good timing too. After learning Billy Walsh had played him for a patsy, he couldn't have felt much lower. Then he made it worse by arguing with Sunday and storming out of the pub. He'd driven straight to Angie's place, sat across from Theresa at the small kitchen table and updated her, told her about Billy's visit, including the fact that Sunday refused to go to the police.

Theresa had shaken her head at him. "It's not up to you. You need to let it go or you're just making this harder on her."

"I'm trying to help."

"Sometimes there's a thin line between helping and controlling."

He looked away from those dark eyes that knew him way too well.

"Do you think it's true?" she asked, her hands cupping a mug of decaf coffee. "That your dad had an affair?"

He finally gave voice to the doubts that had seeped in. "Some of the things Walsh said are hard to ignore. My dad was gone a lot when we were in high school. I mean, the business was growing, I know he was really busy . . ." But that just didn't quite explain it all, how often his dad was absent, how not present he was even when he was home. "My mom was depressed and sick all the time. She was tough to be around." After school or practice, Denny had never been in a rush to get back to a house cloaked in his mother's misery, which always felt like a rebuke for not doing enough for her.

"Maybe she was tough to be around because your dad was cheating on her."

A shudder rippled through him at the thought that his mother might have known about the affair. But he shook his head. "No, she was like that long before then."

"Did your dad ever get her any help? Take her to see someone? Some therapy or medication would have helped with that."

Therapy and pills never would have entered his father's mind. "I remember Sunday asked him a few times to take her to a doctor, or at least a priest. But he said it was up to Mom, and she would never go."

"Yeah, but did he offer to go with her? Did he ever talk to her about this stuff? She found out her youngest son had a developmental disability, you said she blamed herself for being too old when she had him. What did your dad do to help her through that?"

He stopped himself from saying what came to mind: He helped her through it by being a good provider. Because that's not what Theresa meant. The truth was his dad hadn't done much else to help his mother. He spent less and less time with her, always claiming work demands.

"Nothing," he finally said in answer to Theresa's question. "Nothing that really mattered."

He saw it now. His dad had believed his job was to provide financial security, and he'd done that. He'd given his family a nice home, a comfortable existence. When his wife said the house needed fixing up or his kids wanted some walking-around money, he was happy to oblige. But he didn't know how to respond to a woman who was trying to demand love through psychosomatic illness. So he shut her out.

Denny looked across the table. He'd done the same thing with Theresa. He'd pushed her away because he was so used to being the one who made things happen, the one who instilled confidence. He wasn't sure who he was without that.

But he didn't want the kind of marriage his parents had, one where they avoided their pain by avoiding each other, lived separate lives under the same roof. He didn't want that for him and Theresa, and he didn't want it for Molly.

"Have Molly's nightmares really stopped?" he asked.

She nodded. "It's been almost three weeks."

His little girl was so worried about the adults around her it had affected her sleep. She reminded him sometimes of Sunday, the way she wanted to take care of everybody. But it wasn't healthy.

He reached across and took Theresa's hands. "I understand why you left."

Her eyes drilled into his. "You shouldn't have kept me in the dark about the money problems. You end up feeling like you're in it alone, but it's your own fault. You got to give trust to get it, Denny."

"I know I'm not alone." He shrugged. "I don't know why I act like I am."

"'Cause you're a thickheaded Irishman and your mother made you think you could walk on water." But she laid a Theresa grin on him and a big piece of his unsettled world fell back into place.

"Son, I need to talk to you."

Denny turned from his bathroom mirror to see his dad standing in the doorway. He'd done a good job of avoiding his father the last few days, because whenever he saw him a rush of angry questions wanted to pour forth: *How could you betray Mom like that, betray all of us? Do you realize what you opened us up to? Did Mom know what you were doing?*

His father had dressed up for the grand opening, navy-and-green sweater-vest over a blue button-down.

"What do you need, Dad?" Denny moved past him into his room to finish getting dressed. He and Kale had spent the day prepping the new place. They were scheduled to open the doors at five o'clock and word was out. A large crowd was expected, thanks to several announcements on the local radio and TV stations advertising food and drink specials, and live music later that night. They'd left an enthused crew at the restaurant, putting on final touches, so they could both run home and clean up. He wanted to get back. Theresa and Molly were meeting him there, driving separately because he'd be working late. He would finally have his family back home in three days, after he was certain Billy Walsh was gone.

His dad shut the bedroom door. "I want to know what's going on."

"What do you mean?" He pulled his shirt on and started buttoning. "Can we talk about this later? You remember Clare's coming to pick you, Shane, and Sunday up in about an hour, right?"

"This can't wait. Are you in some kind of trouble?"

"Nope, everything's good." He moved to the mirror, running fingers through his damp hair. This night had been a long time coming and was essential to getting on safe financial ground again. For the first time in months he was hopeful it would all get back on track.

"I know you're all keeping things from me, Denny."

Apples must not fall far. "I don't know what you're talking about." He was surprised to feel his dad's grip on his upper arm, pulling him around to face him.

"I heard you talking to your lawyer last week. You owe someone a lot of money."

Denny pulled his arm away. God, he was eavesdropping now? "You don't need to worry about it."

His dad crossed his arms and pulled himself up to his full height, which was Denny's height. "I went to the bank today to see about a loan on the house. Come to find out one's already been taken out. In my name."

Shit. Denny scraped a hand down his face. "We're going to have to talk about this later on—"

"God damn it." His dad's eyes narrowed. "Don't put me off."

Denny tried to take a step back. But he was boxed in by the wall behind him.

"You had no right," his dad said. "I took care of this family for thirty-five years, never missed a day of work, put food on the table, saw to it you all had what you needed."

The words were close to coming out—*Really? Is that all you were doing?*

"Then I find out you've been lying to me," his father said. "You put this family at risk. I want to know who you owe money to. Tell me right now."

You put this family at risk. That was rich. Denny clamped his mouth shut.

But then he thought about the two people that had been most hurt by his dad's selfishness and his secrets. Denny thought about his mother and his sister, and his blood began to boil.

"I borrowed the money from Billy Walsh."

His father's whole face twitched. "Who?"

"Billy Walsh. You remember that family, don't you, Dad?"

"Yes . . ." His face started to sag, his arms slid down to his sides. "I remember that family."

"I thought you would. His father was on your crew, right?"

"Yes, but . . . I thought the Walsh boy went back to Ireland, years ago."

"He came back. He's living with family in Katonah."

His dad held up a finger. "He means you harm, Denny. No doubt about it."

Denny offered a harsh chuckle. "Yeah, well, you're a little late with that. But hey, you were right about one thing. The problem at the new place, it wasn't old pipes." He gave it a moment, let his father put it together.

"Walsh caused that damage? And then lent you money?"

"He was after Brennan's. And he almost got it." Denny leaned his face close to his father's. "Now why do you think he'd want to do that to us?"

His father blinked several times, his lips moving like he was reaching for words.

"No idea?" Denny asked. "No clue why Billy Walsh would want to hurt your family?" That was as far as he was planning to go. All he wanted was some recognition of the pain his dad had caused them all. Just an inkling that he felt some responsibility for the wreckage he'd brought to their door.

But there was defiance in his father's pale eyes as he crossed his arms again. "You've no right to judge me. I was a good husband, and a good father. My conscience is clean."

"You sure about that, Dad?" Denny stepped around him and grabbed his jacket from the bed. "Because I'm not the only one he went after. He hurt someone else in this family, a lot worse than me."

His dad's eyebrows pinched together.

"Five years ago," Denny said. "Right before she left town."

The puzzled wrinkle in his dad's forehead cleared and his jaw went slack. Any defiance was gone from his expression. There was only dreadful understanding now.

Denny turned and walked out of the room, leaving his father standing there alone. Looking far older than he'd ever seemed before.

He was rattled on the drive to Mamaroneck after that conversation. He hadn't intended to get into all that, but his dad had forced it. Just once Denny wanted him to know—really know—that he wasn't fooling anyone, that the very people he had always professed to take care of knew better. And he felt like he'd achieved a small measure of justice for his mother.

He hadn't allowed himself to think much about her since finding out she knew what happened to Sunday. Difficult as his mother had been, they'd had a special connection. She was his biggest fan, always, but she had lied to him for years. Between his mother's deception and his father's adultery, he wasn't sure how well he'd ever really known them.

But this weekend would be a turning point for his family. Everyone would be at the opening tonight, except for Jackie, who was heading up operations at the home location. He was coming back on permanently now that his probation officer had given the all clear, and he'd started to look for an apartment. Sunday was applying to master's programs in the area, and she had assured Molly she could move to the upstairs bedroom by her fifth birthday in two months as promised, which meant Sunday was also looking for her own place. He'd been seeing glimpses of the sister he remembered from years ago. Lighter of heart, more optimistic, like she was healing, shedding some of that mental deadweight.

They all just had to make it to Monday, until they were certain Billy Walsh was gone. Kale was bringing the money to Michael the following day, and then Michael would be meeting with Billy's lawyer. By Monday morning, he was supposed to leave town.

Seeing a boisterous crowd waiting to get in the front doors of the brand-new Brennan's lightened his mood, brought on a rush of pride and excitement. When he entered the back door the place was buzzing with last-minute prep. Yelling in the kitchen, tossing of ice in bins, clinking of weighty silverware being wrapped in linen napkins. A sense of calm took over as he made his way toward the front doors. He knew in his heart the night would be a success, as would the future of this place. It felt good to let everything else go for a while and concentrate on work.

Kale was up front, meeting with the young hostess—this place was large enough to warrant one. He stepped away and met Denny by the front doors. "Ready for this?"

"Yeah. You?"

They looked around at waitstaff running to and fro, the raised bar and cocktail area that dominated the center of the restaurant, empty tables and booths, and the crowd outside that would soon fill them. "This was your vision," Kale said. "You did this."

"Yeah, well, I almost didn't."

"It's all going to work out."

Denny was grateful; Kale could have said a lot more. He'd had every right to walk away from their partnership, wash his hands of the whole mess, but he didn't. As always, he had Denny's back.

The music was turned on—they were kicking it off by streaming Irish Pub Radio—and everyone headed to their stations.

Denny leaned forward to make sure he was heard. "I'm sorry I lied to you, man."

Kale's eyebrows went up. "Wait." He reached into his back pocket and held up his cell phone. "Could you repeat that into the camera, please?"

"Shut the fuck up and unlock the doors."

CHAPTER SIXTEEN

Kale

C ould you repeat that into the camera, please?"

They laughed, which made a small dent in the tension that had wedged between them for months. Maybe it would be possible to get back to a normal place with Denny. Or at least a new normal place.

The crowd was nonstop from the moment they opened the doors. Tables filled and the bar became standing room only. Vivienne, her mother, and Luke stopped by early on. Kale took them on a tour, carrying Luke on his shoulders, and introduced them to some of the staff, but other than that he was slammed with a long dinner rush. They couldn't have asked for a livelier grand opening. The atmosphere hummed with rowdy conversation and loud laughter, sounds of people out to eat and drink on a Friday night. They hit a stride by five thirty that didn't begin to lull for almost three hours.

The Brennans came in around six and commandeered a corner table. They all showed up, including Clare. Shane hated crowds and sat with his back to the room, close to Sunday. Mickey seemed preoccupied, staring into his beer and saying little. Theresa and Molly were in good spirits though, and they stood by Denny with pride while he took them around and showed them off.

Kale gravitated to his typical station in the back, fielding waitstaff questions, traying up plates, troubleshooting software issues. Denny worked the floor, helped deliver food and drinks while chatting up customers, shining in his natural element as host with lots of jokes and glad-handing. This was why they were a good team, the division of labor, complementing strengths. It was invigorating to be in sync again, exchanging glances and hand signals, their own sign language developed over the years.

Paul was in the weeds for a while, three deep at the bar, so Kale jumped in to help. When the crowd was under control again, he strolled through the restaurant, looking for potential problems, but so far, so good. He headed for the back, planning to check the night's receipts thus far, but when he got to the office he found Sunday and Shane there. Sunday was working on her laptop at the desk while Shane watched a video on his phone.

"What're you guys still doing here?"

"Denny asked me to check totals so far, which are a little above target," she said. "But the others took off a while ago. Molly was falling asleep at the table, and Dad had Clare drive him home early. He wasn't feeling well."

"I wanted to wait for Sunday," Shane said. "But I'm tired."

"You guys want a ride home?" Kale asked.

"Oh boy," Shane said, shutting down his phone. "Yes."

"That's okay," Sunday said. "We'll wait for Denny. You can't leave." She gestured to the noise coming from behind him.

"The dinner rush is over and this place is a well-oiled machine." He grabbed his jacket off the coatrack. "Denny's got it under control. No one's going to miss me."

Shane stood. "That sounds good to me. Come on, Sunday." He was already halfway out the door. "Time to go home."

It would have been a quiet car ride if not for Shane. Sunday offered him shotgun and sank into the back. Kale had the distinct feeling she was keeping her distance. Twice now he'd tried to ask her the singular question that was eating away at him, and twice she had dodged it.

Shane told Kale the new Brennan's was nice, but mostly talked about how good it was to see Theresa and Molly again. "Denny promised they would be home in three days," he said several times. "Right, Sunday?"

"That's right."

As soon as they got to the house Shane said good night and headed straight up to his room.

"I'm going to take a look around," Kale said.

"You don't have to do that," Sunday said. "My dad's been home for a couple hours."

"Yeah, but he's probably been asleep for a while." So he did a walk-through, checking locks and darkened rooms, while she waited at the bottom of the stairs in the kitchen.

"All clear," he said.

"Thanks for the ride. I think the new place is going to be a hit." She started to head up the stairs.

But he couldn't let it go at that. "Sunday."

She stopped on the first step and her hand dropped from the railing.

After a moment she about-faced and raised her eyes to his. "I know you want to understand why I left. Why I didn't tell you what happened. But nothing I say will be enough. I won't be able to give you a satisfactory explanation. I can't even give myself one."

She'd had five years to come up with an answer.

"That might sound like a cop-out," she said. "But you have a beautiful family now, Kale. And dredging all this up . . . It's just a bad idea."

She sounded tired and shaky. He felt unsteady himself. This was not a simple question and there was not a simple answer. Getting into all of it would be messy and involved. Not a conversation a married man should have with an old girlfriend.

But Sunday was not just an old girlfriend.

She took a deep breath and looked at him head-on. "Just know that none of it was your fault. I'm so sorry I hurt you the way I did." He could hear naked remorse in her words, see it in her expression. "It's the worst thing I have ever done."

He blinked back a sting in his eyes.

"The rest doesn't matter anymore," she said. Then she sagged like she'd expended all her energy. "I'm going up. Good night."

He watched her climb the steps until her legs turned and moved out of sight at the top. She'd owned it, offered a heartfelt apology. Maybe that should be enough.

Glancing out the kitchen window in the direction of his house a few blocks away, he thought about what to do next. There were several shoulds: ask if Denny wanted him back in Mamaroneck, check in with Jackie at the pub, go home to his family. That last one was the biggest should of all.

The rest doesn't matter anymore. The thing was, right then it very much mattered to him. He was stuck somewhere between their past and his present and didn't know how to get unstuck without the answer to that question.

He took the stairs two at a time. When he got to her room he didn't knock for fear of waking Mickey down the hall. He just opened the door, walked in, and shut it behind him.

She was standing by her bed, kicking off her shoes.

"I'm sorry," he said. "But it matters to me. Make me understand why. Why you couldn't tell me."

"Kale . . ." Her tone said it all. *Let it go.*

"Just *try*, Sunday."

"I can't!"

"Yes, you can." When she started to look away he leaned toward her to keep hold of her eyes. "You broke my heart. Don't you think you owe me this much?"

She brought her fingertips to her forehead. "I was scared."

"Of what?"

"Of everything."

"Of me?"

"No. Not exactly."

"What does that mean?"

She started pacing the space between them, her hands in front of her like she was trying to get hold of the right words. "I couldn't tell my family. My mom said my dad and Denny would lose it—they would go after Billy. I was afraid if they found out it would become this huge thing, and someone would get hurt."

Kale wouldn't have put that past Mickey and Denny. And certainly Maura would have used that kind of psychological aggression to frighten Sunday into staying quiet. "I can understand why you didn't want to tell them." He pulled his hands to his chest. "Why couldn't you tell me?"

She stopped pacing and faced him. "Because you were part of them."

"If you didn't want them to know, I would have respected that."

"Do you really think you could have carried that around? Been with them every day and *not* said anything to my dad or Denny?" Her eyes bored into his. "You wouldn't have pressured me to tell them?"

"No!" Though he immediately knew it was plausible.

She tilted her head in doubt.

If she had told him what happened to her, Kale wouldn't have known what the hell to do with all that rage, and he would have been worried about how to take care of her.

"You're right," he said, holding up a hand. "I would have wanted to tell them, I would have wanted their help figuring out what to do. But I would not have forced it. I never would have betrayed you like that."

Her eyes filled but she didn't say anything.

Maybe she had been right. He had his answer, but it was so disappointing. She hadn't trusted him enough to be in her corner above all else. He rested his hands on his hips and dropped his head. "God, Sunday, I was the one person you should have trusted. We would have been in it together."

She paused long enough for him to give up on a response. "I know that now," she finally said. "But I was so ashamed, Kale."

He had to lean in a little. Her voice was timid, like even now she was afraid to lay bare the words.

"It was all my fault. I should have known I was pregnant." She blinked and the drops streamed down. "I was feeling sorry for myself when I went there that night. I drank way too much, was too friendly with him. And then I provoked him—I was so fucking stupid."

He watched her gulp for air and use her sleeves to swipe at tears that just kept coming.

"I lost our baby and I thought it would always be there. Every time you looked at me." Her face fell into her hands.

Kale pulled his head back as he absorbed the meaning of her words. She hadn't assumed he would violate her trust or side with her family. She left because she hated herself for what happened and she was afraid he would too.

He stepped close and wrapped his arms tight around her shaking body. Her hands slid up his back and she sobbed against him. He shed a few tears of his own, but it felt so good to hold her again after so long. They stayed that way, clinging to each other, until her weeping calmed and he felt her speak against his shoulder.

"I'm so sorry, Kale." Her voice had that nasally quality that set in after a hard cry.

He leaned back far enough to take her face in his hands, gently skim his thumbs across her wet cheeks. "Me too." In the back of his mind those shoulds were still there, but they'd grown very faint. He let his eyes roam over the features he still knew so well. Green eyes with brown flecks sprinkled in, the soft hollows in her cheeks where her dimples lived, scattered freckles that were a little more distinct now.

She looked up at him through moist eyelashes. When she twitched with an involuntary hiccup the shoulds faded to black and he pulled her face to his.

Their lips met and moved like they were getting reacquainted at first, tentative and light, and he could taste salt from her tears. But then her hands gripped his face and the back of his neck, and he pressed her body tight against his so they were touching head to toe. Sunday wrapped her arms around him and he was lost.

He could not hold her close enough while his hands tried to be everywhere at once. In her hair, along the hips of her jeans, on the warm skin of her back. It was like memory recall kicked in and their bodies knew exactly how to move together. They made their way onto her bed, not caring when the box spring groaned its old grievance. It felt to Kale like something in the universe was correcting, a terrible wrong was being made right.

But on the heels of that very thought, Luke's face appeared in his mind. Kale was able to push it aside at first, but a sensation had moved in along with the thought of Luke, a heaviness in his chest, and it lingered. As much as he wanted this with Sunday, if they did this now it would be another secret, something shameful and ugly between them. That thought, the idea that this might drive her from his life once and for all, made his decision.

He pulled away from her, sitting up, instantly regretting the space between them. "I'm sorry. I can't."

After a stunned second she sat up as well, scooted back a bit, pulling her arms and legs together, closing in on herself. "I know."

He moved to the edge of the bed and dragged his hands down his face. "There's nothing I want more right now—"

"No. No, it's okay." She smoothed tangled hair back from her flushed face. "I'm sorry."

That's all she needed, more to feel bad about. "You really need to stop apologizing."

She folded her arms around her knees. "Right."

"Look at me, Sunday."

She did, with glassy, red-rimmed eyes.

Every instinct wrenched at him to close the gap again. But he wouldn't be able to break away a second time. "This isn't your fault. You are not responsible for my marriage."

Her answer was a weary nod.

If he was leaving, he had to go now. He stood and moved to the door. "Everything's going to be okay," he said.

Her smile was painfully sad. "Promise?"

"Promise."

He turned and left before his resolve ceased to exist.

. . .

He made his way down the dark hallway, avoiding the creaky floorboards he'd long been familiar with. When he neared the top of the stairs, though, he heard movement down in the kitchen—fridge opening and closing, jars on the counter. Denny.

This wouldn't look good. Kale could duck back into Sunday's room to wait, or head down the other stairs and out the front door.

The decision about what to do was made for him when Denny's cell rang. Kale had just heard him take a seat at the kitchen table when the phone started to vibrate. Next thing he heard was Denny picking it up and grunting to himself. "Shit." A moment later: "Vivienne?"

Vivienne was looking for him and Denny wouldn't know what to say. Far as he knew Kale had disappeared over an hour ago.

Denny again: "Really?"

Kale had to show himself. He started down the stairs.

Denny looked up from his seat at the table, hunched over a sandwich with the phone to his ear, and his face morphed from confusion to understanding. "No, it's fine you called," he told Vivienne. "His phone's probably on Do Not Disturb because he's driving."

Kale nodded at him to go with that. He'd left his phone in his car.

"You know, Viv, we had a couple guys hanging around the bar who were pretty blitzed. Kale offered to drop them home." Denny stared at him while he listened to her response, a recriminating flatness to his expression. "You know your husband. He's a Boy Scout." He chuckled at something she said. "He wasn't far behind me. He should be home soon."

Crisis averted. Guilty relief.

"Talk to you later." Denny pulled the phone from his ear and ended the call.

"It's not what you think," Kale said.

Denny shoved his plate away and stood, face stiff, hands curled up. "You have the money for Michael?"

"Yeah. I'll get it to him first thing tomorrow."

Then Denny headed down the hall to his bedroom. "Go home to your family, Kale."

. . .

"How did we do last night?" Vivienne asked. She was working at the stove the next morning.

"Pretty good, I guess," Kale said. "Early in the night we were ahead of target."

"That's great." She dished up eggs and toast on three plates.

"Yeah. Bodes well."

"What are your plans today?"

He had to be at Michael's office in an hour with the cash. Cash he had borrowed against their house without her knowledge, sending him further down the slippery slope of lying to his wife. He hadn't even needed her signature. The house had always been in his name. "I'm supposed to be out in Mamaroneck first thing," he said.

"Hi, Daddy." Luke came down the stairs in spaceship pajamas, hair askew, and climbed his little warm body up onto Kale's lap.

Vivienne put the food on the table and joined them. "I like the new restaurant. It's so much bigger than the other one. And it's more modern, you know?"

He nodded and eyed his eggs. He wasn't hungry.

"There's so much potential," she said. "Mamaroneck is a much bigger, younger crowd on the whole." Her eyes were on him, waiting for some kind of response.

"Yeah. Could be big for us." It better be big, considering the hole Denny had dug. He pulled crusts off Luke's toast. "But it'll be a ton of work too. A lot more employees to worry about, new vendors to deal with. And the maintenance on that place is going to be a killer."

"God, Kale, these are good problems to have. It's an amazing opportunity."

He perked up. "For sure. You want some ketchup on these eggs, Luke?"

"Ew! No, Daddy."

Kale smiled and held the ketchup upside down, out of Luke's reach, while the sauce moved toward the mouth of the bottle. "Uh-oh, here it comes."

"No, Daddy!" He giggled and reached for the bottle.

Vivienne cleared her throat. "There's something I was hoping to talk to you about."

The ketchup was close to dripping out. "You sure you don't want ketchup?"

"Kale."

He started switching hands now, laughing with Luke as they fought over the bottle.

Vivienne stood from her chair, reached over and grabbed the ketchup, set it on the table. "Eat your breakfast before it gets cold."

Startled by her response, Kale and Luke gave each other wide eyes and Luke moved to his own seat.

She took a breath. "I wanted to let you know that I was offered a promotion."

"You were?" Kale asked. "That's great."

"What's a pro'tion?" Luke asked.

"A pro-mo-tion," Vivienne said. "It means they offered me a better job for next year, an important one." She turned to Kale and smiled with pride. "Lead administrative assistant in the main district office."

"Congrats!" This was a big deal for her, going after a sizable promotion and getting it. "I'm proud of you." He meant it but everything he said that morning felt false, like he was an imposter husband and father.

"Thanks." She sipped her coffee. "So, I think we should talk about moving to the other side of town."

He stopped his forkful of eggs halfway to his mouth. "What?"

"It would just make sense. I'll be working full-time and Luke will go to school right next door. Right, Luke?"

"Uh-huh." Luke pushed eggs onto his spoon.

"Besides, with the extra income we can afford a house in Manor Hills." She put her hand on Kale's arm. "It's a gated community, with its own movie theater, health club, and pool."

Kale knew all about Manor Hills. It was the trendiest place to live in town right now. Transplants and telecommuters from the city loved it. Everything was brand-new, state-of-the-art, uber-contemporary. Right up Vivienne's alley.

"A pool?" Luke asked. "Are we moving?"

"No," Kale said.

"Maybe," Vivienne said.

She'd planned this out well, sprung it on him, and he was ill prepared to respond. Low-level panic flared up. He'd known she wanted a different house, but he had no desire to live in some Stepford Families subdivision where everyone focused on keeping up with the neighbors.

"We're in a good position to sell this house," Vivienne said, firing the next shot. "You would be closer to Mamaroneck. Denny would probably love that."

"Are we getting a new house?" Luke asked.

"We should talk about this later." Kale nodded toward Luke.

"We never planned on being in this house forever," Vivienne said. "I don't know what there is to talk about."

"Vivienne—"

"Can you think of one downside?" Her gaze was unflinching.

This was a pop quiz and he was failing. "It's a ways out of town, and more expensive. There's a lot to consider." But it sounded feeble.

"Luke, honey," she said, "why don't you go start brushing your teeth and I'll be up to help you in a minute."

With increasing desperation, Kale watched Luke head up the stairs.

She folded her hands on the table. "Look, I think this is important for our family. For you, me, and Luke. It's not like I'm asking you to leave town, for God's sake. You'll only be fifteen minutes away from them. But I really believe this would be best for everyone. Including Sunday."

He hadn't expected that.

"She needs to move on with her life, Kale. That's not going to happen while you're four blocks away and she sees you every day."

That might be true, but she was using it to stack her case for a new house. "I didn't realize you were so concerned about her."

"She's the least of my concerns. But it doesn't mean I'm wrong." She sat back in her chair, shoulders squared, ready with more comebacks if he asked for them.

He should be clear with her that he was not on board with this decision. But how could he explain that the very thing she wanted distance from—the Brennans—was the very thing he needed to make it through this marriage at times? They reminded Kale of the importance of family and being a good father when he lost heart because she just didn't seem to *get* him.

"Will you at least think about it?" Her eyes went back and forth between his.

"Yeah, I will." He didn't know if he meant it or not.

Michael Eaton's office was in a contemporary two-story structure a few miles southeast of downtown that housed a dozen various professionals. The building was lots of glass, cement, and clean lines, with a large treed parking area. Kale pulled his old Honda in next to Michael's newer BMW, the only car in the lot on a Saturday. The interior of the building was airy but warm, with plush carpet, earth tones, and intentional decorating. He made his way up the wide floating staircase to Michael's second-story office.

It was no surprise Eaton was successful. They'd been quasi friends in high school and Kale had kept loose tabs on Michael's career. Dartmouth undergrad, Yale Law School, worked at some big firm in Boston for a few years. But, according to Denny, Michael had quit the rat race to move back close to home and hang a shingle. He checked several boxes where Kale fell short—highly educated, self-assured, making his mark on the world. Kale used to worry about losing Sunday to a guy like Michael, someone that promoted confidence and would not have needed a loan from her dad to start a business. The guy who would have known exactly how to handle her mother and could offer up twenty grand in cash without borrowing against his house.

The guy that would have made damn sure she was on that trip to Ireland.

When Sunday left New York, Kale had been convinced that was part of what she was looking for out there in California. Someone that could take care of her while making her world a bigger place.

There was a small reception area outside Michael's corner office. His door was ajar and he sat at his desk, working on a laptop. No suit, but even on weekends he wore chinos and a polo shirt. When Kale knocked Michael stood and waved him inside. Neither of them sat.

"Here it is." Kale tossed a thick envelope on the desk between them.

"Great. I'm supposed to meet his lawyer this afternoon so we can get that piece of shit gone by Monday morning. He's planning to head to Seattle. Has a distant cousin or something out there."

"You need to get some kind of reassurance. He paid Sunday a visit the other night."

"*What?*"

"Caught her at the pub. He wanted to say some nasty things before he left town."

"She shouldn't have been there alone."

Kale ignored the accusatory tone. "She pulled a gun on him."

Michael's face fell forward. Then he half smiled in disbelief. "She did?"

"Yep. Scared him pretty good, I think."

"Good for her."

The day Michael had come to the bar, he'd been visibly shaken after having to dicker over money in such a deal. But he'd done it. For her. "Thank you for doing this," Kale said.

Michael's forehead pulled up in surprise. "Sure. It'll be good to wrap this up." He bounced on his toes and looked down at the envelope. "You think she'll be able to get past all this now?"

"'Get past all this'? Like it never happened?" He sounded snide but Michael didn't seem to get it. What happened to Sunday wasn't an illness she could get over. It was part of her, part of who she'd become.

Michael shrugged. "It's hard to let go of the past, but she deserves to move on, you know?" Without a doubt he wasn't just talking about Billy Walsh any longer. "Seems like this is a chance for her to start over."

Kale stood up a little straighter. "I suppose you'd like to help her do that."

"I wouldn't mind. I think I have a lot to offer . . ." He waved a hand around, indicating his office, his car outside, or maybe just his general person. ". . . including the fact that I'm single. But really, I just want what's best for her."

Kale gestured to the cash. "Just let us know when it's done." He walked out, hurried back through the pristine building and out to his car, angry with Michael. Not just because he wanted to go after Sunday. What really pissed him off was the truth in what he said.

While he drove to Mamaroneck he thought about the idea of a fresh start for her, the chance to get on with a new life. Kale wanted those things for her too. Maybe she would choose someone like Michael, someone who wasn't sullied with complications or inextricably tied to the pain of the past. Michael and his untroubled vibe could be a clean slate for her.

But Kale didn't think so. He still believed he knew Sunday, knew her in his bones. And a cocky country-club type with a fancy office and expensive car was never going to win her heart.

The crowd was strong for the second night in a row and Kale stayed in Mamaroneck well past dinner. He, Denny, and Sunday had received a text from Michael earlier in the evening, letting them know he'd handed off the money, so there was that. Presumably Billy Walsh would be gone in less than thirty-six hours, to the other side of the country.

Denny came in the late afternoon and planned to close, which allowed Kale to leave before ten. It was a relief; disapproval radiated from Denny whenever they were in close proximity.

But Kale was not looking forward to going home. With Luke asleep, Vivienne would likely broach the next round of discussions about moving. He expected a two-front battle: a slow and steady badgering combined with more indirect hits, like selling Luke hard on the idea. Part of Kale was afraid that if he did go home he'd find himself agreeing to it out of guilt. What had happened the night before with Sunday—and what had almost happened—had been foremost on his mind all day.

So when he pulled into town, he didn't even hesitate. He drove straight past his house to the pub. It was almost closing time, it would be near empty, and he could sit in the quiet and have a drink. Or more than one.

When he walked in Jackie was working on cleanup, his hair pulled back in a band. "Hey, dude. Come to check on me?"

"Nope." Kale tossed his jacket in the office and poured a beer and a shot, took them both to the far end of the bar, and planted himself on a stool. As a policy, he no longer drank at his own bar during business hours. Tonight he was making an exception.

A few minutes later Jackie wandered down his way. His eyes traveled up from Kale's drinks to his face. "Sunday?" he asked.

Kale didn't answer.

"Figured." Jackie turned and strolled away, leaving him to round-and-round thoughts about problems that had no good solutions.

CHAPTER SEVENTEEN

Jackie

Figured."

Of course it was Sunday. Why the hell else would Kale be such a downer. Jackie went back to closing prep and left him to stare into his beer. Denny had mentioned Kale was at the house last night. Whatever had or had not happened between Kale and Sunday at this point, they obviously still had a hold on each other. And an emotional mess might send her away again. Just when they were past the worst of it.

He could not have been more relieved when she came clean with Denny and Kale, like digging into the root of a cavity that had festered for years. And he hadn't realized how much he wanted the chance to explain himself to them, make them understand that he hadn't sat back and done nothing after he found Sunday in that seedy bar, balled up on the floor. He was scared shitless by the blood, and she wouldn't say a word on the way to the hospital. But Jackie got some info when she answered the ER doc's questions: She'd been struggling with a man and fallen down the stairs. No, she didn't want to file a police report. No, she didn't realize she was almost two months pregnant. Yes, she understood she'd suffered a miscarriage. Her answers had come in fits and starts because tears flowed the whole time.

Once he got her home that morning, he gave her pills the doctor had prescribed and got her in bed, where she assumed the fetal position and pulled her quilt up to her neck. Then he sat in her desk chair and waited, watched as the drugs took effect, her body uncurling a bit, her grip on the edge of the blanket loosening. When he was sure she was half-asleep, he knelt down next to the bed and asked the question that was screaming in his brain and drowning everything else out.

"Sunday, who did this to you?"

Her eyes shot open and he felt like shit because she needed to sleep. But he had to know, and if he didn't get the answer now he probably never would.

"I won't do anything," he said. "I swear." An empty promise if he'd ever made one, but he didn't care. Someone had been with her when she fell, maybe even caused it. And whoever it was left her there alone. Passed out and bleeding.

She shook her head against the pillow. "Jackie . . . please . . ." Tears started to fall.

"Tell me who it was so I can make sure he doesn't come back."

Her eyes darted to his, bald fear in them. Jesus, how low he would sink to get this name.

She spoke so softly he had to lean close. "It was the bartender. Billy Walsh."

Walsh. Vaguely familiar. Irish guy, thick accent, couple years ahead of Jackie in school.

"He . . ." She was a mess, the pillowcase wet, her body coiled back up tight, hanging on to consciousness. "He said he had an old picture of Dad so I went upstairs with him . . ."

Jackie's entire body started to shake with rage and he clenched his fists to bring it under control.

Her forehead creased. "When I tried to leave he got so angry. He hates us." Her lids drifted shut.

While she slipped into a sedative-induced coma, he stayed close, half baking a plan. It started as a "What if" game. Sticking to hypotheticals freed him up to think through the details. *What if I grabbed the gun from the bar and found this guy, waited to get him alone somewhere? What if I started to hurt him and couldn't stop? What would Denny do if he were here?* None of the potential consequences weighed much in his mind, and doing nothing wasn't an option.

So after she passed out he went to Brennan's, slid the gun out of its holster behind the cooler, and tucked it into his jacket pocket. Then he drove to the Penny Whistle. A disgusted old-timer behind the bar told him Walsh had cleaned out the register and disappeared during the night. "According to the mother," he'd said, "the bastard's already on a plane back to Ireland."

When Jackie promised Sunday he wouldn't tell anyone what happened, it never occurred to him she wouldn't change her mind. He assumed once she got a little distance from that place and felt safe, she'd tell their family. But when he tried to talk to her about it she was a stubborn wall of resistance.

Then Denny, Theresa, Kale, and Dad had come home full of cheer, bearing stories and gifts from relatives. An onslaught of activity took over their days as they prepared for Denny and Theresa's big church wedding and no-expense-spared reception at Brennan's, bringing new color and animation to even his mother's face. Claiming the flu had been the perfect excuse. It explained away Sunday's confinement to her bedroom, dark bags under her eyes, weight she dropped overnight. The way she dragged and spaced out over the next few weeks.

When she agreed to talk to their mother, he was certain she would help Sunday get honest with everyone and, in the process, lift this burden from his shoulders. He'd been a breath away from spilling it to Denny a couple times. It would have been easy to let him take it on, figure out what the hell to do. But Jackie had promised Sunday, she had trusted him with her secret. As much as he believed she was hurting herself by hiding it, he didn't think he had the right to make that choice for her. Maybe he was also afraid of setting off a chain of events that could get out of hand, impact his whole family in unknown ways. And Sunday had sounded so rational when she told him she just needed a little space so she could focus on recovering. When she said things were working out for her in LA, he told himself it was all for the best.

He'd never talked to his mother about it, never told her he knew what she did. It was there every time she came down on him for being lazy or wasting time on painting, and every time Sunday's name was mentioned. He'd blamed her for so long. Now it seemed his dad deserved just as much blame, if not more. Whatever. He was tired of blaming people, including himself. He'd forever question how he handled things back then, but it felt good to step up lately, be an active part of the family. For the first time in a long time he was looking forward.

When Kale went for his second round—beer and shot—no one else was in the place and Jackie was pulling up the floor mats, the last task of the night.

"You don't have to stay," Kale said. "I'll lock up."

"Why don't you head home, dude?" Jackie said. "It's getting late."

"No, I'm good. You go ahead."

He was saved from deciding when Denny came in, flicking a cigarette over his shoulder into the darkness before the door closed. He was apparently getting his last smokes in before Theresa came home Monday. "Saw lights on. What're you guys still doing here?"

When Jackie rolled his head toward Kale, Denny walked behind the bar. "We had another big night in Mamaroneck," he said.

"Great." Kale downed the last of his shot.

Jackie held up two fingers when his brother gave him a questioning brow.

"That's not gonna help, Kale," Denny said. "Is this about last night?" He leaned his hands on the bar and shook his head. "What the hell were you doing in her room, man?"

"We were talking," Kale said. "I just wanted to understand."

That, Jackie could believe. The person most deserving of a thorough explanation from Sunday had definitely been Kale.

"Did you get the answers you needed?" Denny asked.

Kale nodded. Jackie couldn't have felt much worse for him. Whatever had gone down five years ago, any resentment on Kale's part about what Sunday did seemed to have been put to rest. And with that out of the way, it was clear as day that he still very much loved her.

"Vivienne wants us to move to Manor Hills," he said in a toneless voice. "She got a job over there. Said I'll be closer to the new place."

"That sucks," Jackie said. Manor Hills was full of transplant douches who lived in cookie-cutter houses and wanted to bring in big-box stores.

"Shit," Denny said, his eyebrows pulling up. "But I guess I can't blame her. Maybe it would be best, for everyone."

There might be truth in what Denny said, but they all knew it had the ring of a death sentence. Kale would only be a few minutes away but his life would drastically change.

Denny pulled his cell phone from his back pocket. "Did you guys get this text from Grail? She sent it like fifteen minutes ago."

"My phone's in the office," Jackie said.

"So's mine," Kale said.

"She wants to meet us all here now, including Sunday." Denny looked up at Kale. "Vivienne's on here too."

"What?"

Jackie set a glass of water in front of Kale, who was about to sober up real quick. "Drink that."

They didn't even have time to speculate about what Grail wanted before Vivienne walked in seconds later. Even at midnight her appearance was just so. Smooth hair, tight rippy jeans, one of those no-shoulder gypsy shirts.

"Where's Luke?" Kale asked as she approached the bar.

"He's asleep. I asked Mrs. Nalty next door to stay with him. Do you know what this is about?" she asked.

They all shook their heads.

As if they'd been waiting for a cue, Sunday and Grail came through the door.

"Good," Grail said, turning to lock it behind them. "You're all here."

• • •

Jackie could tell right away his cousin was all business. It was the arm-pumping fast-walk she used to make her way across the room. And she was wearing one of her lady-detective suits with the comfortable shoes.

She stopped near the bar and planted her fists on her hips. "We need to talk. I'm here off duty and off the record because we all have to get ahead of something." She sat down at the nearest four-top, thumped her elbows on the table, and brought her hands together. "We've been investigating a crime today and there's evidence to indicate people in this room might know something about it."

Jackie walked around the bar and took a seat next to Grail, across from Sunday.

Denny, Kale, and Vivienne stayed on stools by the bar.

When Grail spoke again, it was with deliberation, like she was measuring each word. "At least a couple of you will be questioned in the next few days." She shook her head, visibly uncomfortable with this cop-versus-cousin conflict of interest.

Jackie had no clue what she was talking about, and it didn't appear anyone else did either.

"A man was shot in the head and killed outside Katonah last night," she said. Her eyes started skipping from face to face, like the detective in her was already gauging reactions. "His name was William Walsh."

The room spun for a moment. *William Walsh. Shot and killed.* When Jackie checked around to see if he'd heard correctly everyone was staring at Grail in plain shock. Except for Vivienne. She looked more bewildered. "You mean Billy Walsh?" she asked. "Who lived here years ago?" But no one answered.

Grail leaned toward Sunday. "We met this guy once, a long time ago. He was a bartender at the old Penny Whistle. You knew him from school."

Jesus, she was talking about that very night. Jackie fought the urge to reach across to Sunday, whose eyes were frozen to the table, her mouth a tight line.

"I know you remember this dude," Grail said. "Irish guy, strong accent. He was chatting you up all night."

Sunday shrugged a shoulder. "Vaguely."

"Vaguely?" Grail asked, her voice overflowing with doubt. Then, to Denny, "How about you? Did you know him?"

He crossed his arms. "Don't ask me a question if you already know the answer."

The only sound Jackie heard while Grail considered her next move was the low hum of the cooler behind the bar. The cooler.

She flipped her hands up in frustration. "You guys know I'm trying to help, right? Is it true you borrowed money from this guy, Denny? And before you answer, we talked to his lawyer."

"We signed a contract. He gave me a loan. That was it."

"So you didn't default on this loan?"

"I got behind a couple of payments, but we worked it out through our lawyers." He shrugged, like it was the most natural thing in the world.

Grail's eyes jumped to Kale. "You knew about the loan? That Denny put this place up as collateral?"

Vivienne's eyes jumped to Kale.

"Yes," he said. "I knew."

"He's known for less than two weeks," Denny said. "He had no part in it."

Grail studied them for a moment, then turned her attention back to Sunday. "So you don't remember Billy Walsh? Because his aunt reports that he met with you a few days ago."

Sunday finally turned to her.

Seizing on what amounted to an admission of sorts, Grail asked: "Did he do something to you—"

"Leave her alone, Grail," Jackie said.

She flashed that penetrating gaze to him. "Did you know him?"

He shook his head.

She swiped a hand down her face. "Let's try this. Where were you all late last night?"

"You know where we were," Denny said. "It was opening night. Every-body was there."

"Until what time?"

When Denny shot Kale a quick look Jackie knew they were wor-ried about where this questioning would lead. Jackie hadn't seen anyone last night. He'd gone home around midnight after closing up and went straight to bed. For the first time he wondered if Denny and Kale might have actually done something to Walsh. And he was itching to check the back of the cooler.

"I was there with Paul till close to eleven," Denny said.

Grail turned to Sunday: "What about you?"

"I left the new place around ten, with Shane."

"How'd you guys get home?"

Sunday tried to silent-message Grail right then, with a glare and slight shake of the head.

"I drove them home," Kale said.

"Did you go back to Mamaroneck after you dropped them off?" Grail asked him.

Sunday stood abruptly. "Can we talk about this tomorrow? I'm tired."

Grail rose as well. "I'm trying to establish if you and Denny have alibis for last night. They don't know the time of death yet, but they will soon. If someone can corroborate that you two were either in Mamaroneck or back home, they'll rule you out."

"I stayed at the house after I drove Sunday and Shane home," Kale said, a note of resignation in his voice. "I was there when Denny came in about eleven thirty."

It got very quiet. Jackie could sense the implications sinking in around the room. Kale had been alone at the house with Sunday for a while last night, and chances are they weren't building models with Shane. He couldn't help but snatch a glance at Vivienne, who seemed to absorb the info with a stoic expression.

Grail cleared her throat and tugged on the hem of her jacket. "Okay. That pretty much covers you all until at least twelve thirty or so be-cause of the drive. You should just make sure you have your timelines straight." She paused. "I'm sorry if I upset everyone. I just wanted you to be prepared . . ." She raised her shoulders, asking for forgiveness.

Jackie stood. "It's good you told us. Thanks, cuz."

She seemed to study him for a moment, looking for answers she would not get, likely never feeling less a part of the family than she did right then. "I'll let you all know what I hear tomorrow," she said. Then she turned and walked out.

Vivienne was the first to speak. "You borrowed money from Billy Walsh?" she asked Kale, her voice bursting with disbelief.

"I did," Denny said. "It was all me."

She eyed Denny with open contempt, then slid off her stool, shaking her head at him. "You. Idiot. Didn't you realize how much he hated your father? Your whole family?"

Every head in the room swiveled her way.

Her gaze swept across all their faces. "You really didn't know, did you? None of you knew what your father did."

Jackie exchanged glances with Denny and Sunday. They looked as unnerved as he felt.

Vivienne's hands flipped up. "How could you not know? Everyone else did—it was the worst-kept secret in town!" She barked an incredulous laugh. "You were all so caught up in the idea of how special your family was that you never realized your father was cheating on your mother for years."

"That's enough, Vivienne," Kale said.

It was ugly and humiliating, but her words had the undeniable ring of truth. And Jackie could tell by their downcast eyes that his brother and sister felt the same way.

Vivienne turned to Kale and jabbed her finger toward Sunday. "*She* left you high and dry after eight years. *He*"—finger shifted to Denny— "could have lost this place, he still might. He put you in that position, and lied to you about it." She thrust her face toward Kale's. "Do you see it now? Do you see they're all just a bunch of liars who hurt the people around them?"

Kale held her gaze but didn't say anything.

What could he have said? She was right. The only person in their entire family who wasn't in the business of keeping dark secrets was Shane.

"We need to get back to Luke," Vivienne said, an inkling of righteous victory in her tone, in the way she gathered her huge purse from the bar and squared her shoulders. Jackie had never clicked with Vivienne, could never decide whether she wasn't trying at all or she was trying too hard. But it hardly mattered now. Whichever way the dust settled after tonight, they'd all crossed lines, and Vivienne and the Brennans were done with each other.

Kale followed her, which had to be tough after hearing the news about Walsh. Or maybe not. Maybe he was relieved to get away after his wife's brutally honest dressing-down of his adopted family.

Everyone avoided eye contact as the Collinses headed out the door.

That left the three of them standing in the quiet.

"He's dead," Denny said.

"I guess." Sunday's expression was a cross between confused and weary.

"You okay?" Jackie asked.

"I just want to go home."

"You guys go ahead," he said. "I'll lock up, be right behind you."

Denny followed Sunday out. Jackie left less than five minutes later. But first he checked behind the cooler.

When he got to the house they were sitting across from each other in the kitchen, jackets still on. He took the chair at the head of the table so they were huddled around one end.

"I can't believe he's dead," Sunday said.

"Neither can I." Denny turned his palms up. "But, I mean, it's kind of good news. Right?"

"Yeah," Jackie said. Billy Walsh was gone for good. He would never be in a position to hurt their family again. Unless his murder came back to one of them. "It's just the timing's . . ."

"Suspicious," Sunday said.

"That's the word."

"Listen," Denny said, "Walsh had a record, he was probably mixed up in a lot of bad shit. He had to have enemies."

"That's right." Hope edged into Sunday's voice. "Michael said he didn't want to go back to Belfast. Maybe it had something to do with that."

It was possible. But Jackie had checked the cooler. "The gun is missing," he said.

They both turned to him.

"I checked behind the cooler before I left just now, and the gun is gone."

Denny looked at Sunday. "We saw Kale put it back the other night."

"Are you sure about that?" Jackie asked. "No chance he took it with him?"

"What are you suggesting?" she asked.

Jackie turned to Denny. "Who else knew about the gun?"

"You two, me, and Kale."

"You don't think there's any way . . ." Jackie let it trail off.

"*Kale?*" Sunday asked.

"I don't know. You guys were with him last night. What do you think?"

"No," Denny said. "He had other things on his mind." He gave Sunday the raised eyebrows.

"Well, if four of us knew about the gun . . ." Jackie allowed the thought to finish itself.

"Wait," Sunday said. "Billy knew about the gun because I pulled it on him. He knew it was somewhere behind the bar."

"You think he came back for it?" Denny asked.

"I don't know. I'm just saying he knew it was there." She stood up in answer to the whistling kettle, walked over, and poured steaming water into the teapot.

Maybe there was a scenario where that made sense. Walsh came back for the gun and then somebody ended up using it on him. But that was a pretty complicated explanation compared to the other one that kept presenting itself. The scenario where one of the people who knew about the gun, all of whom had motive, used it on Billy. The only suspect Jackie could unequivocally rule out was himself.

"Wait," Denny said. "Why are we assuming it was our gun that killed him?"

"If it wasn't," Jackie said, "that's a hell of a coincidence, don't you think?"

Sunday spun from the counter and held up a hand. "*Shhh*. Did you hear that?"

Then Jackie did hear it. Footsteps coming down the stairs. Dad's leather slippers and plaid pajamas descended on the other side of the railing.

"Well, now," he said near the bottom of the stairs, standing up a little straighter. "What have we here?"

No one answered him for a moment while they tried to determine just how much of their conversation he might have heard.

CHAPTER EIGHTEEN

Mickey

W hat have we here?"

He hadn't meant to spook his children, but he'd heard hushed voices and they looked like they would look after burying a dead body. Denny hunched over the table. Jackie with the wide eyes. Sunday standing near the sink, hands stopped in the air like she forgot what she was doing.

No one said anything for a moment.

"Do you want a cup, Dad?" Sunday asked.

"That would hit the spot." He took the seat across from Denny but wasn't sure where to rest his gaze. He hadn't talked to his eldest since their awful discussion opening night and he couldn't risk catching that look of accusation in Denny's eyes again. But he dared not look at Sunday for more than a quick moment either. Every time he went near her the last twenty-four hours, he thought he would collapse under the weight of shame.

He laid his knobby old hands on the table and focused on them. "How was the new place tonight?"

"Busy," Denny said.

"Imagine that. Another pub, even bigger than the first." Mickey was proud of Denny, despite everything. But he'd never been given to gushing, and saying that now might seem like groveling. So he came the closest he could. "Did you take pictures to send back home?"

Sunday placed steaming cups before him and Jackie. "Already texted them to Cousin Barry. He'll make sure they get around." She brought over another cup for herself and sat beside Denny.

"You can text photos to Ireland, can ya?" he asked.

"Yep." She stared into her tea.

His children's silence and averted eyes felt like a condemnation of the highest order. Had everything good he'd ever done for his family been washed away in their minds forever?

He took a sip from his cup. Two sugars, splash of milk. Sunday always got it just right. He swallowed the lump that was forming in his throat and grabbed for a lifeline to break the oppressive quiet. "When are we going to have Theresa and Molly back home?"

"Day after tomorrow," Denny said.

"Now that's good news to be sure."

Nods all around the table.

"I think I'm going to head up." Sunday stood and lifted her tea to take with her. "Night, everyone."

They mumbled good night as she climbed the stairs. After he heard her bedroom door close, Mickey pulled himself up in his chair. His sons might be angry with him, but this was too important. "You boys sure your sister's doing all right?"

Denny didn't speak.

"She's fine," Jackie said, pulling the band from his hair so it fell out of that silly-looking knot.

They could give him the cold shoulder all they wanted, but he needed to see their eyes when they answered this next question so he could measure the truth in their words. He slammed his hand down hard on the table.

Both their heads snapped up.

"She's not thinking of leaving again, is she?" Mickey asked, training his eyes on Jackie first.

The startled spark in Jackie's eyes faded and he shrugged. "I hope not."

For the first time in two days Mickey turned directly to Denny and waited for a response.

"Not if we can help it," Denny said, without looking away.

Which gave Mickey hope, because, at least in this, they were still on the same side.

They headed to bed after that. The boys looked ready to drop their heads on the table and were probably lights-out within minutes. But Mickey tossed and turned, wide awake, dark thoughts chasing sleep away. He had lived with regrets for a long time, but the list had grown mightily in length and depth during the last couple days.

As much as he hadn't wanted to believe what Denny told him about Billy Walsh hurting Sunday, even while he stood alone in Denny's room and told himself it couldn't be true, it had explained certain things. Sunday had seemed to change almost overnight five years ago. Mickey didn't know what Billy had done to his daughter, and he would never ask for fear of the answer. But whatever it was, it had driven her away.

They'd all been shocked when she left, but, really, half of her had already been gone. He had talked to Maura at the time, assumed she'd have some idea what was going on with her daughter. "Do you not see it?" he'd asked. "She doesn't look well. It's been going on for weeks now."

"Sure she's still a bit under the weather from that flu. Maybe feeling a little sorry for herself. Having to stay home with me, Denny and Theresa getting all the attention with the wedding."

"I don't think that's it. It's like she's here, but she's not really here."

"What're you on about? 'She's here but she's not here.'" Disagreeing with Maura was like leaning into a brisk wind. "Don't be foolish. If anything's wrong with her, it's because you all spoilt her."

Mickey had pushed it hard, stepping in front of Maura so she couldn't avoid his eye. "That's nothing to do with it. I think there's something you're hiding from me."

She had cackled and pulled out the trump card she'd had on him for the last six years. "Now isn't that rich," she'd said. "Coming from the likes of you." Maura had found Lynn's green scarf under a seat in his pickup shortly after the affair ended. They'd had one conversation about it, Maura demanding answers and details in a cold, dead voice, and never spoken of it again.

That had ended the discussion. Four days later, Sunday was gone.

He bolted upright in bed, faster than he had moved in a long time, as questions sprang into his consciousness. Had Maura known what happened to their daughter? If she had known what happened to Sunday, and who hurt her, she would have been petrified of the truth coming out. Had she let Sunday leave so people wouldn't know their dirty laundry? Heavy dread settled in his chest, the way it did when an unwanted truth is the simplest explanation.

Maura had always been sharp-tongued, quick with biting sarcasm, but she made him laugh and early on he knew she was a woman capable of guiding a family. No nonsense, perpetually practical, so sure of the right way to do things—save money, buy a house, raise children. They'd been a good team for a time. He provided financial security while Maura was the center of the family universe, the sun that showed them the way.

When she shut down after Shane's diagnosis, he assumed she just needed some time. It wasn't until the school counselor called Mickey to report Shane wasn't getting to his classes in second grade that he finally confronted her.

"I can't," she had said, sitting at the kitchen table, one hand along the side of her face. She'd lost weight the last few years, sharp angles poking out where soft curves had once been. "I can't bring him to that classroom anymore. You're expected to volunteer two days a week. All those children . . . It's very loud. And they get so close."

That night Mickey asked Denny and Sunday to help Shane get to and from school until Mom was feeling up to it. For the next ten years they got him to classes, activities, sessions with his therapists. They made it work. And Mickey gave up trying to talk to Maura about anything. She responded to any challenge with physical complaints, and he had no clue what to do with that.

He reached over and turned on his bedside lamp, moved to his closet with care, not wanting to wake anyone. After lifting the floorboard with a shoehorn he pulled out his notebook and sat back down on his bed. He used a small pencil to tick off an item on his list because he'd taken care of it earlier that day: *Call Barry about Walsh*. The doctor had been right. Writing things down helped with the spotty memory. Although he wouldn't have had any difficulty remembering the name Walsh.

He'd known Frank Walsh almost since coming to the States. They'd met while playing for the Gaelic Athletic Association, and years later Mickey had hired Frank on as part of his crew. Everyone had warned him against Frank—he wasn't the full shilling, serious problem with the drink, unreliable. But Frank had come from Belfast, and Mickey was known to give a fellow countryman a chance when he could—that's how he'd gotten his own start in construction. Frank had lasted ten years, despite countless tardies and absences. But when showing up to work half in the bag became his norm, Mickey had no choice but to let him go.

That would have been the end of his interaction with the Walsh family, if he hadn't decided to deliver Frank's last paycheck in person. He'd heard Frank was on a bender and figured the wife could use the money. Better to give it to her rather than have it pissed away on drink or the horses by Frank.

From the moment she met him at the door there was something about Lynn Walsh that Mickey couldn't shake.

"Wasn't it kind of you to come all this way, Mr. Brennan." She'd accepted the envelope in the entry of her small but tidy row house on the edge of town, wearing a modest plaid dress, long auburn hair in a loose braid. "Won't you come in for a cup?"

He hadn't intended to stay, but the lyrical lilt to her voice had drawn him in, along with her smile. By then Maura was so steeped in her misery that he'd forgotten what it was like to have a simple conversation with a woman, have her ask about his day, what his work was like. Just take an interest. He enjoyed Lynn's girlhood stories and lively laugh, and sharing experiences of living through the Troubles that defined Northern Ireland while they were growing up.

The idea of committing adultery seemed ludicrous, and when he showed up at the dry cleaner's where she worked a week later, he told himself it was because he'd heard of a temporary crew hiring men and wanted to pass the tip along to Lynn, rather than hurt Frank's pride by going to him directly. The time after was to bring her a coffee-table book he'd come across, quite deliberately, on the mountains of Ireland. "People don't think we have mountains in Ireland," she'd said. "But we surely do." She spoke with a wistfulness and his heart went out to her. Like so many women in Ireland, she'd been rushed into a young marriage by parents with too many mouths to feed. She'd left her home and family for a small, ugly life with Frank and that wayward son of hers, Billy, who seemed to suffer from a double dose of original sin.

For a while it was just meeting for coffee, always on the pretense of job tips or sharing news from home, always at a diner in another town. The affair didn't start for a few months and, once it did, they saw each other sporadically, only when they believed it was safe. Never did they talk about the future. They were both Irish Catholic enough to know they didn't have one together, they were just finding comfort where they could. The first time Mickey offered Lynn money—the Walshes were again behind on the rent—she'd really gotten her Irish up. "Don't be offering me money like a common whore, Mickey Brennan," she'd said, hands on hips and hazel eyes aglow. He hadn't made that mistake again, but he found discreet ways to help, like having groceries delivered or slipping cash in her purse. Lynn knew where the money was coming from, but she could only accept it if they didn't talk about it.

When Lynn realized her son knew about them, they both agreed it had to end. Billy had thrown it in her face during an argument, told her they were fooling no one. The neighbors had seen him drive her home at night, including men who worked for Mickey, as well as that gossip Sharon Martin, with her loads of makeup and shameful clothes that were too young for her. If that many people knew, how long would it be before his own children knew? And Lynn was racked with guilt.

So they ended it. Mickey badly missed those precious reprieves with Lynn, a woman he'd come to care deeply for, but he continued to find ways to provide relief for her because her story only grew more dismal. Frank never held down a job again, and no one was surprised to hear he met a nasty end with cirrhosis of the liver a couple years later. The last time Mickey talked to Lynn Walsh in person was one afternoon when she came to his office to ask for help. The affair had been over many years by then, their interactions limited to sightings in town or on the road, sad smiles and waves.

"I don't want to be putting you to any trouble now, Mickey," she'd said. "You've done quite enough over the years. Especially after Frank died."

She meant her house. Mickey had bought it for her. "Lynn, there's no need to be getting into all that. Just tell me how I can help."

When she looked him in the face he could see it had been six hard years of living for her. "My son went back to Belfast a few months ago. It was for the best, you see. He was getting into some trouble here, drunken fight with a girlfriend, some petty theft. And he said he had people after him." She shook her head and fiddled with her purse straps. "But I'm still his mother and I'd like to know how he's faring back home."

Mickey managed to get reports now and again from his nephew, Barry, who was on the Belfast police force. Unfortunately Billy dipped into a life of drug crime, getting himself arrested a couple times. Mickey kept Lynn updated periodically until she passed away. She was taken by a weak heart no one knew about while working at the cleaner's one afternoon. He attended her funeral in Katonah from afar, happy to see her sister made suitable arrangements. Mickey assumed the house went to the sister after that. He heard it sold about a year ago. By then Billy was nowhere to be found. According to Barry, he'd caught the ire of some drug kingpin and had likely gone to Dublin or Liverpool to hide among the masses.

But at some point Billy Walsh had come back to the States and loaned Denny money. Probably the money from Lynn's house. Billy was responsible for hurting his family and it was Mickey's own fault.

He hadn't been there for his children for many years, but he was determined to lift some of their burden now. First and foremost, he didn't want Sunday to leave New York again. There was a new toughness to her since she'd left for California, he could see it. The way she took no guff from Denny, how she was making plans and bringing order to the house. He would do everything he could to make it possible for her to stay.

He put his notebook away, laid it on top of Lynn's Kelly-green scarf—his only keepsake of her—making sure to wedge the floorboard snug in its place. That hidden compartment was his memory vault.

Before getting back in bed he set an alarm clock, something he hadn't done in many years, so he could catch his daughter before everyone else woke up in the morning. There were things she needed to hear.

Then he did something else he hadn't done in a very long time, since he was a lad. He prayed to God for His understanding, and asked to be forgiven his grievous trespasses.

He'd forgotten the peace that came with being up so early, the preternatural quiet. Clean-slate moments when he was alone with fresh thoughts and the promise of the day ahead. Previous sins weren't erased by any means, but there was the hope of redemption.

As expected, Sunday was downstairs, making strong coffee. Pale sunlight streamed in through the windows and washed her in soft rays while she moved about the kitchen.

When she noticed him, she poured a cup and set it on the table. "What're you doing up so early?"

He took his seat. "Thought I'd catch you before the day got away. Would you sit for a minute?" He was wasting no time, wanted to say things to her before anyone else appeared.

She stiffened momentarily, uncertainty in her eyes. Then she grabbed her coffee and sat across from him. "What's up?"

"I have a couple things I want to tell you."

If he squinted, blurred his vision the tiniest bit, he could see her twelve-year-old self sitting there. T-shirt and jeans. Face clear, hair pulled up high. She leaned forward and sat with one leg folded beneath her, a position she'd favored since she was a little girl. He always figured it was about raising herself up and being counted in a house full of boys.

He took a deep breath against the swell of emotion so his words would be strong and clear. Whatever she might be thinking of him right then, he needed her to believe what he was saying.

"I know you've been through a lot, Sunday. And I'm sorry for it."

Her eyes became moist and he heard her swallow.

He forged ahead because if she started to cry he wouldn't get through this. "I know there are things you're worrying about. But I want you to trust me when I say that everything is going to work out."

"All right. I'll go with that."

"Good. Now there's something else you need to hear." He smiled at her. "You deserve to be happy, Sunday."

She dropped her gaze.

"I know you want to do the right thing by everybody. You've always been that way. But no good comes of it when your only motivation is shame and guilt." He shook his head and chuckled. "Shame and guilt are like plagues. And we Irish wield them like weapons and wear them like medals."

He could see confusion in her pinched brow, as she tried to ferret out his message.

"What I'm saying is, if you can be happy, do it. If you know what you want in life, don't wait for someone else to give it to you. Go after it, and don't let anything stand in the way."

There was movement behind her on the porch. Kale stood at the back door, waving, with Grail beside him. "Well," Mickey said, "speak of the devil and he shall appear."

Sunday rose to open the door. "What're you guys doing here?"

"I would love a cup of coffee," Grail said, gusting in and bending down to give Mickey a hug from behind. She was dressed for work. "Hiya, Uncle Mick."

He patted her arms and watched Kale move near Sunday at the counter.

"Sorry," Kale said to her. "She woke me up and said I needed to come with her right now."

Sunday handed him a coffee. "That's okay."

"Is Shane here?" Grail asked.

"No," Sunday said. "He's working morning shift at the market today."

Grail yelled down the hall and up the stairs. "Denny! Jackie!"

"Christ on a bike," Mickey said. "You're like your mother, screaming like that."

"Sorry. But speaking of, she's got breakfast waiting for you over at her house. She said you promised to mow her lawn this morning."

Had he? Or maybe they were just trying to get rid of him. Either way it seemed the young people had things to discuss.

"What do you want?" Denny asked Grail, entering the kitchen and heading straight to the coffeepot. He'd thrown on dungarees and nothing else.

"Morning, sunshine."

Jackie wasn't far behind him, coming down the stairs in an undershirt and sweats.

Mickey stood to make his seat available. He took a couple steps back, crossed his arms, and watched for a moment. He watched Denny bring Jackie a coffee and drop into the chair next to him, still grumbling about being woken up in such a manner. He watched Grail reach over to ruffle Jackie's mussed hair before he swatted her away. And Kale and Sunday, side by side in their old seats, as they avoided eye contact but kept snatching looks at each other.

"I'll be heading to Clare's now," he said to no one in particular.

"See you later, Dad." Sunday gave him a small smile.

He winked at her and hoped with all his heart she'd remember his words.

CHAPTER NINETEEN

Sunday

"See you later, Dad."

She tucked away the things he'd said to her, knowing she would pull them out later for further examination. She was in a weird place with him, not sure how to feel about what he did. It wasn't black-and-white to her, unlike Denny, who told her he'd confronted Dad about Billy Walsh and his family. She didn't excuse her father for checking out of their family all those years. But maybe more than most she knew how impossible it had been to please her mother, how the suppressed anger and shame about not having a perfect family wound its way into her biting words, actions, even her eyes, filling her up until there was room for nothing else. Could she really fault her dad for finding some kind of love where he could?

There were times lately when he prattled on with no real direction, but this morning he had seemed purposeful, as if he'd thought about what he wanted to say to her and how he wanted to say it.

Kale leaned sideways toward her. "Are you doing okay?"

She looked into eyes that were full of concern and nodded.

"So listen up," Grail said, straightening in her seat. "I have to get back to work soon—I'm supposed to be on a coffee run. We got some more info this morning."

It felt like the whole table collectively held their breath.

"The official autopsy report won't be released for weeks, but based on body temp the medical examiner said the time of death was most likely between nine P.M. and midnight, which is supported by the aunt's account of his activities. If that's the case, you all have alibis."

They let out their breath. Sunday exchanged quick looks with her brothers. This was good news, but it didn't solve the mystery of the missing gun.

"And another development came in overnight," Grail said. "We got a call from a Belfast police detective. Seems Billy pissed off some very bad men. He skimmed a lot of money while peddling their drugs. They've been looking for him since he left. The police on the ground over there heard it might have been a hit." Grail's face and hands were animated. Her excitement seemed ghoulish, but West Manor didn't often see Irish mob murders. "I guess they have some serious drug cartels over there."

"Holy shit," Denny said.

"I know. And if that's what happened, they said whoever did it would have been on the first plane back to Belfast or Dublin. They'll still question you, because Billy had so few contacts here—he was really laying low—but they have a working theory now."

It might be a bad idea to ask, but they had to know. "Did they find the gun that was used to kill him?" Sunday asked.

"Not yet. We should have a ballistics report in the next couple days, maybe we'll get the caliber of the bullet. But that's not helpful without the gun." She turned to Denny. "They might question your lawyer too, to verify the details of the loan he gave you. Which also makes sense, by the way. If he had people after him he had to get inventive about where he put his cash."

Michael. He probably didn't even know Walsh was dead yet.

Grail watched them all with an expectant look on her face. She was waiting—hoping—for some kind of compensation. Not gratitude. Sunday knew that's not what she wanted. She wanted to know what they were keeping from her.

"Thanks, Grail," Sunday said. "We know you went out on a limb here."

Grail frowned at her. "Maybe someday you guys'll fill me in." She stood and gave Kale a hangdog tilt of the head. "I'm sorry about last night. I guess I shouldn't have texted Viv. I was just trying to circle the wagons, you know?"

"It's okay."

Grail looked at Denny. "You should put a shirt on, dude. You're not eighteen anymore." She dropped her coffee cup in the sink before heading out the back door.

Sunday looked around the table after Grail left. No one seemed to know what to say. There was relief floating in the air, but also lingering questions.

"Did you do something with the gun?" Denny asked Kale.

"What?"

"The gun at the bar. It's missing."

Kale held up his hands. "It wasn't me."

"Did you ever tell anyone else it was there?" Jackie asked him.

"No. No way."

Denny tossed his hands up. "Well, somebody did something with it. Maybe it was Walsh . . . Or one of the staff found it?"

There were doubtful shrugs and "maybes."

"I'll look around the pub some more," Jackie said. "Keep my eyes peeled for anything unusual."

"I'll talk to Michael today, fill him in," Sunday said. "In case they do question him." Kale turned to her, maybe thinking about all that money he'd just given Michael the day before.

Denny nodded. "That's a good idea. I'm going to head out to Mamaroneck in a little while, see what the after-church crowd is like. You can stay local today if you want," he told Kale. "Shouldn't get too crazy out there."

"Thanks," Kale said. He focused on his coffee mug. "I have some stuff to take care of at home."

God only knew what was going on there after what Vivienne had heard the night before. Sunday wanted to tell him she was sorry he had a mess to clean up. She wanted to thank him for not even hesitating before speaking up to Grail. She badly wanted to tell him how much it meant to her that he'd wanted to understand what happened five years ago, that he'd given her the chance to try to explain. But that would make everything harder for him.

They all stood and pushed their chairs in, drifted off in various directions without further conversation.

She offered to get a ride to Michael's office late that afternoon, but he told her to pick a coffee shop in the neighborhood because he didn't trust her not to drive again. He was dressed down for the weekend, khakis and a polo, probably about as casual as he got.

"I'm sorry to bug you on the weekend," she said.

"Not at all. I was glad you called." He smiled wide, and once again she regretted having to darken his day. Felt like she did that a lot with Michael.

She recapped everything they'd learned from Grail the night before. Michael stayed quiet, but she could see the growing disbelief, and then concern, while he listened.

"Did the police question you? Or Denny?"

"Not yet."

"If they question you, call me. Right away."

"I think we'll be all right. We have an alibi for when it happened."

"What kind of alibi?"

"Kale. He was at the house with us that night."

Michael sat back, his lips pressed together like he was holding fast all the questions he wanted to ask but knew he shouldn't. When she explained the police might question him too, he said it wouldn't be a problem, that it helped they made such a big payment just the day before. Why would anyone fork over twenty thousand in cash to a dead guy.

She lowered her voice. "No one outside my family knows what happened to me that night . . ." It was difficult to meet his eye. She might be asking him to do something unethical, or even illegal.

"Hey, all of that's privileged. You don't have to worry about it. And his lawyer's not going to offer up those details."

She felt her whole body relax. "Thank you."

He nodded, looking a little bewildered. "Wow. Well, at least it's all over."

"Yeah." As over as it could be.

"So, what are you going to do now?" he asked.

"I'm hiring another bookkeeper for the pub so I can get a job and find my own place. Jackie, Shane, and I are working on a children's book. And I'm applying to master's programs."

"That all sounds good."

It sounded good to her as well, building a new life here. But she just didn't know if it was possible. After everything that happened lately Vivienne would—rightly—put as much distance as she could between Kale and the whole family, especially Sunday. And the thought of a life here without Kale in it made her heart hurt.

Michael leaned forward on the table, one hand twirling his cardboard coffee cup. "I'm sure you need some time, Sunday. But when you're ready, maybe we could . . . hang out."

Her face began to burn and she didn't know what to say. She was so bad at this.

"And not as lawyer and client." He laughed and it took some pressure off. His smile stretched to his eyes, which were honest and kind.

She said goodbye to him shortly after because it was hard to know where to go from there. On the walk home she thought about him though. Michael was a nice guy with a quick mind, successful. The thing was, she didn't really know him. And other than a dark, painful secret, he didn't really know her.

There was a logical argument to be made for that very thing, a new beginning with someone outside all the history. But she'd already spent years trying the "fresh start" option, and she'd failed miserably. All she wanted, that entire time, was to get back to the people who knew her best. Bailing on them was the most chickenshit thing she'd ever done in her life.

"You can go, dear." An older lady gently elbowed her on a corner because she was still waiting for a crosswalk light that had already turned green. After crossing the street she took a turn into Hollis Park and found the bench by the pond. She dropped down beside her bag and forced herself to sink into those memories.

When Kale had first returned from Ireland, she was so relieved to see him she convinced herself she could just treat that night like an awful nightmare that would diminish until it had no power over her. She bought some time with the "flu," and then it was easy to hide among the chaos of wedding prep. But it didn't fade; quite the opposite. What happened that night flooded her thoughts and made it nearly impossible to deal with the mundane activities of everyday life. And with Denny moving out, everyone was leaning on her more and more. She couldn't eat or sleep, felt out of step with everything happening around her, she became jumpy and abrasive. Kale tried everything, but she would tell him to give her space and get off her back, using words and a tone he'd never heard from her before. She didn't know how else to regulate her emotions. It was either that or tell him the truth, that she'd gotten wasted, gone to another man's room, and then lost their baby. So she pushed him away, and the longer it went on the more she hated herself.

When Jackie all but threatened to expose the truth, Sunday chose to tell the most difficult person in her life because she was more afraid of everyone else's reaction. So she sat her mother down at the kitchen table one morning when no one else was home and told her what happened.

"How could you not know you were pregnant?" was her mother's first question.

"I just thought I was late. It's happened before . . ." But it sounded so irresponsible, even to her own ears.

"Jesus, Mary, and Joseph." Her mom had kept her stiff brown hair cut close to her head after her chemo and she had an anxious habit of pulling at it on the side of her neck. "What were you thinkin', going up to a strange man's room?"

"I told you. I thought he had—"

"Oh yes." A withering eye roll. "To look at a photo."

"As soon as I realized, I left."

Her mother narrowed her eyes in question. Or doubt.

"That's when he tried to stop me, Mom. That's when I fell and lost the baby. The doctor said—"

"The doctor? You went to the hospital?"

"Yes." Sunday was leaving Jackie out of this.

Her mom started tugging at her hair again. "Did you report this to the police?"

"No. I don't want to. Besides, I found out he left town right after."

"Who? Who was it?"

What Sunday wanted to do was rewind to five minutes ago and stop this interrogation before it started. "It was a bartender at the Penny Whistle. His name was Billy Walsh."

Sunday would never forget her mother's reaction in that moment, the way her face had gone beyond white—almost gray. Like she recognized that name.

"His father worked for Dad for a long time, but I guess Dad fired him—"

Her mother shot out of her seat, one fist on a hip. "You've told no one else?"

"No, but maybe I should. I'm making a mess of things, especially with Kale."

"No, no. You did the right thing. What good would it do now?" She threw a hand up. "You were drunk, you can't even be sure of what happened. He's gone away, what's the point?" Her eyes drilled into Sunday's. "You know your father has to watch his blood pressure. God forbid he finds out. Or your brothers or Kale. None of them would rest until they found him." She crossed herself to ward off such a thought. "Besides, these things have a way of getting out. And you know how it goes, there'd be talk about you. Pregnant and drinkin' at the bar, going to the bartender's room . . ." She shook her head. "It would be a stain on the soul of the whole family."

"But I feel like I'm lying to everyone all the time."

"You're just right. This is no one's business but yours." She tapped the table with her finger. "Mark my words. If you tell Kale, he'll never look at you the same again."

If her final decision to leave could be traced back to a single moment, that was it. She couldn't tell her family. She couldn't tell Kale. And she couldn't stay in control of herself around them.

When Sunday mentioned the idea of California, her mother offered to pay for the plane ticket.

Five years later, a realization slid into place. Given her mother's reaction to the name Walsh, she'd likely known about her dad's affair and couldn't chance the scandal. People knowing her husband had been unfaithful with the mother, and her daughter had been tempted by the son. The world had just asked too much of Maura Brennan and she wasn't up to it. Instead, she had shut herself off from everything, even her family.

Like mother, like daughter.

A peaceful crowd was scattered throughout the park. Parents with young children, a few runners and dog-walkers. It was one of the first truly warm days of the year. Sunday tilted her face up and soaked it in.

She was stalling though, putting off thinking about the most agonizing part of that whole time. The morning she left.

Over dinner the night before her flight, she told Kale and the family she'd received an unexpected job offer in LA to write content for blogs and websites. Eating around the table ceased and flatware was laid down while she went on about what an opportunity it was, a good résumé-builder. She remembered rushing her words, trying to inject excitement, willing them all to just accept what she was saying.

At one point Denny had turned to Kale. "Did you know about this?"

Kale, who seemed more resigned than shocked, had shaken his head.

"This seems a bit sudden," her father said.

"You can't leave, Sunday," Shane said. "Dad, she can't leave."

She remembered gulping water then, forcing down the lump that was threatening to close her throat.

"I would think you'd all be more supportive." All eyes turned to her mother. "Sure it's only temporary."

Until that point Jackie had said nothing, just sat in his chair, gripping his arms like he was trying to contain himself. But he glared at her. "Suddenly you've decided to support her writing?"

"If she's a chance to make a go with the writing, of course she should try it. Isn't it what she went to school for? She'll be back before you know it." And somehow that deceptively logical support from a highly unlikely corner had ended the conversation.

The next morning she called a taxi to take her to the airport. Kale showed up at the house to say goodbye—they hadn't slept in the same bed for weeks at that point. When the cab arrived, he carried her bags out, loaded them in the trunk. She fought off tears that would come very shortly by thanking him for understanding. "I just want to see if I'm any good at it—"

"Don't." He shook his head. "I know this isn't about some goddamn job."

"I just need some time," she said, "to . . . figure things out."

He glanced at the cab. "I think you already have figured things out."

She bent down for her backpack, knowing she had to get in that cab or she wasn't going to be able to leave. When she stood back up she stepped forward and hugged him.

He was stiff for a second, but then he hugged her back and said, "I hope you find what you're looking for out there, Sunday." He let go and walked away without looking back.

The only reason she could get in the taxi that day was because she told herself she'd be home soon. She'd go to California, get her head straight, maybe see some LA therapist. Figure out how to get past that awful night. Reset her brain, her emotions. Then she'd come back to him.

She still didn't know whether she really believed that at the time or if it was just what she had to tell herself to get in the cab. Maybe there was no difference.

A faint breeze whispered through the park, across her face, and she realized her cheeks were damp so she searched her bag for a tissue or napkin. Coming up empty she made do with her sleeve and stared at the small interior pocket of her bag. She hadn't opened that pocket since the night she slipped their postcard in there, the night Vivienne found it and assumed it was Sunday's. She'd zipped it away and refused to look at it again, not even long enough to move it from the bag to a drawer.

But it seemed a good time to do it now, sitting on their bench in the park. She was already steeped in self-flagellation, what was one more lash of the whip.

She unzipped the pocket and slid the card out with two fingers. It was worn, soft with age. Corners tattered, colors faded, small wrinkles and indentations. But there was the beach, the waves, the palm trees. The place where the two smiling stick figures in the corner were supposed to start their grown-up life together.

She flipped it over because she wanted to read the name again. Magens Bay. She would always know it by heart, but she wanted to lay eyes on it, see the letters in solid form. When she turned it over something was wrong. There was writing that didn't belong there, and for the tiniest second anger flared up at the thought that someone had used it to jot some random note. But then she recognized his handwriting.

Booked. Promise! June 2, 2012

So many realizations hit her at once she became dizzy while she tried to put them in some kind of order. Kale had booked their trip. He'd been planning to surprise her with the postcard. He would have given it to her or had her find it somewhere and waited for her to notice, to understand. When he was in Ireland and she couldn't find it . . . He'd taken it with him because he'd already written the note and didn't want her to find it without him. That's why he'd been so angry when she stayed home. He was planning to give it to her on that trip. She knew all this to be true because it would have been so Kale to do it that way.

And when she was such a mess after he got home, her behavior erratic, he would have waited, and kept waiting, not wanting to start out that way on the road to their marriage. That last morning when she left . . . Had he thought about telling her? Doubtful. By then she had him believing she wanted something else.

She leaned forward, her arms on her knees, as she stared at the card and made one final connection that cut to her core.

He had planned for them to elope on June 2. She had left New York on May 19. Just two weeks before.

She didn't know how long she stayed that way, bent over and staring at the card. She was half-aware of passersby while she fully grasped the discovery she'd made. Kale had done it. After two years of talking about it, despite the backlash that would come from her family, he had booked the trip.

She felt the bench shift as someone sat on the other end. Why they had to choose this particular bench out of all the available ones in the park was beyond her, but she figured it was time to pick up her head. Feeling protective, she covered the postcard with her hands. Then she took a deep breath and sat up, planning to grab her bag and go. She was not in the mood for small talk with a stranger.

When she turned toward her bag, she saw who was sitting there.

"Pardon me," he said. "You're sitting on my bench." His hands were folded in his lap and he looked sideways at her, clearly as surprised as she was.

CHAPTER TWENTY

Kale

P ardon me. You're sitting on my bench."

Sunday had been so lost in whatever she was thinking about, he had managed to walk up behind her and take a seat without her noticing.

When he spotted her there, sitting on the very bench he was headed for, he had stopped in his tracks for a moment. He didn't necessarily believe in signs from the universe, but, given the timing, this had to mean something.

He was at the end of a strange and terrible day.

The night before, when Grail had forced the conversation about everyone's whereabouts on opening night, he never considered stalling. His first concern was that Denny and Sunday could actually be suspects. His next concern was further questioning would bring painful secrets to the surface for Sunday. If he could head all that off, he was going to do it. But he'd essentially told his wife, in front of an audience, that he spent time alone with Sunday at her house that night. So when they got home he expected a confrontation—Vivienne's rage, tears, questions. But it never came. She just said she was tired and went to sleep.

He lay awake next to her for a long time, her words still ringing in his ears—*Do you see it now? Do you see they're all just a bunch of liars who hurt the people around them?* There was no denying it. Denny had lied to him for months, risked his very livelihood. Sunday had left him rather than tell him the truth. Jackie had been lying to him for five years. They had all kept harmful secrets, from him and from each other, for a long time. Vivienne wasn't wrong.

When he returned from the Brennan house that morning she met him with coffee and a smile, and asked that he take a drive with her and Luke. He agreed and she directed him to Manor Hills, past several houses that were for sale. That was when he understood what this was all about. She was still planning for a move, trying to seal the deal, despite what she'd heard last night. Or because of it, because she had some leverage.

They walked the upscale neighborhood, with its flat roofs, monotone HOA-approved house colors, and themed street names—Van Gogh Court, Renoir Drive. They toured the health club, infinity lap pool, and eco-friendly playground. Kale did his best to be interested yet noncommittal, which was tough because Vivienne worked hard at getting Luke excited about it—*That yard's big enough for a tree house. This house is right across from the park. There are lots of other kids on this block.* Kale tried to see himself there, in an alien neighborhood. Living in one of those houses, meeting new people. Maybe shaking up his world would be enough, in time, to unlearn what made him truly happy.

They had an early dinner out and when they got home Luke ran up to change out of the nice clothes she had him wear that day. Kale sat at the kitchen table, slumped in his chair, hands dangling between his legs. He was being carried away upon Vivienne's momentum and had to get a handle on it. She only confirmed it when she joined him at the table with a pile of house listings.

"I'm exhausted," he said. "Do we have to do this right now?"

She spread out the flyers on the table. "Yes, we do."

The whole day had felt like it was funneling toward this painful moment, the one when he had to take some kind of stand. Because Vivienne had spent the last eight hours laying out what the path forward with her would look like.

"These are the places I think we should consider," she said.

He understood why she was drawing a hard line in the sand. She couldn't stay in this house, in this situation, any longer. But it meant there was no more time to think about it. He was either staying with Vivienne in this half-hearted marriage or doing the thing he thought he'd never do.

"This one is my favorite," she said, pointing to one listing. "Can't you just see us here?"

He stared down at the photo. A new house on a corner lot with a perfectly manicured lawn. No, he couldn't picture himself there at all, and the fact that she could just confirmed how little she knew him. Or how little she cared about what he wanted. If their marriage was this flatline after four years, what would get them through the next forty? She would never really know him, not the way *they* did, the complicated lot he'd thrown in with twenty-five years ago. Vivienne wasn't wrong about the Brennans. The whole family was a mess. But they were his mess. He was part of them.

"We drove past it today," she said. "I talked to a real estate agent last week and it sounds like prices are staying pretty firm, especially with summer coming up."

He heard Luke moving around upstairs. How does someone explain to a three-and-a-half-year-old that his family is going to change? No one had explained it to Kale, his mother just left one day, and all his father ever said was that she was unhappy. Kale had vowed never to be like her, yet he followed her footsteps into a lifeless marriage. Part of it had been obligation. He'd tried to kid himself that he could be content doing the right thing. And part of it had been because, after Sunday left, he didn't want to be alone.

"These three are all the perfect size," Vivienne said, sliding papers around. "All in our price range. Assuming, of course, we sell this place."

His gut flipped as he thought about living separately from Luke, going whole days without seeing him. But it was possible to still be a good father. It wasn't ideal, it wasn't fair to Luke, but Kale would not disappear. Of course he'd have to make room for another man in Luke's life at some point. That thought was accompanied by such an acute pang of alarm he squeezed his eyes shut with his fingers for a moment.

"I don't think there's much to do to this place before we list it," Vivienne said. "We've kept it in pretty good shape . . ."

"*You've* kept it in good shape." And she had. Part of what made this so hard was that he didn't have any of the more convenient complaints people cited to end a marriage—adultery, neglect, constant arguing. They just lacked a fundamental intimacy that kept someone from feeling alone in the world. Kale had forgotten what that was like. Until Sunday came back and he realized she was still the voice in his head.

"Thanks," Vivienne said, studying the flyers. "Anyway, it should be a close trade."

Kale didn't know if he had any future with Sunday. But this marriage was shortchanging him and Vivienne both. He couldn't let her go any further. "I think we should—"

"The agent is coming Monday to do a walk-through so we can decide on a selling price." Her eyes widened. "Oh, and I already got a line on some good babysitters. They have couples events in the clubhouse each month. It would be nice to start going out once in a while. I met some people—"

"Vivienne."

She stared at him for a long moment, then took a breath. When she let it out her shoulders sank and a slow blink seemed to wash a feverish hope from her eyes.

"I'm so sorry," he said. "But I can't do this with you."

Her mouth tightened and she looked down at the flyers again.

"You deserve someone who wants—"

"I knew it." She shook her head. "I *knew* you were going to do this. After everything they've done to you, you're going back for more." She curled her lip in disgust. "Figures. You've been a Brennan groupie your whole life."

Kale didn't look away. Whatever she needed to say, she was entitled to say it.

Her face scrunched in disbelief. "She's back a couple months and that's it? Seriously?"

With a rush of sadness he thought back to those early days with Vivienne, when she'd helped him pull out of an alcohol-fueled haze of loneliness. He was grateful to her for that, and for giving him Luke. He wished he could explain it all to her, why Sunday left. But it didn't matter, it wouldn't change anything. He shook his head. "This isn't about her—"

"Bullshit."

He stopped.

She drummed her fingernails on the table, considered her next words. Then her fingers slowed and stopped. "The postcard I found that day in the desk. She's not the one who kept it all these years, is she?"

He didn't respond. He didn't want to lie to her.

"Un-fucking-believable." Her laugh was riddled with scorn. "You know she's just going to hurt you again, right? It's in their blood, Kale."

He thought about pointing out that, Sunday aside, they just didn't want the same things. But the blaze in her eyes said he'd only be feeding her fire. So, instead, he said, "I'm sorry. I never wanted to hurt you." As true as those words were, he could hear how hollow they sounded.

"Whatever." She waved off his pathetic platitude. "I can do a lot better than this."

"I know you can."

"Luke's staying with me. And we're still moving to Manor Hills." She arched her eyebrows, daring him to challenge, even though she had to know that was unrealistic now.

"We'll have to figure all that out. I'll do whatever I can to help you get what you want—"

"Don't pretend to give a shit about what I want." She started yanking the house listings into a pile. "I don't care what your plan is, I'm selling this house."

"This house is half yours. We can sell it if you want." He debated for a moment, but this was all about telling the truth. "You need to know I took out a small equity loan on it. Twenty thousand."

"*What?* Why did you . . . Wait. Don't tell me. You did it for them."

"It's my problem, it'll come out of my share."

"Yeah, well, you might as well hand over the rest of your share too because I'm going to need other help." She crossed her arms and flung one leg over the other. "Child support, money for groceries and bills. Even after I'm full time in the fall."

He leaned toward her on the table. "I promise I will not leave you in the lurch." In that moment he didn't care if he ended up sleeping on a cot in the office at the pub. "We'll work together to make sure you and Luke are taken care of."

Her hostile eyes zeroed in on his. "So when do you plan to tell Luke you're abandoning your family?"

All the air was sucked from his chest. He dragged his hands through his hair to take a moment to recover. "I'll talk to him now."

Her arms were still crossed tight. "I'll tell you one thing, Kale. When he asks me what happened, I'm not going to lie to him."

He nodded and stood.

"Might as well pack your shit while you're up there too," she said. "I want you gone." Her look and tone were venomous, but Kale knew underneath she was feeling the special kind of pain that came with rejection. He knew it from experience.

He'd climbed the stairs to Luke's room then, with a heart so heavy he had to stop halfway to shore himself up. But he'd opened this door and he was past the point of no return. He found his son sitting on the floor of his bedroom in his underwear, playing with blocks. The same wooden blocks Kale had played with as a child. He sat beside him and Luke showed him the house he was building. He'd managed to pile blocks together in a rough image of their house, two stories with a simple roof.

In a calm voice Kale told Luke that he was going to be leaving the house. That he wouldn't be going far, but he would be staying in a different place.

Luke kept working, started to add the garage to his house. "When will you be back, Daddy?"

Kale clenched a square block in his hand, letting the corners dig into his palm and fingers. "You'll still see me every day, but I'll be sleeping in a different house."

"Where?"

"I'm not sure yet, but wherever I go, that will be your home too."

Luke stopped playing with the blocks. "What do you mean?"

Kale was confusing him. "Well," he said, stacking a few blocks together, "from now on your mom is going to live in one house . . ." He pointed to the house Luke had built. ". . . and I'm going to live in a different house." He pointed to his simple square structure. "But we'll both see you all the time, and you'll have two homes."

Luke's eyes went back and forth between the houses. "But why?"

"Because we decided that would be best." Kale wanted to keep it simple, reassuring. But he cringed on the inside when he thought about how Vivienne might answer that question. *Because your daddy left us.*

"But why?"

Kale picked up a block and added to Luke's garage. "Sometimes things change, and change can be good." He put his hand on Luke's head, twined his fingers in the soft curls. "But one thing that will never change is that Mommy and I both love you very, very much." He gripped the small block in his other hand again, until it felt like the dull edges might break the skin.

Luke was working on the garage again.

"Do you understand that, buddy?"

"Uh-huh."

But he didn't, not really. Luke would wake up tomorrow morning and Kale wouldn't be there. How many times would his son look for him or need him only to find him gone? Luke would have questions for a long time, Kale would have to explain this again and again. And at least half the time it would be Vivienne who would be answering his questions.

After a few more minutes he left Luke to his blocks and packed a duffel bag. Downstairs he told Vivienne about their conversation. She stayed at the kitchen sink, her back to him while he spoke. When he was finished, all she said was, "You and that family deserve each other."

Then he left.

He hadn't thought beyond that, beyond walking out the door. Once he reached the corner he called Paul. Last week Paul had mentioned he was looking for a renter for the small carriage house on his property, which was only half a mile away, on the other side of Saw Mill Road. Funny how certain tidbits planted themselves in the subconscious, even if they seemed irrelevant at the time. Paul answered the call and said the place was available, but the current tenant wasn't out until tomorrow. Kale said he'd take it.

He hung up, feeling light-headed, as if the momentous life changes he'd just set in motion were about to catch up to him. He needed to find a place where he could sit down and figure out his next steps. So he'd slung his bag across his shoulder and headed to Hollis Park.

"I thought this was my bench," Sunday said.

He gave her what felt like a very tired smile.

She tucked her hands between her knees, like maybe she was chilly. "I was just on my way home from meeting Michael."

"How'd that go?"

"Okay. He doesn't think there's much to worry about. Right now, anyway."

Kale nodded. "He's a good guy. Michael." Some self-punishing part of him was fishing for how she felt about Michael.

"Yeah, he is."

When she didn't offer any more, he looked out into the fading light that was settling across the wide green lawns. A few stragglers remained in the park. He needed to figure out where the hell he was going to stay that night. He couldn't stomach the thought of a hotel room in his own town. He was so tired the park bench would probably do the job.

"What's that?" Sunday asked, nodding toward his duffel.

Staring straight ahead he said, "I left."

He heard her soft gasp.

"I had to. She forced it after last night. I tried to explain it to Luke . . ." His voice caught and he stopped for a moment. "It wasn't her fault, maybe

I never gave it a fair chance. But I couldn't pretend it was working any-more, that we were making each other happy." He hesitated but decided on the most truthful explanation. "It was never going to be the way I know it should be."

Out of the corner of his eye he saw her head drop. Maybe she was thinking about how to tell him they were finally over, that everything had been exorcised and she was ready to move on. That it would be best for both of them.

After a minute she lifted her head up and laid something on the bench between them.

Their postcard. With his note scribbled on it.

They exchanged sad smiles. He picked it up and held it in his hands.

She leaned back against the bench and they sat in silence for a bit. It was that time of night, right after the sun sets, when the air feels thinner, and scattered light seems to wash everything in a soft violet hue.

"Sounds like you have a lot to figure out," she said.

He rubbed the back of his neck. "Yeah."

"Do you know where you're going to be living?"

"I'm renting Paul's carriage house starting tomorrow." From owning a house to renting an employee's outbuilding.

"So, you're homeless for the night."

"I guess I am." Homeless, financially strapped, on the road to divorce.

"Well, does it make you feel any better to know I officially have a crim-inal record now?"

He turned to her in surprise. "A little."

She smiled. And the tiniest weight lifted from his shoulders.

"I know a place you could stay tonight," she said, "if you're interested. It's a little crowded at the moment. But there's a cozy extra room in the attic that's yours if you want it." A nearby lamppost created a point of light in each of her eyes.

"That sounds really nice."

Above them the sky was darkening, transitioning to indigo. The first cicadas of the evening began to announce themselves with soft chirping throughout the park.

Sunday pulled her bag on her shoulder and stood. Then she stepped in front of him and slid her hands in her jacket pockets. "Let's go."

They walked their old route in a silence so comfortable Kale didn't want it to end. A thousand difficult questions nibbled at the edges of his mind: How could he best support Luke through this? Would he and Vivienne be able to work together or would it always be contentious? How was he going to pay for two households for a while? He didn't have answers to those questions yet, but he didn't feel alone.

Sunday followed suit when he stopped on the sidewalk outside the Brennan house. The first two stories were lit up, warmth emanating from all corners. It was the place Kale had been coming to since he was five years old.

The front door swung open and Denny appeared, squinting into the darkness. He stepped out onto the porch, getting a closer look. Then he crossed his arms up high. "For fuck's sake."

Kale tensed up. There was no gloomier feeling than the idea that he might no longer be welcome in this house.

But then Denny tossed up his hands. "Might as well come inside."

He turned and went back into the house, leaving the door wide open behind him.

CHAPTER TWENTY-ONE

Denny

"Might as well come inside."

He'd been surprised to see Kale and Sunday standing out there together. But, then again, not really.

His gut reaction had been to lecture them about marriage and parenthood, letting go of the past. But he knew Theresa would say something along the lines of "Who the hell are you to know what's right for anybody else?" And he decided to keep his mouth shut.

He headed back to the kitchen table, where he'd been making arrangements to move his wife and daughter back home the next morning. A moment later Jackie and Shane walked in the back door.

"Look what Shane brought from the store," Jackie said.

Shane dropped a large paper bag on the table and started pulling out pints of ice cream. "Mr. Newman gave me ice cream because I stayed to help with inventory. I said he didn't have to, but he wanted to."

"Nice, Shane," Denny said, checking out the flavors. "Good work."

Jackie grabbed a handful of spoons from the drawer, dropped them on the table. "I call the mint chocolate chip first." He sat down and peeled off the lid, started eating out of the container. "The pub was busy tonight. It's time to close later, at least through the summer."

Denny nodded, digging into some kind of chunky chocolate.

Shane sat down, studying his options, lining them up so he could make an informed decision.

"What's going on around here?" Jackie asked.

"Dad's still at Clare's. She had some priest over for dinner and asked him to come."

Jackie chuckled. "Poor bastard's probably being subjected to the un-abridged Brennan family history."

When Sunday rounded the corner from the living room with Kale in tow, Jackie's mouth fell open. Shane didn't seem to take much notice.

"What's going on in here?" she asked.

"Shane brought home some treats," Denny said. "We're having an ice-cream social."

She and Kale took their seats at the table.

"Kale's going to spend the night here," Sunday said. "He's set up in the extra room in the attic."

"Next to me?" Shane asked.

"Yeah," Kale said. "If that's okay with you, Shane."

"That's okay with me."

Jackie held up his spoon. "Is anyone gonna ask if it's okay with me?"

Denny, Sunday, and Kale all said, "No," in unison.

Shane full-body laughed. "No one's gonna ask you, Jackie."

"Don't worry," Kale said, reaching for a carton and two spoons. "It's just one night. I have somewhere to go tomorrow."

Denny raised his eyebrows at Kale, who gave him a solemn nod.

So Kale had left home. What a shit show. And it was only a matter of time before Sunday got sucked into it. She and Kale would wait awhile, they had stuff to work through. But as far as Denny was concerned, their fate had been sealed the night Kale asked to read her story in high school.

He glanced around the table in the quiet. Shane, at one end, dug into his dessert with purpose. Jackie, opposite Shane, scooped ice cream into his mouth, glancing at Kale and Sunday, as if confirming they were really there. They sat across from Denny, taking turns eating from the same carton.

Two months ago he had sat at this table, feeling utterly alone, about to get a phone call from a cop in LA.

"Theresa and Molly are coming home tomorrow," Shane said. "Right, Denny?"

"That's right, bud."

"Everybody will be together then." Shane scooped more ice cream. "When I was helping Dad park his truck in the garage, he told me everything will be okay now." He looked across the table. "Jackie, can we swap?"

Jackie slid his container across. "Why were you helping Dad park his truck?"

"Cuz it was really dark and the light in the garage is still broken. He didn't want to hit something like last time." He started in on the mint chip.

"Dad was driving at night?" Denny asked. "By himself?"

"Yeah. He woke me up to help him park."

Christ. Dad had gone out driving alone late at night, without any of them knowing. He could have hurt himself or someone else, or gotten lost far from home. Maybe it was time to start hiding keys to the vehicles.

"When was this?" Jackie asked.

Shane scratched his head and then stood, spoon still in his hand. He walked over to examine his calendar on the fridge. "It was one, two . . . two nights ago." He pointed to the day with his spoon and shook his head. "I missed a Yankee game. Cuz we had to go to the new Brennan's."

Opening night. The night Denny had come home to find Kale at the house.

The night Billy Walsh was killed.

"But Dad was at the grand opening," Denny said.

"Only for a little while," Sunday said. "He had Clare take him home around six thirty."

"And he stopped in the pub back here around seven thirty," Jackie said. "I assumed he was walking, but maybe he was driving the truck."

Anxious looks ping-ponged across the table while Shane took his seat again. They were getting used to small memory lapses and repetitive questions. But taking off by himself for a drive at night? This was a whole new dimension of their dad's aging that would make it difficult to keep him safe.

Jackie jerked up straight in his seat and dropped his spoon on the table. "Wait a minute . . ." He stood and jogged upstairs.

"Where the hell did Dad go?" Denny asked Shane. But he knew right away there was too much edge to his question.

"Oh boy," Shane said. His eyes got huge and his hand went to the side of his head. "I wasn't supposed to tell."

"It's just us," Sunday said. "It's okay."

"But Dad said once three people know it's not a secret anymore."

She placed a hand on his arm. "He probably just felt like going for a drive."

"Yeah, he said . . . he said he went for a ride."

"Did he mention where he went?" she asked.

He shook his head.

"Or if he met anyone?"

His features squeezed together while he thought about it. "I don't think so. But I was sleepy. It was late." He went back to work on his ice cream.

They heard the front door open and close. "'Lo? Anybody up?"

"Oh boy," Shane said. "We're in here, Dad."

Denny watched his father come around the corner and backstep. "What's all this?" He smiled when he saw Kale at the table beside Sunday. "Well now."

"Dad," Shane said, his fist closed tight around his spoon. "Sorry, Dad. But I told these guys about, about the other night. With the truck."

A spark of panic lit up his dad's eyes and died down just as quickly. He pressed his lips together and shook his head. "Fair play to you, Shane. That's all right. Sure I didn't want to worry yous just because I felt like driving around the neighborhood a few times. Won't happen again, you have my word." He bowed from the waist, hands up in contrition. Then he went to the sink, grabbed a glass off the dish drainer, and filled it. "Clare's was good enough. Father Pat's a nice fella. Patience of Job listening to her natter on the way she does." He looked to Heaven and drank his water.

Jackie came back downstairs and took his seat.

"You want some ice cream, Dad?" Shane asked. "Mr. Newman gave it to me."

"Thanks, but no. I'm just after some of Clare's soda bread pudding." He patted his stomach and stepped closer to the table. "Does my heart good to see you all sitting here together."

Denny looked closely at his father, who didn't seem to notice the uneasy glances coming his way from around the table. What the hell had he done the other night? But there were no answers in the bright eyes and beaming smile.

"Well," his dad said, placing his empty glass in the sink. "I'm off to bed. See you all in the morning." A final salute to the table and he headed upstairs.

"Me too," Shane said. "I'm tired." He pushed his chair back with a loud screech and stood, took his empty carton to the trash and his spoon to the sink. "Good night, everybody." An energetic wave before he climbed the stairs, untroubled by the whole conversation.

Denny's gut started to churn. His father had gone somewhere the other night, just hours after Denny told him that Billy Walsh had hurt Sunday and was coming after the pub. But, seriously, a clandestine trip to Katonah to take someone out?

No one said anything or touched the softening ice cream in front of them. After they heard two bedroom doors close upstairs Jackie reached behind him, under his sweatshirt, and pulled out a solid object wrapped in a vivid green cloth. He laid it in the middle of the table with a soft thud. When he folded back the scarf, there it was.

Fuck. A fifth person had known about the gun. His dad had been the one to buy it for the pub all those years ago.

"It was in his hiding place," Jackie said.

"Oh my God." Sunday's voice was laced with dread as the truth descended on all of them.

Denny looked up. They were all staring at the gun. Jackie with his hands plunged into his hair, Kale with a fist to his mouth. Sunday sat very still, her hands clasped in front of her. But the expression on her face was one of weary resignation, like she'd already gotten over the shock.

Denny understood. In many ways this ending seemed inevitable. She had delayed it, but really it had been set in motion one terrible night five years ago.

"Well," she said, taking a deep breath and pulling herself up in her seat. Her eyes swept around the table and landed on Denny. "We need a plan."

He slumped back against his chair, feeling the entire weight of those words, the complications and risks involved. As if the old man hadn't given them enough to deal with already . . .

But she was right. They would do everything they could to protect their father, and each other, because that's what family did. They all screwed up, made mistakes, and hurt one another. But in the end they came together.

Even his parents had done the best they could. As misguided as they'd been, they thought they were protecting the family. Both of them had missed the mark, just like Denny had for a time. Family didn't mean hiding the hard stuff from each other, it meant facing it together. And it meant forgiving each other.

Making some kind of peace with it all caused an uplifting in his chest, and he imagined his mother looking down on them now, sitting together at the kitchen table where so much of their lives had happened. In the big white house she'd always loved, a few blocks from the neighborhood pub she helped make possible. In the tranquil town she'd chosen as the best place to raise this family.

There would be a plan and, whatever happened, they would figure it out. Together.

Acknowledgments

I will be forever grateful to the people who believed in this novel and were essential to getting it out into the world:

Stephanie Cabot, my amazing agent, for seeing the diamond in the rough and helping me improve the book by miles. Your guidance and support are invaluable to me.

The incredible team at Celadon: Deb Futter, for challenging me to find a different plot twist that got us to the same place and made for a much richer story. Randi Kramer, for all the spot-on editorial suggestions and being there to pull me out of rabbit holes. Rachel Chou, Christine Mykityskyn, Jaime Noven, and Jennifer Jackson, for working so hard on behalf of this book. Anne Twomey, for creating the most perfect cover. Rebecca Ritchey, for making social media less scary. I am thankful every day to be working with all of you.

Deborah Johnson, my talented instructor and early draft reader, for assisting me with bringing this story to a whole new level by asking all the right questions.

My crew, the people who keep me going through this solitary endeavor and add so much to my work and my life: Jessie Weaver—available at all hours to talk me off the ledge—Steve High, Carol Merchasin, Bob Murney, and Kim Young. This book would not have seen the light of day without you, and every time I read it I see your influence on the pages.

Angie Dail and Sue Deitz, who were excited for me when I couldn't get there yet.

And biggest thanks to my family:

Louis O'Hare, my father, for always keeping us tied to our deep roots in Ireland, and for sharing countless stories about your upbringing and your immigration to the States almost sixty years ago. Also, for knowing this part of New York so well and answering all my nitty-gritty questions. Kathleen Murphy, my mother, for reading early work and being a cheerleader every step of the way. Kevin O'Hare, my brother, for being a sounding board when I had tough decisions to make.

And greatest thanks to my guys, Fred, Will, and Ben. I wrote this novel in our kitchen, which has always been the heart of our home, and the perfect place to write about family. I welcomed all your interruptions, which fed my soul, and this story. Thank you for believing I could never fail.

WE ARE THE BRENNANS
READING GROUP
DISCUSSION QUESTIONS

1. Long-held secrets play a central role in the plot. Do you think important secrets can ever be kept without causing some kind of damage?

2. What caused the Brennans to be a family of secret keepers?

3. Why do you think the author chose to tell each chapter from a different character's point of view? Do you think it was effective?

4. Which member of the Brennan clan do you relate to the most?

5. Do you think Billy Walsh caused Sunday to fall down the stairs?

6. As Denny decides what to do about Billy after his unexpected reunion with Sunday, Theresa tells him, "Sometimes there's a thin line between helping and controlling" (p. 200). What do you think of this, given the situation?

7. What do you think are the most important themes of the book?

8. How did learning about the history between the Brennans and the Walshes change your view of Billy?

9. What roles do mothers play in this book?

Submitted by Hidden Hollow Book Club (West Chester, Pennsylvania)

10. Do you think Sunday coming back into Kale's life was ultimately a good thing for Kale? For Sunday?

11. What do you think about Kale's relationship with Vivienne?

12. Did you expect the ending to unfold the way it did?

13. What do you think will happen next for these characters?

Submitted by the Kolvig Literary Club (Minneapolis, Minnesota)

CELADON
BOOKS

Founded in 2017, Celadon Books, a division of
Macmillan Publishers, publishes a highly curated
list of twenty to twenty-five new titles a year. The
list of both fiction and nonfiction is eclectic and
focuses on publishing commercial and literary
books and discovering and nurturing talent.